Early Praise for Seize me From Darkness

"There's something classic about captives falling in love through mutual suffering, but Cari Silverwood finds a way to twist all you believe will happen. From a dirty, painful hell to one with nicer surroundings, but you still aren't free. And may not want to be."

Bianca Sommerland – author of the Deadly Captive Trilogy

Seize me From Darkness

Book 4, Pierced Hearts

Cari Silverwood

New York Times and USA Today Bestselling author

Published by Cari Silverwood
Editor: Nerine Dorman
Proof reader: Donna J.
Cover Artist: Thomas Dorman aka Dr. Benway on Deviantart and Facebook
Formatting: Polgarus Studio

About Seize me From Darkness

This book is part of a dark erotic fiction series and may disturb readers who are uncomfortable with dubious consent or graphic violence.

If you've processed that and are headed onward, strap yourself in and hang on tight. The twisted fantasies in this story will take you to the edge of the abyss.

In this dirty, bloody world we live in, the answers to prayers aren't always pretty angels.

Retaken by human traffickers, Jazmine's one hope is ex-cop, ex-mercenary, Pieter, a man with a glower that stops lesser men in their tracks.

She prays he can save her.

But this savior is far from perfect, and his flaws may prove as devastating to Jazmine as the torture of her captors.

The fire of dominance never dies.

Disclaimer

This book contains descriptions of BDSM themed sexual practices but this is a work of fiction and as such should not be used in any way as a guide. The author will not be responsible for any loss, harm, injury or death resulting from use of the information contained within.

ACKNOWLEDGMENTS

My great thanks goes out to my beta readers Shannon Wichman, Jennifer Zeffer, Bianca Sarble, Tequila Rose, Sorcha Black, and Jody Rhoton. I pestered them all endlessly and they gave me so much of their time. I love you all and I hope I've not scarred you for life. Free kittens, hugs, coffee, and spanks – whichever you choose. Just no feet kissing.

A special thank you to Nerine Dorman, my South African editor, for looking out for goofs to do with Afrikaans and her country.

Chapter 1

“Head down, cunt up, until I say you can look at me.” The growled command and smack on the back of my head by a rough hand was enough to make me snap my gaze to the gritty concrete. My bare knees hurt. My torn and stained dress concealed almost nothing. Tears slipped down my sticky face and shivers wracked me despite the tropical heat.

Out there, beyond, were men. I could see their shoes and the legs of their jeans, hear their soft laughter.

I was helpless, alone, shaking.

I knew where I was. On the way here, curled on the floor of the small plane, men had spoken. Even with the bag on my head and the drone of the engine, I knew my destination.

In Australia, I’d been desperate to escape but the concrete I knelt on was in Papua New Guinea. I hadn’t a clue as to where I could go. Had no friends. I didn’t even have Pieter, the strange guard with the Good Samaritan tendencies. He was probably dead. I squeezed shut my eyes, as if that would make my memory of him go away. I’d messed up, like half my life, by getting him involved.

My hopes of escape had become nothing. I was nothing. I was so lost.

My heart hurt from beating too fast for too long – fight or flight response, but I could do neither. Being scared for days on end was exhausting.

Run. Run. Run. The single word popped up unexpectedly. It would go round and round in a loop in my thoughts until I slept or something distracted me. I couldn't *not* think it, even if its meaning had evaporated as soon as they bundled me like an express package onto the plane.

We must have crossed the sea to the north of Australia. I'd lived with the fact that if the plane had gone down in the ocean, I'd have been unable to do more than sink with it.

"They tell me you tried to get away. No more of that. You try and you get punished. Badly. I know who you are, little miss posh bitch. Jazmine. Hey? My name, you don't need. If you have to talk to me, you call me Sir. Nod, so I know you have ears."

Fear had slowed my thoughts to a sluggish drag. In the few seconds it took me to figure out what to do, he hit me. A single swish and whack sent a stripe of fire across my ass. I gasped but didn't speak. My nods were jerky, swishing my hair, as I prayed he'd not hit me again.

"Good. You behave and we'll get along. For your sins, you're being sold to the meanest bastard on our books. Three days, give or take a day, and he'll be here to claim you." His stick tapped the backs of my thighs. "What a pretty cunt. Hmmm?"

I squeezed my legs in closer.

The man nudged my chin with his stick. "Up."

I raised my head to find him squatting a few feet in front of me. Jeans, neat blue short-sleeved shirt, heavily muscled thighs and arms. Shaven scalp. A man who could do what he liked with me.

Like some sort of macabre decoration theme, the walls of the room were hung with instruments of torture – pincers, floggers, ugly leather masks, whips, and handcuffs. I couldn't fathom the use of some of the devices. This surreal place could have been just another made-up location for a magazine shoot. If only. I didn't fool myself for long.

There was a long, dark-glassed window and on the other side, were the vague shapes of richly upholstered chairs as if, perhaps, there was sometimes a classier audience than the three hulking men now propping up the walls with their shoulders.

At my whimper, one of them grinned and licked the remains of his lunch from his fingers.

If I had a chance, if I could and did run, would they shoot me?

They'd just catch me and beat me, again. My bruises throbbed. I was too chicken to volunteer for that, even if death seemed to beckon.

This man's dark gaze swept from my bodice, where my breasts spilled, to my face. He spoke softly while staring into my eyes.

"You're pretty. The ladies with black hair make me think they're wild women. Quick to anger. Feral. Yes?" With the tip of the stick, he stirred the loose hair that fell over my ear – picking it up and letting it slide away. "Even if you are wild, I doubt you'll be that way long. He wears out slaves fast. To be fair, he doesn't ask for training or a perfectly intact woman. Obey me and I won't need to hurt you before he does."

His smile was a miniscule upward tilt of his lips, as if he couldn't be bothered doing a proper smile. He poked his stick at the chains wrapping my wrists, traced the line of my arm to my neck, then skipped to my face and let the tip rest near my eye.

"Nod."

I swallowed in my dry throat then nodded. The stick slid closer to my eye. Cold, I was so horribly cold.

Chapter 2

The back of the truck had been left open, as if my guards no longer cared who saw the trussed, chained, and beaten man inside. I tasted the blood from the last blow. My ear rang. Being whacked on the side of the face while your ear is against a metal floor wasn't good. I snorted back some of the blood in my nose. In the bright rectangle between the two sides of the door, I observed green, big-leafed jungle, as well as a motley collection of men, bearing machetes and pistols, from a local raskol gang.

Three of my guards were there too – they'd jumped out when we slowed and stopped. From the chatter it was just a meet-up of friends. Pity. If they'd had a fight, I might've had a chance to…

I strained against my bonds for the umpteenth time, felt the ropes tighten on my biceps at my back, the metal cut my wrists, and I gave up. My uppermost arm stung from the injection I'd just been given.

A chance to do fuck all. Who was I fooling? They'd locked my wrists and elbows behind me with handcuffs and chain and rope, as well as done my feet and thighs. My one bit of fortune was the hogtie link between hands and ankles had been left off since they'd hoisted me off the plane at some tiny airstrip.

I was in Papua New Guinea, back in my old haunts, and from what I'd heard of Vetrov, soon to be tortured to death for my misdemeanor of helping a woman to almost escape from his little slave house back in Australia. Wherever Jazmine was, I prayed she was better off than me.

Not likely, but I could hope.

Sweat dribbled into my eye and I blinked it away.

Maybe I could sweat away all my muscle bulk and slip free like a skinny Spiderman instead of the Incredible Hulk people liked to compare me to. From my para-military experience I was all too aware that muscles or even fighting skill didn't mean invincibility. Men died from being shot and macheted and burned all the same – skinny, superfat, or superfit.

Yeah, I was slightly fucked.

Never give up, never give in.

I resumed my watching of the proceedings outside on the dirt track. Birds whooped and whistled up in the trees. I counted five raskols armed with homemade pistols and various knives and machetes. Plus three of my guards, all ex-mil like me, and armed to the fillings in their teeth. Wasn't legal at all here, to carry, but they did. Their shotguns and shiny Sigs and Rugers were pretty weapons the raskols would be drooling to get their hands on.

The minutes ticked by. I was in no hurry. At the end of this drive might be my death.

Then a little girl in a grimy dress hopped up on the back of the truck and smiled at me. Nine, ten years old?

What the… I blinked. Still there. I wasn't tripping out on dehydration or concussion or whatever drug they'd injected me with a few minutes ago.

I croaked out a sound, then licked my lips and swallowed, tried again. "Hello."

Her smile widened.

Here was someone who might be innocent enough to help. I knew some of the pidjin English they spoke here. "Want gut moni?" But would I get her in trouble?

If I told her an address, would I get my friends killed? They were…

My surroundings fuzzed out, my tongue thickened.

Drug…

And fuzzed back in. And she was gone. *Fuck.*

My windpipe gurgled as I breathed and I coughed. Then the girl was back again, screaming and running from a snarling beast of a dog. She leaped into the truck and scrambled to me, the dog's jaws snapping shut just a few inches shy of her leg. With my tied-together feet, I booted the mutt in the jaw and sent it sprawling back a few yards. A young man yelled at and kicked the dog then chained it up.

He levelled his gun at me where the girl huddled quivering my side.

Typical New Guinea justice. They'd probably trained the beast to attack but that didn't help its case. Not that I wanted the girl mauled.

Last I saw of the boy was a scowling face as he hauled her out of there. A sheathed knife fell from his belt and I stared stupidly at it, almost scraped it to me with my heel before he snatched that up too.

"Fluck it," I slurred, my tongue now thick enough to use for toast. Missed a chance. And goodbye world. I could feel myself going.

Blackness swirled in.

I awoke staked out, flat on my back, in an open yard. Glaring sun above. Dirt all around me. My sight was still hazy. Damn it. Who was paying for this trip? I wasn't even getting an in-focus view of my holiday resort.

"Who is this?" someone asked from just beyond my vision. Male or female? They could've been Martian for all I could tell.

I swung my head, dirt grating against the back of my head. My thick lips were stuck together. My eyelids too. But I kept that one eye open a half an inch.

"Pieter. A traitor. He let us down, helped the Jazmine girl escape, got men killed."

My hearing seemed filtered through a ton of mud.

"He's acceptable in appearance. I like him. I don't know why you thought you could get rid of the girl without my agreement. She's special to me. I need to see her damaged and humiliated, slowly. Clean him up. I want to see him play with her. Maybe more if he does well."

"He's dangerous."

"Then take care with him. I pay well. Vetrov will agree."

The crunch of boots came closer and someone blocked out the sun.

Time sludged past, the blue sky fading in and out.

He leaned over me. "You lucky bastard. I don't get to see you die today. We were filming you today too. One last kick for luck."

His boot thudded into my side and the world fuzzed out again.

Chapter 3

On the second day, a guard yelled through the door, "The manager will be seeing you later."

Overnight I'd heard others, outside, speaking to this *manager*, the man who wanted me to call him sir. They called him sir too. Or sometimes Gregor. I decided not to try calling him that without permission. It seemed likely to earn a punishment. How easily I slipped into the mind-set of the conquered.

His weird, stilted accent sounded Scandinavian, and already I could imagine that voice haunting my nightmares.

I'd not seen anything when they delivered me, but the wind brushing through the trees and the animal noises betrayed that on the other side of that high-up window was the outdoors. I'd also heard the cries of women, their screams of pain, and some general all-purpose sobbing. There were other captives. If anyone here was having fun, they disguised it well. I'd thought this was some sort of way-point before they sent women elsewhere, after selling them. Maybe I was wrong.

Or maybe just some of them got to stay longer, have other things done to them?

The awfulness of this place never failed to impress me.

My memoirs, if…when I got away, would get me a nomination for horror writer of the year.

I sat on the edge of the bed with my hands tucked into my armpits and hugged myself. No one had left me so much as a nail file, let alone a way to tunnel out.

My room was simple. One single bed. Clean sheets. Across from the door was a deep alcove containing a toilet with a push-button flush and a sink with no taps, just a big button for cold water. A shower was next to it, also open to anyone walking in the door. I had a curiosity streak wide enough to embarrass a cat. I'd stared at my tapless sink and shower for a few minutes before it clicked. Taps could be unscrewed, made into weapons perhaps. Though I couldn't imagine a woman overcoming any of the hard men policing this place, I guess they were being thorough.

I rose and went to the sink to stare in the steel mirror. Just the steel collar on my neck said I was in deep trouble. Though I wore a clean black dress, with my red-rimmed eyes, streaked face, and messed-up hair, I looked like death warmed up. Where were all the other women I'd been grouped with in Australia? Had that been some of them screaming last night?

I leaned my forearms on the sink and though I stayed calm for a while, I wanted that release, here, now, when nobody was watching. The first tears merely dribbled down my face. I waited some more, my forehead throbbing, for the dam inside me to break. A sob cracked from my aching chest. I lowered my head and cried my heart out. The tears pattered into the sink. My sobs grew weaker. My legs trembled and gave way. I ended up on my knees, hanging onto the sink, still crying in silence.

Least when I was done, it wasn't far to go to wash my puffy face.

I was drying my face with my dress when I heard the small hatch in the door being slid aside. Then the door unlocked and I turned to look. Mr. Gregor himself. Where some big men stalked, his steps were careful and calculated. The blond stubble on his head looked unchanged. I imagined him beginning each day staring in the mirror, seeing his own incisive blue eyes, while he painstakingly scraped a razor over his scalp.

A chill shivered through me.

"Come here." The door shut behind him as he beckoned.

I hated that he could see I'd been crying. Hated my weakness showing. But I took a breath, pressed my forearm into my eyes and did a quick sniff as if it was nothing and maybe I'd had something in my eye. I walked to him even though hugging the wall was where I wanted to be.

Whenever I was close to one of my captors, fear kicked in. I'd been in their hands for long enough to have memories that haunted me. Zoe being made to sit still for the knife as Scrim taunted her – that was one of the worst.

"If I do this." He clicked his fingers. "You're to kneel." Again he clicked them.

I kneeled and felt the skirt of the dress settle on my thighs. I waited, staring at his shorts. The man had bright green surfer shorts on today and it was so weird seeing those, and his hairy knees. *Slice* was the brand name. How apt.

"Give me your arm, Jazmine."

I held it up and tried not to flinch when he took my wrist.

"This is yours now. Wear it every day." He slipped a silver bracelet on my wrist and fastened it – something tiny, with petite wings, dangled from the chain, catching the sunlight streaming from the one tiny and barred window high up on the far wall. "If I see you without my angel, I punish you. If I ever take it off you, it will be because you've been very bad. Okay?"

I nodded.

"Say yes, thank me, and kiss my hand." He put the back of his hand near my mouth.

Even in this there was menace. His eyes narrowed as I leaned forward.

As if I wouldn't. I kissed his fist. "Thank you, sir." *You utter pukeworthy bastard. Your mother was a fucking pig and so are you.* I put on a fake smile.

"Good." He patted my head. "You're a lucky, lucky woman. Someone has taken a liking to you. You're going to be part of a show that should last a few weeks. As long as you perform."

Perform? My fear spiked up a notch. "What does that mean?" His hand drew back as if to slap me and I hurried to add, "Sir?"

He chuckled. "You will see. Tonight, perhaps, is your first time."

My throat closed. I held my breath and rested my laced fingers in my lap.

"Be good, remember? Hmm?" He ran his fingers down to my cheek. "You have to be an angel for me. We mustn't disappoint the customers, must we? Not like the last girl."

Slowly, I shook my head. The bracelet on my wrist was cold, as if it had recently come from a fridge. A tiny red spot on a link speared my attention. *Oh fuck.* My reply was soft. "No, sir."

I prayed he didn't have the final say in this – in assessing whatever I was to do. Someone liked me. I shut my eyes. *Liked.* Maybe they just wanted me to dance or do a striptease?

Panic was there in my mind, coiled up, ready to explode. I screwed it down tight. *I mustn't. I mustn't.*

This wasn't going to be a dance.

Late that afternoon they came for me.

Their standard procedure, I discovered, was to have my wrists cuffed together before me and a heavy bag over my head – strapped around my neck over the top of the steel collar. The only light and air came from some neat round holes down near my mouth. When I breathed, the bag sucked in. I'd had asthma as a child. It'd left me with a fear of being unable to breathe. A little desperate, but trying not to draw attention, I plucked at the fastening strap.

If they tightened it, I might choke. The potential for pain, for death, for nastiness, was so ripe in the air here that I might suffocate from that alone.

Someone breathed, from an inch beside my ear. I froze. They were watching me.

"That's so you can't see. Leave it alone, my angel."

Him.

I lowered my cuffed hands, shut my eyes, and tensed. Even my pussy clenched in. I had no underwear on. Also standard operating procedure with these men, like the bag, like the ever-present danger.

"Walk," he added.

They drew me onward down some maze of corridors until we entered a room. I could tell from the openness, the echoes. My attempt to see through the holes at my mouth revealed the concrete block on which they'd displayed me when I arrived here.

He'd done nothing to me that time. Only scared me. This time...

From somewhere in front of me, he spoke. I raised my head.

"Jazmine, we have a rich client who wants to see things done to you. I don't have all the details, but I think they want to see you hurt, in stages. You might think this is bad, but it's not. Do you want to know why?"

Fuck, no, I don't, you asshole. I curled my toes in, feeling the hardness of the concrete.

He poked my breast with his stick. "Nod, girl."

I nodded.

"Most of the clients love the sex with the girls, along with the power games. They like having a slave who will do whatever they ask. The ones who like to watch shows can be a little different. In this one, I sense, maybe anger? You must give them screams and crying. Give them a *big* show. Yes?"

A show? Was he crazy? Tiredness sifted into my flesh, weighed down my limbs.

"Are you wondering why, Miss Jazmine? It's because I think, at the end of this, you will not be happy." He clicked his fingers. "You must make it last."

Was he saying they meant to kill me...after? At the end? Fuck this. My heart knocked hard and fast. But, he'd clicked his fingers. His harsh sigh and the *whoosh* of a stick being drawn back made me drop to my knees.

Make it last? If I made myself not scream, would that get it over with quicker? Or slower? Which did I want? That was the question. Such an evil,

evil question. Was that why he'd told me? To make me agonize over impossible decisions? I was sure he didn't do it out of goodness.

Did I have the courage to not scream if I was hurt badly?

Images slipped into my head of me bleeding, writhing, of my hands cut off. *God.* I shuddered and swallowed acrid bile.

"Stay kneeling. Put your palms on the floor."

I did so.

What were they going to do?

Last time, I'd been in here, I'd shaken. I was wondering why I wasn't shaking, feeling separated from myself, eerily unemotional, when it began. My arms shook, then my legs until, like a cartoon character, even my teeth chattered.

After fiddling with my wrist cuffs, he picked me up with his arm slid between my legs and supporting my weight. My palms stayed on the floor while he turned me like I was the dial of a clock, set on the wrong time.

The pressure of his forearm there, on my most intimate place, was casually invasive. I'd been demoted to the level of a piece of furniture.

He put me down. With his palms, he pushed my thighs a little farther apart.

"There. Now we can see you properly." His stick he laid across the back of my neck, pressing me down. "Stay there unless someone tells you to get up. If you're wondering why the concrete, it's so we can hose it off afterward. Sometimes the girls get a little...messy. Your friend will be here soon. You might want to relax. He's a big man."

I heard his footsteps then the close of the door. Subtle tugs confirmed he'd locked my cuffs to some anchor point on the floor.

Kneeling there on the hard floor made my knees ache. I shifted my weight from one knee to the other, afraid to budge more than a few inches from where he'd left me.

The door creaked open, clicked shut, and there were more footsteps – shuffling ones and firm ones, then the mutter of low voices.

I was all too aware of my vulnerability and of how the dress had ridden up my back when Gregor had moved me. Whoever was at the door behind me could see everything. I shuffled my legs together and concentrated on sucking air through the mouth holes. It was dark in here, but not as dark or terrible as whoever was out there, or what might be about to happen to me.

I don't want to hurt. Please, let it be fast.

A speaker squealed as someone turned it on. "Testing, testing. Okay, you can hear me?"

Someone in the room answered yes.

"Good." This time, despite the overriding buzz of the speaker, I recognized the voice. That was Him again. Who was in the room with me? "Pieter. Our client says one rule only today. Make it last. You can do what you want to this woman, as long as you fuck her, but no permanent damage. This is our little trial run to see if you are...suitable. Make it entertaining."

The words spun through, like dry leaves tossed by a silent wind. I could hear them repeating, the vowels, the consonants, the assembled sounds, but not understand. Those words couldn't be about me. They just couldn't.

Couldn't. Couldn't. Uh-uh.

Pieter though? Him? He was the only man who'd shown any kindness toward me since my abduction. The last time I'd seen him had been after my recapture and he was being beaten. He was alive and they were going to make him...fuck me.

Why? Was he in on this? Had he always been? Had it been a lie? Not that I hadn't lied to him. But I'd needed to. Maybe he'd found out.

The pressure in me built. In my attempt to not make a noise, one sound escaped my throat. I bit back the terrified half-swallow, half-squeak. I wanted to be little, to be so small they wouldn't see me. I wanted to hide in this bag and never, ever, be seen by *them.*

Behind me, metal clinked.

"No. No, no," I whispered, clawing into the floor with my nails. "Go away."

They didn't. Of course.

Chapter 4

The speaker fell silent.

They'd fed me and let me shower under guard, given me pants and a shirt. I stood there, still dog-tired from the combo of beatings and drugs, but also furious and blind. The sack idea was a sound one. Unless you were some superhero who could sense the drop of a hair from ten yards away with your eyes closed, being blind made the strongest man into a victim.

Now, they were setting me free for the worst of reasons. The fuckers. I flexed my muscles covertly, clenched and unclenched my fists, getting ready for when the last restraint fell away. Kicking somebody's head in was always on the menu, if they gave me an opening. If they made a mistake. If you waited long enough, everyone made mistakes.

I couldn't see the room with the canvas sack on my head but I could smell it. Beneath the scent of cleaning fluids was a thick aroma of sex, blood, sweat and, yes, fear. Whatever had been done in here, the consequences had leached into the walls.

You could smell fear. In my days in South Africa, I'd had my fill of being scared shitless while enforcing the law, while shooting soldiers in the bush when I could barely see a few yards ahead of me and they were shooting back. I'd smelled the stench of fear and adrenalin from a crowd as they hacked to death a man in front of me. Fear and me were drinking buddies from way back.

As they unstrapped and uncuffed my arms, leaving only the chain-linked manacles on my ankles, I ran through what Gregor, the manager of this house had said.

"Remember. Your job is to make love. To make her suffer, a little. If she makes no interesting noises, *hmm*, we will take you off the job. For her sake, do it right."

Damn, that creep deserved to die. For calling it love, for starters. What they wanted from me made me want to vomit.

The strap around my neck was unbuckled and the sack removed. I squinted, adjusting to the bright fluorescent lights ten feet above.

"I am watching you from behind bulletproof glass. Do not make us shoot you, Pieter. Do not harm the young man who has freed you."

I did a circle on the spot and I watched the man back away toward the door then lean against it. He wasn't armed and he was the only person in here – apart from me and the woman kneeling, facedown, in the middle of the room. If I attacked him, I was certain I wouldn't get out of this room alive. They wouldn't be stupid enough to give me someone they weren't willing to sacrifice. Poor bastard.

I grinned at him wickedly, to let him know that on a bad day, I might use him to decorate the walls with red.

The woman.

I inhaled, let it out. *Kak.* They hadn't said her name, at least, I didn't think they had...but I knew who this was, even with her head covered – Jazmine. The waves of ebony hair cascading over her shoulders were unmistakable. *She* was unmistakable.

The blatant display of her cunt shocked me. I should have expected such things, here. To my dismay, my cock stirred though I knew it was pure physical reaction. It didn't make me a bad man, just human.

In Australia, I'd helped her escape because she'd impressed me in many small ways – her courage, her selflessness toward the other women. She'd said she had a baby waiting for her and that had tugged at my better self too. But I couldn't hide from myself that her looks had influenced me also.

If she'd been on a beach, or asleep in my bed, I'd have happily watched her for hours.

I hesitated.

"Go to her. Do your job." The chuckle that followed came through clearly on the speaker.

I took that first step to her. What the hell was I going to do?

I'd done so many horrific things in my life that the Devil would have a hard time listing them all. But this *act* was on a whole new sordid scale of its own.

The manacles clinked as I walked. I could hear my breathing then hers and a faint tapping that I belatedly recognized as I stood over her. Her teeth were chattering.

Maybe all those men I'd seen die, who knew it was coming, had also had chattering teeth. Maybe the one with the burning tire around his neck and with the mob using their machetes and bricks on his body had shaken this much? Even if I'd been close enough, I'd never have heard him over the screaming.

I looked down at her.

The men I'd killed close-up were the worst. I couldn't forget them...their faces exploding, the teeth, blood, and bits of bone flying.

At least a man could fight back.

How could a man do this to a woman?

"Pieter! You're boring us. Fail and I have five men who will be happy to play with her."

"*Jou fokken holnaaier poes,*" I cursed Gregor in Afrikaans, under my breath. The man gave swear words a bad name.

She was terrified.

Why had they chosen me? I'd been going to be killed but tortured first. Someone had arrived and chosen me to do this for some reason I couldn't recall, though I think I'd heard them explain. It would be worse for her if I said no. They'd kill me outright. I'd go to my death with a clear conscience with respect to this at least. Even if I couldn't wash away the rest of my dirty past.

That was my easy path, the cowardly one.

But I looked at her and shrank. I couldn't do this.

Never give up. Never give in.

If I died, I'd leave her alone, at the mercy of Gregor and his client. To be gang raped by however many men he decided would do the *job*. To be hurt also – he'd wanted me to do that too.

The speaker buzzed as if they were about to say more. Decide. I dropped to one knee beside her and roughly undid the neck strap of her bag to show them I meant business, that I was doing as they'd asked.

"What are you doing, Pieter?" said Gregor.

"I'm taking off the fucking bag! You want me to get it up when she looks like a rag doll?" I looked over at the dark-tinted window. With the lights on high, I couldn't see who was behind it. "I need my women to look like they're human. Besides, blow jobs from sacks aren't my kink."

His laughter echoed a little. "You are brave if you wish a blow job from her, today. Keep going."

I was an evil man, but I wasn't this evil. I couldn't rape her without trying to comfort her. I slipped the bag off and watched the rest of her hair spill over her back. If I was quiet, maybe they'd not pick up my words.

"Hey." I smoothed my palm up her back to her nape, sadly admiring the flow of light as her hair shifted under my touch. She was exquisite, like a butterfly trapped in a jar about to be chloroformed and pinned down with needles.

Was it to be me, or them?

Some days you had to be bad to be good.

I pretended to gather her hair into my fist. In truth, I held her hair loosely, but I dragged her head back.

Pretty eyes, gray-green, and her face shone with the tracks of tears. "I'm so sorry this is happening."

I bent down closer until our faces were inches apart. I brushed her forehead with a light kiss. I wasn't a gentle man, normally, but I could fake it.

"You have to be brave. I'm Pieter. You know me. I'm going to do what they ask me to because if I don't, they'll get other men to do it. Understand, me, *bokkie*?"

I waited for her reaction, prayed I could get through to her that I didn't want to hurt her, that I was still on her side.

"Yes." Her answer was so soft. More tears slipped down her cheeks. "Thank you."

My heart broke more than a little then.

How I needed to kill somebody.

I shook her head with my fist. "I have to pretend to be hard on you. Trust me. I'm going to…" Not fuck, don't say that to her you *domkop*. "To make love to you. No matter what I say or do, remember, I care."

That was the best I could do, the most delay I could risk. Dying now would be a mistake that she would regret, not me. I'd be gone from this earth.

I pushed her face into the floor, stopping a fraction short of her hitting it with her forehead.

"Keep your *fokken* head down!" I stepped back as I unzipped my pants then nudge-kicked her thighs apart. "Open those legs."

She yelped as my toe dug a little too deep into the back of one thigh.

Every movement was calculated to look violent but stop short of hurting her too much. Yet I couldn't fake it totally or they'd know.

Thank god I had an erection, or close to it. Disgust vied with the necessity of this act. I had to do it. I grabbed my cock and massaged up and down, never more aware of needing to perform in my life than now.

Forget them. Forget they were watching.

Impossible. No, doable. Look at her. I concentrated on her, on the soft curves of her body. The swell of her breasts. Luckily my cock wasn't governed by my rage. I soon had a hard-on good enough to at least enter her.

Fok. They wanted pain. I stared at her there, on hands and knees, tense as hell, sobbing with each breath, and with her wrists chained to the floor. I steeled myself to hurt her. They probably expected me to grab one of the whips off the wall. My ex had liked pain and I'd given it to her when she asked for it and not just because I was a kindly husband. *I can do this.*

Every time I went to make myself go to the wall, I froze up. I shook my head.

I pushed her dress to her waist and smacked her butt a few times, enough to leave red hand prints and make her squeak. Then I stopped and said fuck them in my head.

I simply could not hit her more than this.

"Be good, *bokkie*. I'm doing it."

"Okay." The quaver in her word said I still scared her. Nothing would make this fine.

I knelt between her legs, centered the head of my cock on her slit, and guided it in. I sucked in air, mesmerized by the heat of her and the wet glide. *Fuck.* In that riveting moment of penetration, I let my gaze traverse her body and my hands caress the sweet swell of her hips. I was going to enjoy this, I knew it. I couldn't come and not enjoy it. My cock pulsed inside her.

She wasn't that wet. But if I tried, I'd make her like it too.

I did little rough shunting moves inside her, probing for the right spot. I moved into her to make her open her legs more then I sneaked my hand beneath and searched for her clit.

"I'm going to make you come too. Just…" I thrust in. "Squeal some more. For them."

"I'll try."

Try what? To come, or to squeal? Still dry. Fear maybe. Of course. Of course it was that.

"Forget anything but us. You're a beautiful woman, Jazmine. Pretend this is a date night. We've been to the movies and –" I gave up. I was no actor. I kept thrusting and working at her clit, her nipples, feeling for the reaction if I hit her g spot. Nothing. What did I expect? To my cock, this was just a fuck like any other fuck, but to her it was terror central. I might have to use spit for lubrication or it'd start hurting both of us.

Determined to make her happy, I altered position, then the strength of my thrusts. They wanted me to make this last, well, it was lasting.

"Jazmine. Relax."

"I can't," she blubbered.

I kept trying and got nowhere with her.

Overcome by the awesome feel of being sheathed high inside her cunt, I powered in, fucking her harder for a few seconds, and her breathing…stopped. Was that good? Bad?

"You like that?" I moved over her, one arm to the floor in support, the other wrapped around her breasts, hugging her to me. No answer. Was she still holding her breath? An inch from her ear, I asked again. "Jazmine?"

"Umm."

Damn, the scent of this woman, having her under me, being in her. I groaned and couldn't resist. I licked around her ear once then I bit her hard at the back, over her nape, and followed up with another firm, locking bite on her neck while I speared into her, smacking in hard, rocking her body back and forth. My teeth were anchored in her flesh. My cock had her at the other end.

Possession was an aphrodisiac that beat anything.

Her pussy walls clenched in and she groaned, her lower back bowed in a clear sign of a female inviting the man in, and her juices welled around my cock. My balls grew wet as I slapped into her.

Was it the firm hold I had on her? The pain of the bite? The altered angle? Did it matter?

"That's it." I did some little jabbing shoves with my cock, smiling as I heard the wet sounds of her pussy. "Take me. Fucking take me. You like it now, don't you? Say it."

Her *yes* was gasped out loud and clear.

"I'm in you deep. *Fok*, you feel amazing."

Her choked whimpers, the writhe of her hips, and the incredible tight suction of her pussy on my cock, drove me to haul her back by her hair.

I gave up on conversation and fucked her thoroughly.

At the end of it, she quivered under me, still moaning a little. They'd come to separate us soon. As I caught my breath, I stroked where I'd bitten.

"It's done. You're fine, *ja*?"

"Yes." She tucked her head under my hand then added quietly. "Thank you."

I frowned. A thank you seemed odd.

My next words seemed a little patronizing and yet also right. "You were such a brave, good girl. I'm sorry I couldn't make you come."

For a few moments, I *had* made her mine. We'd been outside this place, in our own passionate world. I toyed with a curl of her hair, winding it around her ear.

Her reply was even quieter than before, like she only wanted the floor to hear. "It was...good. I think I did come, a little...and I never come...with a man."

I drew back, staring. "What?"

"It was good." She smiled shakily, a small but definite smile.

Were we both crazy? Pride flared and I almost smiled too. Then nausea kicked in. The contrast between us here on the floor, and what was out there, watching us, tore at me.

The speaker crackled to life. "Pieter. You did a terrible mess of that. You made her happy! I think we must sack you."

Crap. My heart stuttered. I shut my eyes for a second then searched for her hands and squeezed them. "I'm so sorry."

Her nails dug into my fingers.

"Wait. Wait. The client speaks and tells me it was okay. Next time you will do better."

The bastard. I couldn't stop looking into her eyes.

I came to a sudden, yet flawless conclusion, as startling as a man finding the moon in his backyard. The danger we were in had burned away all the stupid nonsense that normally clouded men's decisions. I wanted her. Truly wanted her.

Given a clear conscience and a day without this insanity in which we were trapped, I'd have dragged her away by the hair and screwed her until she never wanted to leave my arms. Well, I guess I'd have talked to her as well. Small detail.

But I didn't have that day.

When they demanded I stand still to be restrained again, I let the man come over and do it, though I glowered at him – my arms were again bound behind my back at elbow and wrist.

I believed what Gregor had said. Stupid of me.

After more men entered and held me to the wall, they made me watch while Gregor strung her up from the ceiling and caned her to the count of seven. The thrum of the cane in the air and the thwack as it hit her ass and back, the red and blue marks…damn him to hell. Killing him shot to number one on my list of things to do.

"That was for not making her yell." He waggled the cane at me as his men let down her limp body. "See what you did to her? *Tsk. Tsk.*"

Her screams still echoed inside my head.

Chapter 5

What he'd done to my back…I couldn't look. When they brought me to my room, I couldn't look in the mirror. Not that I could stand anyway. I'd been mostly carried back. The pain from those few strikes with the cane had shocked me, and that someone could so callously strike me. I'd been lucky before. Scrim had concentrated on Zoe.

I'd never been hit like that. Did a human mean nothing to Gregor?

I lay on my stomach for hours, feeling the mixture of bite and throb. Every time I shut my eyes, the pain drew me back into the world of the awake. After inching my dress up my back and shakily feeling for the welts, I wept quiet tears. Then I lay there, just listening to the night. I had no light, only a faint, second-hand moonlight that came in the square window near the ceiling. The jungle sounds soothed me for some odd reason. The flap of wing. The cry of bird or bat. The distant crash of a branch falling from a tree.

It was life. Proof there was an existence without torture. I fastened onto that idea like a leech. I wasn't losing hope that I could have some of that again. I wanted freedom. I wanted normal, gray dull reality, not this insanity.

I wanted fucking boredom so hard that I wrenched my pillow into a ball as if by crushing it I could be like Dorothy clicking her shoes.

Take me back. *Now.*

But it didn't happen. I was stuck here. I could've put myself in one of my exposé articles and had it featured by every news service in the country.

Human traffickers enslave, rape, and torture freelance female journalist. Read all about the depravities she was subjected to.

I bit the pillow until my jaw ached and I rocked into it. *I want to go home.*

He hadn't been told to use a condom. I couldn't bear to deal with the implications of that. Not *now.*

Flashes of what had been done to me carved through my thoughts uninvited. Little vignettes of rape and hurt played over and over. Me, screeching while he whacked that stick on me, my feet not touching the floor, my toes scrabbling for a grip as I swung. The rope above creaking. The new scenes were added to the ones I'd already perfected where I tried to turn back time so that *none* of this ever happened.

If only I'd not gone out for a drink that night. If only I'd turned left for a taxi instead of going right down the alley to the car park and aiming to drive myself home. If only the assholes hadn't decided to add me to their list of women to sell to other, richer assholes.

If only one of those rich assholes hadn't decided I'd make a nice victim for his sadistic pleasures.

The weight of the sheet was stinging the skin on my bottom. I inched it off me, wincing when it tore loose in a few spots. I must have bled. Nothing I could do about it. I covered my head with my poor ravaged pillow. Slowly the deeper darkness let me fall into sleep.

At the tap of footsteps, I jerked awake. Pain blazed across my back and I yelped.

Someone sat on the edge of the bed, bowing it down, and a large hand was laid across my spine.

"Oh dear. What bruises you have. My, my. I'm so sorry it came to this but your Mr. Pieter did not do as he was told to."

Gregor. I gulped. My head was still under the pillow. I felt like a turtle hiding from a crocodile.

"Come out, come out." He chuckled and pulled the pillow from my grasp. "There you are! I have something for you. Ointment. It will be good for your wounds. Stay very still."

I barely glanced at him before staring at the wall beyond the headboard. I heard a jar being unscrewed and he shifted on the bed, rocking the mattress.

As he touched a finger to my back, the cold of the ointment and the burn of pain made me wince and try to fly up off the bed. His hand anchored me in place.

"Stay. I said to stay. You don't want me to spank you now, do you?"

I gritted my teeth, wishing I could do something bad to this man. Eyes closed, I made myself be still as he traced every welt with his fingers, rubbing in the cream with agonizing thoroughness.

If I had a gun under my hand, would I have the guts to shoot him? He so scared me that I knew I might not dare to try. If I failed, he'd do terrible things to me.

"Why are you shaking? Does it hurt that much? Such pretty, pretty bruises. If only you could see them like I do."

I shuddered. Light as the walk of a spider, Gregor's fingers trailed over my ass, venturing close to the divide, then he took a pinch of skin directly over one of the worst spots.

I hissed and tried to claw my way up the bed. Without releasing my skin, he fastened me down with his palm planted on the small of my back.

"It hurts. Let go. Please." I whispered my plea. "Please."

"No, no, no." He waited until I was staying in place, though gasping and crushing the pillow with my hands. "Now. What did you forget to add to the end of your sentences? Hmm?"

Oh fuck.

"You didn't say 'sir'. Yes? I was very lenient, considering your condition. But now I have to punish you. Be good or I will do it twice."

Punish? Not more of the stick?

But he shifted to the end of the bed and dragged me by my legs until I was over his knee with my dress gathered above my waist. I buried my head. I was whining as the first blow struck, crying out by the fourth. If he'd taken a hammer to me, it might have hurt less.

"There now. All done."

I panted, determined not to make more noises. He probably enjoyed them.

The door opened. From the sounds, several people came in.

I turned my head away, embarrassed as well as sore. Tears streamed down my face and I wiped them away with my wrist.

"It's your friend, Pieter! Hop off my lap now, dear girl, and say hello to your present."

Present?

God, I hated how cheerful, how condescending, this man acted. Like a demon babysitter risen up from the depths of Hell.

He'd said Pieter. I struggled off Gregor's lap then pulled down my dress. Sitting on the bed only made me flinch. I stood and pretended nothing had happened. That I hadn't been spanked and presenting my naked butt to these men when they came through the door.

How many of them had seen what had happened in the other room? Did it matter? They were dirt. *Despise them. These men are all pieces of crap. I'm better than them all.* I tried my best to look them in the eyes but I couldn't.

Two guards and Pieter with his head covered.

My muscles tensed.

In front of me was the man I'd been raped by last night. Even if he'd been made to do it…it bothered me. Why had they brought him to me?

They had him wrapped up in chains and leather and handcuffs. Gray shirt. Gray pants. His arm muscles bulged around the straps like he might explode them any minute.

He was big. I'd forgotten how big. He'd been behind me, last night, in the room.

My mind skittered away from even thinking the words for what he'd done.

They were releasing him, all but his handcuffs, and backing out the door.

"You can have him for three hours today. Your client, Miss Jazmine, has asked us to let you two interact." Gregor shook his finger at us both. "Do not have sex. That is a rule." As he spoke he went to Pieter and took the bag off his head. Then he went to the door. "I'm leaving you now. Back up to the door hatch so we can take off the cuffs, Pieter. Each time you leave this room, you will do the same procedure. Understand me?"

They were leaving us together. Alone. And it sounded as if they meant to do this regularly.

The door was closed and locked.

I studied Pieter as he did what he'd been told to do and backed up to have the cuffs removed through the hatch.

No sex. Thank god for that. I didn't know this man, at all. How many times had we spoken alone back in Australia before he'd helped me escape? Four times? I'd never been sure of his reasons for helping me.

If any man could be said to be lion-like, it was Pieter. His head was as substantial as his muscles and his untidy and ragged mop of shoulder-length black hair could've been mistaken for a small runaway pet. The gray streaks might mean age, or that he'd suffered extreme stress. Older than me, anyway.

The one fact he'd told me that seemed to tee up – he'd soldiered in South Africa. But on which side of the law?

Trusting him was the last thing I should do. Everyone had hidden agendas – lawyers, neighbors, boyfriends, everyone. He was simply a better risk than being Gregor's toy.

He looked at me from under his brows while massaging his wrists then he surveyed the room. All without moving from where he stood near the door.

My heart decided to go on high alert and pound away. Beads of sweat popped up on my forehead. Today was going to be hot, but this wasn't the heat. Pieter made me nervous. I shifted on my feet, shrugged. How did I greet a man who'd done what he'd done to me?

I cleared my throat. "I'd offer you tea and scones but…"

"You okay?"

To the point. Was I? Hell no. Stupidly, tears stung my eyes. I blinked them away, stared at my fascinating floor. "I'm, yeah, okay."

"You're not. Dumb question. Come. If you can stand me. Come." He beckoned me to him.

What? I was baffled.

He looked down. Shook his head. "I know you must be going in circles. Things like this mess with your mind. This is my territory. I've seen enough in my life to make this a walk in the park. But you…" He looked at me again from under those thick, gorgeous eyebrows that I was crazy to be admiring. "You need a *fokken* hug."

"Uh. No." I tried to back away and my knees hit the bed.

"No?" His gaze was so searching he probably knew the color of my panties. Wait. I had none on.

I couldn't sit. I wasn't going to lie down with him here. My legs started to tremble and I put a hand out to the headboard and missed. *Shit.*

His sigh was loud enough to make me frown.

"What?" I had to get him out of my face. "Do you think you could lie on the floor, because I… I don't have a chair." And I needed to lie down fast before I fell over.

"What did he do to you? Just now? Did he do something?"

I felt the heat as my face reddened then cold rushed in and prickled down my body. I swayed. "He, umm, hit me, yes." I hurried on. If I fainted, I'd never forgive myself. It seemed ridiculous to be embarrassed before Pieter, but I couldn't help it. "It was nothing."

Go fucking lie down.

That assessing stare of his was going to wear out the room atmosphere.

"You *poepol*," he muttered and he walked toward me.

"What does that mean? What are you doing?"

"Means idiot." Then he opened his arms and slowly, while watching me, as if to see if I was going to punch him or something, he half-closed his arms around me, stopping just short of touching.

I froze. The scent of this man so near…he smelled good. Warm. Intense. It signaled humanity to me.

I should not trust him. He'd been with them, worked *for* them. I hadn't even liked touching my assorted boyfriends, some days. Touching wound me up like a spring.

My eyes, traitorous things, watered and I felt more tears well and trickle down my cheeks. I sniffed. Fuck him.

"Come. You need this, *bokkie*."

"*Bokkie*?" I wiped at the tears. Another stupid foreign word.

"Little doe," he whispered. "It's an endearment in Afrikaans. "Please. You'll make me happy too. I need a hug."

"Little doe?" I giggled. "You need a hug?"

I frown-cried. More fucking tears.

I hung my head and wiped my palms up my face, speaking past my fingers. "This is all so stupid."

I shouldn't. It'd give him the wrong idea, that I liked touching.

But I took a small, shuffling step and I fell into his embrace. Without saying another word, he delicately closed his arms on me, as if I might break. I slipped my own around his broad back and I sobbed for ages, wetting his shirt. He rubbed between my shoulders. High enough, I realized, to miss where Gregor had hurt me. He remembered. And he was right. I needed this. Needed someone to hug.

If he was faking all this caring shit, he was doing it so bloody well.

Chapter 6

When she was done with most of the crying, and her legs seemed ready to give way, I picked Jazmine up to put her on the bed. Her small protests, I ignored.

"I'm not a child." She wriggled as I lowered her then she glared up at me.

"Shush." I put a finger to my lips. "You know you need to do this. I bet you got no sleep last night. Hmm?" I looked about, shrugged. "And like you said, no chair."

Her laugh was dismissive. She propped herself up on her elbow. "It feels wrong lying down when you're…" She nodded at where I stood.

"*Ja*. Well there's only the bed." I thought about joining her. I was tired too.

Despite my comment about this being a walk in the park for me, it wasn't. I'd slept very little. I'd never had a woman in this sort of traumatic situation to worry about before. Never been a prisoner. I was used to acting, to fixing things by violence or by negotiation. The more things got planned ahead, the better too, with multiple contingency plans for when things went wrong.

I had a ton of *kak* to dig up before I could plan ahead here. For starters, why her? Was there a rhyme or reason for this? Or was it random?

I could check out the room first? Her big, frightened eyes decided me. Seeing those did odd things to my insides. No matter how confident she was acting, that hug hadn't been enough. I wanted to be her knight in shining armor and stick myself between her and anyone who might harm her. Fucked if I knew how I was to do that.

If I could've flattened Gregor and his men, I would've.

"Gregor said three hours but I'm not sure I'd believe his word on anything. He might come back soon and take me away."

"I was thinking the same thing." She looked at my knees as she said it, her mouth twitching, her long legs shifting as if she wanted to be elsewhere right now.

Not surprising. I made a note not to say that man's name except when I had to. The fucker.

I needed to gain her trust too. After what they'd made me do to her, I figured I'd lost ground.

"You poor sad –" I almost added kitten.

Uh. No.

Calling her by a pet name might raise her hackles.

"I'm not poor, or sad," she shot back. "I don't want pity, just..." She frowned. "Don't pity me. I'm still me. I need to be *me,* not some horrible lost creature to be pitied."

Her expression made me halt and think as much as her words. There was strength in this woman. Good.

"I like your attitude, but we have to talk and I don't want to be loud. Stay where you are." Without further warning, I climbed over her and lay down.

"What are you doing?" Alarmed, Jazmine looked over her shoulder. I noticed she still wasn't lying on her back.

"I'm lying down before I fall over too." I looked over her lower body, that stunning female curve of ass, and tried not to seem like I was perving.

Spooning was tempting me though it'd get me slapped. I guess I was as pitiful as her. I really did crave that physical contact. The hug had been soothing, warming, like a big bowl of soup for my soul.

"How bad is the damage?"

She sucked in a breath that turned quivery, as if my question had made her remember the pain.

The bed was tiny. Even with my back jammed against the wall, I couldn't help touching her legs with mine and making the mattress sink.

"It hurts. He put ointment on me."

"And then he whacked you again." Asshole that he was.

"Yes." Her lip trembled and she moved to wipe her eyes. "I'm sorry. I can't stop crying. I hate this. It's weak."

"Cry if you want to. There's no shame."

I tried not to breathe steam out my nose. Gregor needed a ton of karma to crash down on his head.

With her distracted and wiping her eyes, she overbalanced and rolled into the dip of the mattress. I caught her with my hand on her shoulder. Then I let go. "Sorry."

Touching her without permission was a big no-no, but my palm tingled where I'd contacted her skin, like she was alive with some strange electricity. Maybe lying down was a bad move. With her this close, my body was reacting in a way I couldn't control.

To my consternation, after a long pause, she quietly inched backward. "Is it okay if we still hug?"

Fokken hell…

"As long as you're okay with it." Her hair was under my nose. A subtle feminine scent. I inhaled quietly.

"Just be careful not to press on my back too much."

"Sure." *Or you on me.* The effect she was having on my ever-alert cock… I cleared my throat. It was surely the height of bad manners to get an erection with her cuddling against me.

Couldn't help it. I prayed she couldn't feel my dick with her back and butt being so sore.

Spooning was body language that screamed *fuck me* in giant throbbing letters, and I didn't know where to put my arm. I fiddled with my position until she took my forearm and drew it over her.

Thank god she'd nestled her own arm beneath mine so I didn't have the mound of her breast there, under my hand.

Okay. I couldn't check the room yet, but I could find out about her. But I waited and I watched her for a while. She was breathing so gently. Quiet at last. At peace in my arms and so little and sweet.

I barely stopped myself kissing the top of her head.

The last time I'd felt this way, it'd been a stray cat wandering into my yard in Cape Town. There was something about her I couldn't quite define that roused my protective instincts more than my other partners had, including Elenor.

It must have been half an hour, at least, before I said softly, "You awake?"

"Uh huh."

"Tell me about yourself. Where you come from."

Her answer was drowsy. "Sydney."

"Job?" I'd ask the easy ones first.

Pause. "A librarian."

"Interesting. And the baby?"

"No. No –" She stiffened.

"You told me you had a sick baby." Clearly that had been a lie. I thought about it. Whatever she said, I didn't really blame her for trying.

"I…don't. I said it to get you on my side."

"*Ja.* I figured that. Don't worry. I'd probably have done the same. So. Not married?"

Another longer pause. "Maybe you can tell me about yourself instead?"

I lifted my head and stared. I was annoyed that she wasn't willing to tell me more. It screamed lack of trust when here I was trying to save her life. Then again, could I blame her?

She shrugged and looked back at me. Her mouth screwed up. "I'm sorry. But you *were* with Scrim. I don't know you, not really. Why you were doing what you were. You were a slaver. You have to give me leeway. I'm not going to instantly give you the address to my house and the key to my grandmother's chastity belt."

I chuckled. "I think I'll skip that last one, and I don't know you either. That's what this is for. If you want my help, I need information. Plus, I think we have to learn to trust each other."

She was getting my help anyway. I wasn't going to give up on her, no matter what she said. If I didn't do my very best to get her out of here, I'd feel so *wrong*. But it wasn't just that it'd be yet another notch on the big stick that recorded all my failures.

What the hell was it that I meant?

I ran through my thoughts and feelings. If I couldn't get her out, it'd be like stamping *evil worthless bastard* on my own existence.

"Okay. I'll go first. I'm South African. I've got family going back to the original Boer settlers hundreds of years ago. My country is still a very conflicted one. High crime rate. I was a policeman."

"Was?"

Shit, now she was asking me the wrong damn questions, but I felt compelled to tell her my truth, such that it was.

"I was in a special part of the police that got called out to control super-violent situations."

"But you left?"

"I did." I shut my eyes. "Due to a stupid mistake I made, my brother was killed by officers of my unit during a political demonstration. That's when I left." And my wife left me. I deserved it, though. "I joined mercenaries in a neighboring country. Fought for a cause I thought was right, for a while. Then I came here, worked here and there for a year or so then a friend introduced me to someone else. They flew me over to Australia and that's how I ended up doing what I was when you first saw me. I didn't know what they wanted of me until I got there. I thought it was to do with people being flown in, not out. Happens all the time."

"Then why didn't you leave?"

I sucked in a breath. "I did. With you. I wasn't with Scrim long. That was my first trip."

"Seriously?" She looked back at me, those pretty eyes topped by a tiny frown. "You expect me to believe that?"

"I do." I found my fingers had entangled with hers and I played with one of hers with my finger and thumb. So tiny. "All of that's true. My brother was called Johann. He died from a bullet shot by a friend." And I'd never forgiven myself.

"That's...so sad."

"Yes. It is. Now. You. I need to know why and how you were taken. It might give me clues as to what they mean to do to you."

Her frown deepened and she pulled her fingers from mine. "I don't think it will. I don't see how it would do that, but I was kidnapped outside a pub, down an alley. I was a bit drunk, I guess. I haven't a clue as to why. Random. I guess."

One of the things I hadn't mentioned to her was that I'd been good at getting the truth from people. What she'd said seemed as if it was skirting the truth. I wasn't sure, though. There was no way to check, unless she contradicted herself. I wasn't keen on liars. Once, sure, but repeatedly? And I couldn't see why she would do it now, of all times. I'd told her my past. Was there something wrong with hers?

"You're not in trouble with the law, are you?"

"Nooo." She edged away and winced. "No."

I let it pass. She was right, anyway. It probably had no bearing on what was happening to her here at all. If it did, I'd just kill her. I half-smiled at my morbid joke.

"I'm going to look at the room. See if I can find anything of use. If they let me back in here regularly, I'll have a better chance at helping you escape." Then I carefully climbed back over her and off the bed. I studied her one more time.

"Why are you looking at me?" She tugged at the hem of her dress.

I smiled. Hell there was so much bleakness here, why not? "I'm looking at a beautiful woman." Then I winked, ignored the way her eyebrows shot up and she seemed to have lost the ability to speak, and I went to check the room.

"Just telling the truth again," I added, peering up at the barred window.

I didn't discover anything of use, apart from a potential to rip up part of the bed to make into a knife. They'd escape-proofed it.

The toilet, sink, and shower were made of parts that weren't accessible, or removable. The window was so tiny only a baby could get through, even if I could get up there and somehow remove the bars. The door was solid metal, solid hinges. The locks looked complex and I certainly had no skills in that department. Maybe a locksmith could undo them, or one of my ex-customers, but not me. Though I'd try, if I could. I needed something to use as a lockpick. The walls seemed solid concrete or brick behind plaster. Give me a year of imprisonment and a secret spot to dig at and I'd dismantle or dig through it. I figured we had weeks, at most.

"Find anything?"

"No. We aren't getting out of here tomorrow, but it was worth it to see your face when I said you were beautiful."

She was rolling her eyes at me when the screaming started. They shut him up fast, used a gag maybe, but we knew. And we could still hear him. Somewhere they were torturing a man.

Jazmine put her hands over her ears. "That wrecked the mood." She sent me a strained look and I could see her hands were shaking.

I strode to her. "Next I get to check your back. Lie on your stomach."

"I will not!"

"Why?" I cocked my head a little.

Her blush was cute too. "I don't have any underwear."

"Ahh. I still need to check the marks from the cane. You need someone to look who is on your side. These things can get infected. I *have* seen all of you already. Please. It would make me less worried about you."

"Oh." Her hesitation lasted all of ten seconds before she sucked in her lip and moved onto her belly.

I was gentle as I pulled up her dress, careful not to look at her form in anything but a doctorly way. Well, close to it. I was a man not a *fokken* physician, and she was gorgeous.

Jesus. He'd used a lot of force. Her skin was split in a few places and the bruises from some of the strikes had spread inches, but they looked clean, so far. "They're okay. But you need to watch for discharge and growing redness."

"Okay," she said quietly. "Can you pull my dress down now? It's hard for me to twist around."

"Sure."

"How do you know so much about cane marks and what to do with bad ones?"

This time I wasn't sure if the truth was the right thing to say.

"Pieter?"

"My wife liked pain. She was a masochist. I used to cane her, flog her, spank her. I did what she liked. Do you understand?"

Her great green eyes seemed rounder than ever. "Maybe."

I could see she hadn't a clue as to what to think. Footsteps were approaching outside the room.

"She gave me permission. That means everything in the kink world."

I neglected to mention that I was a sadist. No point really. It would only freak her out to know I enjoyed making a woman hurt.

I had no more time. The hatch slid open.

"Come here, Pieter. Time to go home."

Fucking Gregor. It hadn't been anything near three hours.

Chapter 7

The sound of footsteps outside faded. I strained my ears to hear. Nothing. No cries either. Had that man died? Or had they stopped hurting him?

The room was horribly empty without Pieter in it. I despised women who couldn't fend for themselves and make their own way in life, but in a miniscule amount of time, I'd been reduced to wondering if the next person through my door would be coming to hurt me or kill me. And I couldn't do a single thing that stood a chance of stopping them.

The bruises on my back reminded me of that.

I was defenseless.

With him here, I'd felt, not exactly safe, but comforted – like I was more than just a thing, like I mattered.

Normally, I hated touching strangers. I stared at my hand where I could still recall the feel of his fingers on mine. People touching you when you didn't want it was creepy and it made me feel all surrounded, closed in. Liking it was weird and not me.

I sighed. I'd get over it. Fear was messing with me.

The man himself was big and scary with all his hard muscles, shaggy hair, and that black glower of his. I shivered, remembering a moment when he'd lowered his head and looked at me like I was maybe an enemy. Pieter had some nasty history but I didn't think he'd meant to scare me, because a second later he'd smiled.

If he'd sat next to me at the movies, I'd have moved away a few seats and checked for the exit.

A scene flashed into my thoughts. I was naked with a man advancing on me, scowling that same way. I shook my head.

Hah. I'd run.

And if he'd grabbed my hair like Pieter had done? Made me look at him?

"Damn," I whispered and pressed my hand between my legs. Crazy. The tiny climax he'd made me have was also messing with my mind.

I'd thought men just didn't have it in them to stir me that much.

"Picked a great way to find out that," I muttered. Then I shut my eyes to relish the spreading warmth from my clit.

They left me alone the rest of that day. The next morning a cleaning lady came in, escorted by a guard. When the unknown man started screaming again, she flinched and swore under her breath. I took a chance and asked her a question when she swept near where I sat on the bed. The guard was bored as could be, watching a fly buzzing against my one window.

"Who is that?"

Fear laced her eyes, but after a second she said quietly, "Polisman." Then she moved away.

The guard twitched his gaze on me.

Shit. The floor at my feet got my attention, fast.

That had sounded like *policeman* but was it? Surely they wouldn't dare?

Around noon, I couldn't be sure of the time as they fed me only breakfast and dinner, Gregor returned.

He was the one person who could send my mind into mouse space. I went blank when he stepped in, his shaved blond scalp had come round the edge of the door about when his boot did, but his fingers had wrapped round the door first. I recognized him even then, I think, just by his fingertips.

My heart thumped erratic beats. My whole body seemed to squeeze down tight – like one of my worst times when someone touched me uninvited.

The excessive reaction was explainable. Gregor didn't just touch.

"Here." He clicked his fingers.

As I stepped quickly over and bent to go to my knees his lips parted and his tongue flicked out. So fast, but I saw it. Did seeing me kneel give him pleasure?

I wanted to hide under the bed.

"Very good, little Jazmine, and how is your back?"

Little. Again that condescension.

My throat didn't work. Answer. I had to answer. His gray eyes dissected me. I forced the word out. "Sir. It's fine." I didn't want him looking.

"Really? Show me, please. Turn." He did a circle with his hand.

I shuffled about on my knees, and faced away, lowered my head before he could think to make me.

"Hmm. I need your dress out of the way. Pull it up then press your forehead to the floor."

Blushing, I did so. I waited with my bottom up higher than my head. A moment later his bug-like hand crept its way down my back, slow and meandering, as if it were tasting me. Spider hands, I should call him, or maybe tarantula, considering the hair on the back of them.

"Nice, but I think you need more ointment. We don't want you looking bad for the next time. A pristine canvas is best."

I swallowed. He could make even art supplies sound evil.

After he'd made me lie on his lap to have more ointment applied, Gregor placed the bag over my head and attached my wrist cuffs to each other. Then he drew me outside and along to somewhere else in the house. I had a moment of panic, as he pulled the bag off. Was I back in that other room?

But no.

I stared at the red, dripping mess, unable to decipher what my eyes beheld.

He clicked his fingers and I knelt on the dark stained concrete. A man. This was a man.

Strips of bloody bandage lay at his feet. They had him standing and fastened to an upside down *Y* shape of timber. His entire naked body seemed to be weeping blood.

I looked at the bandages again. Not bandages. Skin. These were strips of skin. With the stench and this savagery before me, I had to fight the urge to vomit.

His moans were the only noise in this bare room. His body, skin, and blood, a scalpel and a few knives, lying on a table, were the only decoration.

"I am a precise man, Jazmine. I like the mathematics of dividing a man or woman into pieces. This." He took a handful of my hair and tipped back my head, gestured with the other hand at his victim. "This is why you must always obey us. The House is not to be trifled with. This man was about to betray us despite being paid off. Obey and this won't happen to you. Yes? Nod."

I nodded, eyes watering, in his grip.

Oh yes, I understood this terrible threat. Only I knew Gregor by now, enough that I could see this was more than a warning of punishment. This was a demonstration of what he might do. He'd do this to anyone on a whim, if his superiors or his clients didn't stop him. I guess being worth money would be enough to rein him in.

This could happen to me on the day my client grew tired of me.

Blood dripped from the man's big toe and splattered into the small pool on the floor.

The man lasted another day before I stopped hearing him.

They let me see Pieter, a day after that. Fifteen minutes together, just long enough to say hello and sit on the bed to talk a little. After my denial of needing a hug, Pieter gave up. I asked and found out that polisman meant policeman in New Guinea pidjin language.

"If we're lucky," Pieter said, "that may come back to bite him. Cops don't like their own being killed, and if they find out what's happened, this place will be shut down, no matter who's been bribed.

I nodded. That any police would overlook what went on here was appalling. I didn't hold much hope of anything coming of this. "Have you found a way to escape?" I asked, leaning in and saying it softly.

"No. Not yet."

On Saturday afternoon, Gregor arrived to tell me Pieter was coming to see me. I couldn't help but smile at the announcement.

He smiled back in the biggest, broadest smile I'd yet seen on his face. Cold crept up my spine. "It is good to see you happy. Tomorrow too, you have another date with our client and your Pieter." Then he left and the locks on the door clicked.

Happy? If you ever saw an evil clown with its makeup off, I was sure it would look like Gregor. Whatever Scandinavian country he came from, the crime rate probably dropped a hundred percent the year he left.

It took me a while to remember to breathe.

The small fat lizard that had made a home of my room skittered across the wall on the other side of the door. At night it arrived to eat the flying bugs that battered themselves against the light on the ceiling. If only I could walk on the ceiling like it could.

I didn't like it when Gregor was happy.

When Pieter arrived he didn't look at me. The guards left and his manacles were removed via the hatch. I shifted over on the bed to give him room, feeling as if I was inviting over my executioner. The air seemed stiff and filled with prickling tension.

He slouched on the bed and half-turned to study me in that under-the-brow way of his, then he searched for my hand with his own.

I tucked mine in my lap, shook my head. "What is it? Tell me. I know about tomorrow."

"They've given me an ultimatum…again. I have to hurt you tomorrow. Give them a show, and I have to do it worse than last time.

I didn't have the words. I shook my head again and mouthed a no.

His eyes were kind and he looked at me as if to see if I had something to say before he continued. "I believe I can do this in a way that won't be as bad as you think. I can lessen the pain."

Frantic, I watched his face for some clue. "How? You have a drug I can take?" Unwanted tears dribbled from my eyes and I swiped at them. "I don't want to be horribly maimed." I almost asked him to kill me. "I've seen what happened to that policeman. Gregor cut pieces off him. Don't you ever do that to me."

His Adam's apple moved in a quiet swallow. "I wouldn't, Jazmine. No matter what. I want to get you out of here, alive, intact."

Intact sounded so clinical, but I clutched at the hope.

"Can you?"

"Not yet. I'm working on it."

"Oh."

This time when he took my hand, I let him. The squeeze on my fingers made me look up.

"So. What do you mean by lessen the pain then?"

"It's what I did for Elenor. She liked pain but mixed with pleasure. I think if I do the same for you, it'll not hurt as much."

Uh. I blinked, sniffed away the tears. "You mean sexual pleasure, don't you?"

"Yes." He squeezed my hand tighter. "They want me to have sex with you anyway. Whoever is paying for this wants you humiliated as well as hurt. But, to me, it's not that – humiliation. So it shouldn't be to you either. Keep that in your head. You're beautiful and I'm not fucking…doing this to shame you."

Did him thinking I was pretty make a difference when everyone was watching?

I was going to die inside, but if he didn't perform as they said, Gregor would do it worse. Maybe use his scalpel. "I can take it. I'm strong. This won't get to me."

"Good."

I was lying, but I was good at that. Practice makes perfect.

This was why Gregor had let us be together, so he could torture me with dread between now and tomorrow.

The rap on the door came way too soon. Pieter had to pry my fingers loose.

Chapter 8

When they pulled off the sack and I saw her, standing there under the lights waiting for me, I nearly turned around and said no.

I didn't because I couldn't. In those few seconds, I'd flashed through what would happen. They'd kill me. They'd hurt her worse than I would. The consequences ruled out self-sacrifice.

I'd done this before. Each time, would I have to argue with myself? Or would it get easier?

Though it was a new problem that had shocked me. I was looking forward to this, just a smidgeon, just enough to creep myself out.

Fok this.

Her lonely figure in the center, beneath the dangling chains, spoke of the purest of vulnerability.

There was so much room in here and so much equipment lining the wall. Diabolical stuff. Good things, depending on your point of view.

I walked to her, saying, as I drew near, "It's me, Pieter."

The poor girl was quivering already.

They'd left it all up to me this time. No tying her down in position. Just her, standing, with her plain dress, and her head covered by the black bag they used on her. Her wrists were cuffed at the front, but that was it.

Me, I was in suit, pants, black shoes, and tie. My best guess – this client had a fetish for women being molested by men in suits.

The speaker came on. "You have a blank canvas, Mister Pieter. A pretty woman to draw on. Do what you wish to her. But make it good." I could hear the amusement in his voice. "Wait. There is one proviso. Our client wishes you to cut off her dress."

Christ.

I held up my empty hands.

"Harrison, please, a knife for Pieter."

After a heavy pause, my friendly guard, lazing by the door, heaved himself upright and slid a knife across the floor to me. I picked it up by the brown handle and rotated it. Light curled across the steel.

Lekker. Very nice. Pity I couldn't stick it in Gregor.

"And Pieter, no excessive chatting to her this time. The mic registers it. We will know."

No talking? *Shit.*

The edge of the knife was well honed. The guard tensed when I stared his way, but there was no point in angering him. I turned to Jazmine, walked a slow circle around her, while she vaguely followed the sound of my path by tilting her head.

They wanted me to cut off her clothes? She knew I had to be rough. I should do it properly.

Her dress was thin and soft and my grasp of the hem made it ride up the back of her thighs. I gathered it some more until I pulled her off balance and she gasped and staggered into me. The knife carved through the fistful of cloth. Casually, I tossed the weapon in the direction of the guard before I tore the top of each sleeve. The dress slipped to the floor.

Naked and, *damn*, that ivory-white expanse of female skin. No bikini tan lines. I sucked in a long breath. Pervert that I was, I couldn't help looking.

With her head covered, she appeared more of an object, a *thing*, than my wife had ever been in our S and m scenes. But what a cute thing. The slope of her spine as it curved into her waist, the tease of her glossy hair across the small of her back, the tremble of her hip when I rested my hand there and pulled her to me, her ass to my groin.

I held her tighter, fingers digging in. So soft. My fingers dug in more, as if they were obeying another, deeper call, until she squirmed the smallest amount…and whimpered.

"I'm going to show you the other side of pain, *bokkie*."

I recognized the familiar zing of anticipation. Inflicting pain on women did things to me. Before had been different. This time, I had consent, of sorts. She knew what I did. Why.

I needed to allow myself to enjoy the sadism. It gave me a hyperawareness I'd never get if I stayed distant and gritted my teeth. I had to devote myself. All amped up, I was a gourmet and expert sadist, I could *taste* the pain with my eyes, my hands…maybe my tongue.

Ja, she was a meal laid out before me. I circled her, twitchy to get going, to see what toys they had.

This was bad.

Be guilty after.

I had to zone in, see every reaction, every flinch, every blanch of skin and trickle of blood from the strikes. And there would be blood.

I'd realized last night that blood was the only way I'd be likely to convince Gregor and co that I'd done it properly. I hadn't told her that. It seemed wiser and kinder not to.

Zone in.

Just me. Just you.

This was a woman I'd have jumped at the chance to scene with, if she'd ever asked me in Cape Town, when I was young and free and, yes, stupid. Getting my brother killed had proved my stupidity.

I sniffed. *Zone in.*

I must be Master here and dance on the precipice. Pain. Pleasure. Starting now, my little captive. That thought sneaked in and I let it pass. For this to work, she had to be mine in these scenes. Not theirs. Mine.

There was no safeword. No hiding. She was my woman to do with as I wished. My balls tightened.

Such a heady situation, enough to spin me off into space if I wasn't careful.

I'd long ago learnt to disassociate from the violence of what I did for a living. It acted as a buffer though some things still got through. I'd talked to a doctor and it was the same for him and the suffering and death he saw from day to day. Either you took that mental step back, or the stress would pull you apart. I could do this, though it was weird because I also had to keep my emotions engaged as a sadist.

Jazmine had no training, no buffer. She was an innocent. I had to keep that in mind.

I stepped away.

The jacket was uncomfortably tight. I took it off and tossed it aside, rolled up the long sleeves of the white shirt. No protests from Gregor? Good.

Be damned if I'd scene looking like a model from a catalogue.

Should I remove the bag? Perhaps being blindfolded would calm her?

I picked up the rags of the dress and tore off strips then took the bag from her head. After the barest glance at her eyes – she blinked at me and swallowed – I blindfolded her. With a second strip, I tied up her hair, out of the way of any implements.

I risked a whisper. "I begin." From the faint inclination of her head, she'd heard me. "Don't move."

I padded to the wall where a rack stood.

Floggers, paddles, whips, canes, leather harnesses, bondage gear. Nothing sharp or piercing, though you could do damage with any implement, if you wanted. Was this, what they had me do to her, so rare? It seemed as if they didn't aim for the darker, nastier, sadistic acts. Why now? Why Jazmine? Or perhaps they'd taken away some things to keep them from my reach?

I selected two floggers and a whip, then a crop with a rectangular end. The harnesses called to me. I'd never been allowed with Elenor. I'd been her top not her Dom. I had no such limitations today.

Fok. I almost salivated at a shiny black leather straitjacket with what looked like an open front. There were rubber-tipped forceps too. There were *D* rings on the jacket for attaching things like rope. There was rope. If I kept her still, it would be safer. *Ja.* And I'd possibly come in my pants.

For a man with death watching from the other side of the window, I was way too eager. But I'd faced death before and this was for the best. I banged my head with the side of my hand, stared at the stuff. Then I picked it all up.

Wrapping her in the jacket, which did have an open front, then connecting the chains hanging from the ceiling to the shoulder D rings, meant she was bound standing. The jacket encased her arms and, when buckled, crossed them over her chest and beneath her breasts so she was hugging herself. Everything I wanted was still accessible. Best of all, her tits were bulging out, front and center.

I'd found a spreader bar too and I attached her ankles to it so her feet were kept apart.

"Gorgeous," I said softly from behind, cruising my hand over her belly to her mons then downward, cupping her, feeling the heat of her pussy. I recalled how she'd reacted the other time, when I'd held her tight. I barred my other arm across below her bare breasts, squashing in her bound arms. Her breathing deepened and a small, almost imperceptible, shudder ran through her body. My middle finger, when extended, nestled beautifully into her slit.

Very wet. *Good.* I had at least one piece of knowledge.

"So, you like tight bondage?"

Her breathing stalled, and a second later, she shook her head vigorously in negation.

Here, now, I doubted she'd admit to liking her favorite food, let alone bondage. I eyed the dark window. She didn't know I'd set her facing them. I had my reasons, apart from letting the client think it was to display her.

"I don't believe you. But let's see."

Before they could complain about us chatting, I went to my pile of implements and selected the softer, thuddier flogger.

I took one breath, released it, and began on her back.

The wide falls of the flogger laced across her – back, breasts, ass, and upper thighs. I circumnavigated, painting her with red lines. I planned to cover her body with my strikes, sensitizing her to the feel of light pain. But I didn't dare keep this mild play up for long, not when our watchers wanted more. As I increased the zip of the leather through the air, Jazmine tried to turn away, her feet searching for somewhere to go. The chains held her in place. It would be hurting now.

I aimed some blows between her legs, slapping the leather near her clit. Light hits. Heavier ones on her thighs.

Did she spread her legs? Was that a breathy shudder? Eagle-eyed and greedy to both harm and please her, I concentrated on her pussy.

Her lips worked, pursing, pouting, and huffing.

Was it good or bad for her? She was new to this and I was new to her. I had a theory that most could be trained to like pain. It was only a theory. Some serious masochists craved the immediate, nastier, harder stuff, but this woman…I had no idea.

I watched. I studied her to get a fast degree in Jazmine 101. I picked up the stingier flogger and whisked her skin, here and there, then swung it in forcefully. What got her moving and breathing differently? What made her moan?

Ahh. Her face had contorted.

More strikes, more sting, until she seemed crosshatched in red.

I recoiled, just for a second.

What I was doing? This was terrible. Deep inside, I knew it. I walled it off.

Afterward, I can help her.

Now, I had to be her sadistic torturer.

Panting, I admired my work. Her tits heaved. The leather squeaked as it stretched. I stepped in closer until I could feel her exhalations on my chest where I'd undone some buttons. My sexy victim. Her breasts were an all-over pink and her slit showed the puffiness of arousal and my blows.

Sweat saturated the twists of hair that fell across my eyes. It was hot, thirsty work, beating a woman. The tropical atmosphere penetrated even the thick concrete of this bunker-like building. I dried my palms on my pants and tossed my head to clear my view. Then I took her hair in my fist and kissed her.

"Are you liking that? Are you hurting?"

No answer. If I could see her eyes, would they be glazed? I was tempted to remove the blindfold.

I nipped her upper lip, listening to her small sounds of protest. Slowly, I ran my hands over her plumped and warm breasts. A woman trussed like this looked succulent to me. Biteable. Her nipples jutted out, tight, tempting me. I stooped to suck one into my mouth, circling it with my tongue, before sucking some more, then doing the same to the other breast.

"Pieter." She wriggled but I wasn't letting her go.

"Hmm?"

Moans and little gasps accompanied my sucking, as well as a jerk when I grabbed a handful of her no doubt throbbing ass.

But… Pain, remember? I stepped away to my pile of goodies and found the forceps, returned to her to decide where to apply them first. Not her clit…not yet.

I took hold of one areola with finger and thumb, and nudged my thigh onto her slit. Pleasure and pain, always.

As I opened the jaws of the forceps, I warned her. "Keep still." Her little step backward got her nowhere. "You can't leave. I've got this." Her nipple stretched in my grip and went no further. Despite her struggles, the steel jaws closed. The ratchet engaged.

Click. Click. A precision medical instrument. Exquisite pain. *Click.* Her loud squeaks made my already hard cock poke into my pants. I adjusted my length and an idea surfaced.

Why not? This wasn't a playground. I unzipped myself, but left the button done up, then went around behind her, and shoved my cock between her legs.

Bliss. Her thighs were slick with her arousal. When I paused, halfway along, her inner thighs shook. I nudged along the seam, pressing upward, feeling the head dipping ever so slightly into her entrance. Agonizing but amazing. How I wanted to fuck her properly. She tilted her pelvis back at me.

No condoms of course, but I'd been made to get tests prior to working for Vetrov. Why weren't they worried about pregnancy? This wasn't the time. Figure it out later.

My smile was probably evil.

"Want me in there?"

"Nuh-uh." But she gave a small, strangled grunt when I poked at her, and bowed her head. I loved those sexy, funny noises that turned-on women made.

"Going somewhere?"

I trapped her with my hand in a *V* under her jaw. Smelled her neck and bit back a groan. *Mine.* That thought was getting louder. I teased her some more, sliding my thick cock back and forth, in that slippery valley down here.

"Like being caught, hey? By a big bad man?"

When she choked out a *no*, I laughed. I dragged her pussy lips apart with both hands so I could fake fuck her better. Slippery, wet pussy. I closed my eyes to *feel.*

Wait. I had the second forceps in my pocket. Even better. Peering over her shoulder, I pinched her other nipple flat. In tiny increments, I squeezed in the forceps, stopping at the second click.

For a few seconds, her screeches threatened to crack glass, going high pitched and desperate. But still she rocked her body against me.

"Conflicted, much?" I kissed her ear, bit it, then I tapped the forceps to make her breasts wiggle. More of her juices moistened my cock.

Getting bound and flogged had turned her on. Pain too, most likely.

I frowned. Regret pinned my thoughts for a moment. I rested my forehead in her hair, listening to her, avoiding looking at the window opposite.

What I could do with you if I had you for real. Sad.

It wasn't to be.

Taking my cock in hand, I tucked it away, and zipped up. It took a ton of effort, but I managed. Sweat sheened her body and wet my shirt where I'd leaned on her. My own sweat dribbled down the side of my face. I wiped it away with my forearm.

Red lines crisscrossed her body. My fingers sifted over raised welts, felt the heat.

I stood before her, studying her succulent, panting mouth and I rested my knuckle across it.

"Lick me. Suck it inside."

Such hesitation. In the tiny movements of her facial muscles I saw how bothered she was by my command – in the wrinkling of her forehead, in the twitch of mouth.

This wasn't part of the deal, I knew that. Pain and fucking, sure, but this was a direct command...akin to domination. "Take it."

Her tongue emerged and she licked me once, then her head dipped. Her lips softly enclosed my knuckle. I felt my eyes widen and I memorized the look on her face.

I'd never been a Dom to Elenor. But in Jazmine, hell, I saw the possibility written in sweat and tears. If only we were free. If only.

I removed my finger and ran my hands over her, stopping at her hips. "I'm going to make you come now, after I make you hurt some more."

"No, please. Not more pain." The frown showed above the blindfold. She shook her head. In the leather of the straitjacket, her arms writhed as if to break free. "Let me go! Please?"

"Shh. I can't." My mean side wrestled with my good. Mean won. Besides, I knew I hadn't done enough.

I strode to the pile and fished out the crop. I beat her ass and thighs and pussy until her lower lips were as pink and engorged as seemed possible in a woman. I beat her until she was squeaking and dancing. Until she was pressing forward, eager and writhing, into the whack of the crop.

Ready. Ever so ready.

The next three strikes smacked dead center onto her clit.

Entranced, I watched her squirm for a fraction longer.

Every visible muscle on her body strained. She cried out, arching so hard her weight took her off her feet and left her swinging with only the chains keeping her upright.

"One more." I drew back my arm and thudded the crop squarely onto where I could see her little swollen clit peeking from her folds. Her screams as she came kept going for some time. Unblinking, I drank them in.

Like water to a thirsty man. Like meat to a lion. *Be still my fucking beating heart.*

Her last noises died away and she hung in the chains and ropes.

Strait jackets, I decided, had definite advantages, but I'd gotten side-tracked. I hadn't made her scream enough, had I? Not painful ones. *Shit.*

I swept aside my sweat-sodden hair then I undid the last buttons on my damp shirt, peeled it off, and dropped it to the floor.

I hadn't fucked her. Neither had I drawn blood.

Was the mic really that good? I leaned in so my mouth was a half inch from her ear.

"What happens next, you may not like."

Her head rose as she searched for me, as if she could see through the cloth. I wasn't sure why I'd told her that. Hadn't I decided it was kinder if she didn't know what was coming?

I took the forceps off her nipples then I reached around and undid the knot. Without the blindfold, her eyes were on mine in an instant.

It was several seconds before she figured out how to talk. "Why...why'd you take it off?"

She was as puzzled as I.

Then I knew.

"Because." I thumbed her lower lip, rolling it out until I could see her teeth. The tears on her cheek drew me and I wiped them away. "I'm done with pretending."

I hadn't blindfolded her to be nice. I'd done it to hide my nastier side. My sadism wasn't all there was to me, but it was me. I'd be lying if I said otherwise.

The whip was the surest way.

With one strike, I had her shrieking, with the fifth, I had blood shining in the mark. I turned her so her back was on display to the client and retied her to the chains. I'd meant to try to deceive, to smear the blood. There was no point to that when it was plentiful.

Control, I reminded myself. *Remember to stop.*

My never-ending question popped up. Was I liking this too much?

I swallowed and answered myself. Probably.

Chapter 9

Everywhere hurt, but my back and thighs had been fucking napalmed.

My last scream seemed to have scorched the air itself. The echoes rang in my ears long after I'd stopped and all I was doing was panting and hissing through bared teeth and hoarse throat.

A few times, I'd forgotten to breathe.

"Fuck you. Fuck you. Fuck you." My swearing was aimed at Pieter now, not the unseen Gregor.

He'd stopped pretending. Hah. I'd thought that funny for all of twenty seconds. Then the little whip had uncurled in his hand like an obedient snake.

The first hit had been a revelation. Many of the subsequent hits hadn't been as bad because he'd varied the power, but enough of them, definitely enough. I suppose it might have been a plan to stretch this out so Gregor was happy. I still hated him.

Pieter came to my front and flicked out the whip so it tapped my stomach. "It's done."

"Fuck." I gasped then closed my eyes. "Thank god." My sniffling might be blatant weakness but so had been the shrieking and the pleas for him to stop. "Then you can let me go."

A sound made me open my eyes. He was before me, one step away.

"No. Now I get to fuck you."

Somehow, despite the others watching, he'd given me the best orgasms of my life. The only ones with a man. That they'd come simultaneously with pain was mind-bending.

I'd wavered in and out of a strange state where nothing existed but him manipulating me, doing whatever he wanted to my body. He'd made me his puppet. The intensity of that sheer dominance as well as the fiery throb and bite of the instruments he'd used had sent me reeling. Nothing had mattered except what he did.

Now he'd ceased, I could recognize it for what it was – devastating and damn scary. Every time my back pulsed with fire, I was reminded of that.

With Gregor, I knew what he was – pure evil. Pieter had sneaked in and taken over when I thought he was on my side. I'd been ready to bear whatever pain he dished out. But not this, and he still wasn't letting me go.

"You hurt me so much. They won't mind if we don't…fuck." I hated how small and desperate my voice sounded.

The speaker buzzed and I flinched, but no one spoke.

"Shh. Stop talking. It's not worth the risk."

"You're talking!"

"I think they like it if I threaten you. Don't you?" He yelled the last words.

After a second came, "Agreed. We are finding this quite amusing. Keep going."

I flicked my gaze, as if to look over my shoulder. I'd almost convinced myself we weren't really being watched.

Pieter grabbed my chin, crowded in. "Here. Me. I'm the one fucking you."

I stared back, wondering who he truly was inside. Those brown eyes concealed something far more sinister than the average man. All my boyfriends had been wimps compared to him. He dwarfed them in height and muscle but also in something I'd always run a mile from – that *me, Tarzan, you, Jane* attitude.

I tried to shake loose his hold on my mouth but he only narrowed his eyes. "What are you thinking?"

"Nothing." That I'd been right to run from men like this.

He scared me. Yet something about how he held my face was so personal that whenever I relaxed the slightest I felt my sense of danger slipping away. And that was dangerous in itself. I resisted.

"*Ja*, the things I would do to you, *meisie*," he murmured. "'Meisie' means girl, in case you wonder."

I squirmed, the teensiest amount.

It wasn't the Afrikaans word for girl that was making me wonder. He'd already done more than was sane. What else did he want to do to me?

This wasn't just Gregor's game anymore.

My nipples were rubbing on his chest sending crazy, hot signals to my sex. The ache between my legs intensified, intermingling with the throb from the whip marks. The aftermath of the pain was...distracting. Strangely sexual.

I wrenched my mind back on track and prayed he had no idea how his punishment was affecting me. *Scary Tarzan, remember?*

One of his fingers played with the corner of my mouth. "Ready?"

Lips parted, I breathed slower, entranced by his eyes.

Then I heaved in a deeper breath and was reminded of the creaking tightness of the leather. My fingers could barely wriggle in the mittens at the ends of the sleeves.

A little panic reached in and blotted out my thoughts.

"Pleeease, let me –"

After a single shake of his head, he wormed the blindfold into my mouth and tied it on. "No. No. Be good."

He kissed my forehead then began to wind the whip around my breasts in a figure of eight pattern, linking it at the sides with the straps of the jacket, tying it all together in a neat pattern. Knotting it. "Pretty."

Then he went to one knee, took a firm grasp of my breast, and licked me.

"Uh." I could still talk in a gargle, just not well. My eyelids fluttered down. That tongue of his… For all of one second, I wanted him to stop.

The pressure on my breasts made them feel odd, like they'd pop any minute. Supersensitive, achy, but so nice when he sucked there. I shouldn't succumb to this. I didn't *want* to like this man touching me. Self-preservation drove me to wrench myself backward.

Only to be brought up short by the ropes at my shoulders and his tightening grip.

"Be still!"

The growl in his voice then his teeth applied to my nipple had my mouth slackening. I froze, shivering, all too aware of how much I was at his mercy. I was nude except for the straitjacket, my legs were tied apart, and the gag between my lips tasted bitter.

Where had the real world gone? I wanted to curl up on my sofa before my TV.

Wherever it was, I was here, tied up so tight he could use me every which way and I could do nothing. He turned his fierce gaze on me, still with his teeth fastened on my nipple and dangerously close to biting it off.

"Umm." I wasn't sure what I wanted to say, but nothing would come out intelligible anyway.

For the first time I saw humor in the crinkles about his eyes. His other hand had drifted from my back to my stomach and I felt his finger toy with my belly button, circling it.

"Now I'm getting somewhere. I have you quiet."

He released my ankles from the bar. Was Pieter letting me go after all? But he wrapped his hands around my thighs and with his tongue played games with my poor abused clit. He was gentle. I lost count of many times he circled it without touching, blew air over it, tapped it without engulfing it. The bastard. Need grew. I wouldn't cave in to this. But the pressure of lust built. Giving in was inevitable. I gasped out a choked *fuck* through the gag, jerking at the last infinitesimal licks he'd done. A feather would have more pressure. God.

Then I pressed forward onto his face.

Nothing.

He slowly rose, sliding his bare chest up my body to tower over me.

My throat tightened as I took in his male bulk.

The throb from my clit mingled with the ache in my lower stomach, the clawing pain, and the *dub, dub, dub* of my heartbeats.

"Hmm." For ages he watched me and I wavered, swaying, watching him back.

I sank, half aware that he was in some weird way hypnotizing me but not caring at all. His shoulder shifted and his hand pushed between my thighs. I felt the tip of his finger probe upward in the wetness of my slit, then slide effortlessly inside me.

I sighed at the pleasure, rocked back my head, half shut my eyes. There was nothing I could do and it felt so good.

His mouth covered my gagged one and with surprising gentleness, his lips and tongue explored me there, while his fingers below widened me, fucked me, explored my pussy.

"You know I want you. One day, I'll have you stand still, unbound, so I can look at you before I fuck you."

The statement shocked me.

The craziness of that. I had no answer and I was certain my eyes were wide as beacons. I tugged and was strangely reassured to find my arms still wouldn't budge. His jacket. His hand at my waist. His whip tied about my breasts. His gag. In the real world, I was often lost, scattered, running in ten directions at once.

Here, I was pinned in one place.

He smiled.

Everything flipped. Though I wanted away from here and them and their dirty voyeurism. Right now, here, I wanted him in me. And I wanted to be me, myself, I. And I wanted to be his. I wasn't sure they were compatible. If I was his, there might be nothing left of me.

Was this what I had been missing all my life?

"I can see you thinking. Don't."

Since forever, I'd shunned skin on skin. Yet in this moment it drew me, like a dewdrop of good among the horror. I leaned forward and kissed him once, chastely, with my bound lips, like a princess bestowing an honor.

His snarl and the roughness of his answer took me by surprise. He grasped both sides of my ass and hoisted me up to the level of his cock, shoving me back into the creaking hold of the ropes. I could feel the tip center at my entrance. At the first savage thrust, I yelped. Soreness reawakened. My legs were forced apart.

His flesh slapped against mine in that dirty nasty rhythm of sex. Each time he withdrew, his cock almost pulled out, and in that split second when he moved to re-enter me, I wanted to wrench him into me harder. His bites on my neck, migrated downward and he bit my engorged breasts, leaving an exquisite path of pain, of possession, of teeth marks.

Stunned by his onslaught, I didn't try to wrap my legs around him, though my heels bumped on his butt with each thrust.

I was going to have bruises on my bruises. He rode me hard, fucking me until I seemed one second away from coming. His own screaming grunt erupted as I felt his cock swell and cum fill me. I'd never heard a lover cry out. Though I hadn't come, I was panting as hard as Pieter. He rested his forehead in my hair. With my arms secured, I couldn't hug him, but his arms wrapped around me. When I hissed he muttered a sorry and moved his arms. At the *sorry*, I smiled. My thoughts wandered in that hazy zone of the well fucked, marveling that I had brought him to this.

When he pulled out, his cum dripped down my leg.

"Now you," he gasped, his breath warming my ear. "I'm going to suck your clit until –"

A hum arrived at the same time as a new set of lights flickered on.

"Step away, Mister Pieter. Time for me to assess your performance and have a little talk with Jazmine."

Our gazes met. The coldness of this surreal little world crashed in. As did terror. It wasn't possible for me to forget what Gregor had done last time.

Chapter 10

Whatever protection I still drew from Pieter's presence evaporated once he was restrained and towed aside. I knew why he couldn't fight back, yet I was disappointed. Stupid. He wasn't superhuman. The clutch of fear on my heart was unhinging me.

When the first sound of the speaker had died and we looked at each other, I'd glimpsed something unknown in Pieter's eyes. A worm of fear perhaps, or doubt, or anger. One moment he was all powerful, the next he was mute and a victim like me.

I strained to see the movements at the door from the corner of my eye.

Gregor walked over with precise strides, stick resting on his shoulder like a soldier's rifle. If ever a man could be called a shark, it would be him. He probably drank blood and ate the livers of his victims.

The gag was still in my mouth. Nothing more had been removed. I was cocooned here in the middle of the room, my arms strapped to my sides, surrounded by men who didn't much care if I lived or died. The chains above me clinked.

My nemesis paced around me, his stick tapping on his leg or resting on my skin when he stopped to examine a spot. I sucked in pain-laden breaths. My eyes watered. Poking made the throbs from the whip marks turn vividly hot.

"Ahh. He has done well. I had thought perhaps I'd have reasons to hit you but no. The client is happy. I am happy. You are lucky, you know?" He undid the gag and pulled it down. "I would have made you bleed much more than this."

Thank god. I sagged.

"And such wonderful fucking too." His voice rose up at the end in that weird, amazed tone he used. "Next time, whatever can we get him to do that will be better? Hmm?"

He raised his eyebrows and leaned down to kiss my cheek.

My shudder was small but I'm sure he saw it. How could Pieter do worse than this and not maim me?

The march back to my room was an exercise in staggering into walls as Gregor decided to pull me along by a leash. Without sight, I made errors. Though I sobbed after a few of the bumps, I managed to mostly be silent. Being naked was nothing in comparison.

I sat on the bed shivering, hugging myself.

The room temperature would be hot enough to keep a python happy but I was cold. Gregor hadn't stayed to apply ointment. For that I was grateful. When I finally wriggled around, ever so cautiously, to lie on my side, still naked, I fell into sleep.

Every five minutes…

I jerked awake…

Screaming…

By the next morning, I was stiff. My head seemed stuffed with knives. My muscles ached so much I wasn't sure I could sit up let alone stand. But I managed. Naked, I padded over to look in the mirror. There were bruises galore on the backs of my thighs and butt, only a couple on the front of my thighs, and my breasts were unmarked except for one bite mark. Fascinated by this, I stared at it and poked it. His mouth had made that mark.

Most of the bruises higher on my back were thin red and blue lines. Surprisingly, only three or four were cuts. I drank some water and returned to bed, wrapped myself in the sheet. The light faded.

A shuffling awoke me.

The cleaning lady arrived, carrying a tray with breakfast. I saw her through blurry eyes. She came closer and whispered something. Before I could get my fuzzed-out brain to check in, she went over and yelled something through the door. A young guard I'd not seen before hustled in.

A brilliant idea arrived. Pretend to be badly injured. I might get special treatment, even delay the next scene. Anything that might achieve that was worth trying.

I lay there unmoving.

The sheet had stuck to the wounds on my back. A little later, someone sat next to me, peeled the sheets off me, then turned me onto my stomach and cleaned my skin. Gregor, I was sure. The heaviness of their body, the scent, the overzealous cleaning as if every welt had to be swabbed – it all said him.

I kept my eyes closed, only wincing at the worst pain.

"I don't believe you to be as bad as you are pretending, little Jazmine." He lifted my shoulder then rearranged me so I lay on my side.

Fuck. I kept my eyes squeezed shut. Yes, it was Gregor. My stomach churned with horror. If he punished me...

"But, I will do as our client wishes. You will have a roommate from now on unless they stipulate otherwise. Now, open your eyes and look at me."

I edged them open, a little, then wider.

Though his square face and shaven scalp repelled me, his eyes were as blue as a beautiful ocean. Disturbing, that anything about him could be pretty.

His lips curved up. "Very good. Your roommate will be in charge of tending to your back. If you get sick it will go badly for both of you. In a week, we have another scene."

I swallowed, afraid to blink, but I had to ask. I dredged the words from my throat. "What will be done, next time?"

"Ohhh, you will see." He tapped my nose as if a birthday present was coming. "It will be a surprise."

The word *evil* sprang up in my mind, and kept repeating like a mantra, even after the door closed. I shook my head and bit my finger, hard. Then I clawed my hand into my hair and pulled until the sting made the word stop going round and round, and the awful sick feeling lessen. Despite all the leftover pains, I was tempted to sit digging my nails into my bruises. I wanted to hurt to forget. If that was possible.

I didn't do it. I hadn't had such thoughts since high school when an accident with a steak knife had alarmed me. I still had the scar on my leg from that.

Who would be this roommate? Another captive? I hoped so. It must be or he'd not have threatened us both.

He'd left me a new dress. A pale pink one. Plain cotton. No underwear. I pulled it on and found it the same length as the last one – it hit the top of my thighs and barely concealed anything. Bending over, even a little, was going to show off everything I had down there. I tweaked up one side of my mouth. What did it matter here? Zero.

An hour later, the familiar clink of chain and loud footsteps of several people outside made me suspect who my roommate might be. They never bothered with more than one guard plus Gregor when it was me.

Pieter came through the door. My guess was correct. I had no idea how to react.

I was sitting on the bed and I pressed my legs together. The dress was so skimpy. The bruises on my legs and butt ached, reminding me of what he'd done.

When the guards went to leave, I blurted out, "We'll need another bed."

They laughed.

Once freed, Pieter stood in the middle, waiting, looking at me.

Shit, shit, shit. I bit a nail or two then lowered my arm when he arched his brow. Bugger this. I wasn't going to be a wilting flower. What he did to me in that room could stay in there.

Then I had second thoughts, and third ones. Who was I kidding? That would be like ignoring Armageddon.

"They told me your back needed attention?" His question was soft, as if he was trying not to alarm me.

Too late. A whole mess of emotions had tumbled down on me – anger, dismay, shame, fear. These feelings, it was all him, all his doing. Yet he looked so normal. I hated that.

He'd raped me. At their demand, but he had. The first time, I'd understood. This last time, he'd gotten inside my head and fucked around with it too. But I wasn't showing him, this stranger, any of that turmoil.

Stonewall him. Make it a yesterday thing, or a future thing. It wasn't *now*.

I grunted, got halfway through a shrug, then winced and thought better of it. "I'm okay."

"Show me."

Fuckitty. I frowned. Admitting anything to him might be a mistake, but I couldn't be completely silent.

I repeated my idea, hoping to convince him. "What happened yesterday stays in that room. Here, now, it's gone."

"Yes. Now show me your back."

"Gregor looked already." I figured I'd let him look tomorrow. Or never. Now was definitely too soon to let him near me. My skin crawled at the idea.

"Do I have to go through this again? I need to know what it's like so I can tell if it gets worse. If you don't let me see it, Gregor may hurt you. I'm not having that on my conscience."

I scoffed, laughing. "You have one?"

His stare was direct.

He'd agreed with me, though, and smoothly. He'd said yes. Like the room had meant nothing to him. How could anyone think of what we'd done as nothing? Like raping me was nothing? Emotions pecked and pecked at me. I felt bloody and ragged and raw.

Why should I care what he thought of me?

Forget it. Forget. It was yesterday, remember?

I was being irrational. Tears threatened to squeeze from my eyes.

"I can see you're a bit scared of me. That's sensible. But I still need to see your back."

"Scared?" I snort-laughed, dismissing that notion, but when he took a step nearer, I flinched. My body knew what his hands could do.

He held out his palms. "You know I want to help you. Please."

Obviously he thought he was still on high moral ground. Just because they'd told him to do it. I wasn't sure of that anymore. He'd liked what he did to me too much.

My body was so tight; the slightest breeze might crack me. "How…can you be so *fucking* calm?"

Don't swear. It made me look stupid. Fragile.

His brow wrinkled. "Training. Experience. You had a severely traumatic day. You see me as the person who did it, but I'm not guilty. Think it through."

I had. I'd seen a fire blazing in his eyes when he beat me. He'd taken off that blindfold just to say he liked it. He'd fucking told me that.

Swearing in my head was okay, I decided. Just not at him.

He'd liked mind fucking me as well as fucking me, but I wasn't telling him I'd noticed that. He might use it as ammunition…next time.

Calm down. Be like him. Visible unhappiness is a weakness. Assume he's an enemy but act nice. I could do that because, after all, that was the sum of my whole life. Laugh, smile, and inside be like a prison guarded by walls topped with spikes with the heads of your enemies stuck on them.

I glowered then I smoothed that away. Firm but nice.

"You're not seeing my back."

"I've seen all of you, girl."

Girl, again. I hated that. Gregor said it enough.

"Woman. Woman is the correct term."

"Woman." His smile was patronizing. "I'll wait then."

"Yeah, like maybe forever."

At his movement, as if to come for me, my nipples tightened. I flashed into that state where I was bound and waiting for him…

Then he halted and gestured at the floor. "I'll sit there. Okay?"

I blinked. "Okay."

The floor looked so uncomfortable and when, after a few minutes, he shifted his backside, I threw him one of my two pillows.

Awkward. I sat with my hands in my lap. If I lay down I'd feel vulnerable. Just having him in the room was horrible.

I was worse than I'd ever been. Normally I could sit with people, shake hands, and be moderately normal. I eyed him, cross-legged and looking almost as awkward as me. Yesterday, for a strange hyper-crazy moment, I'd craved his touch. I'd wanted him.

I shuddered. Hypnotism or something. Being beaten had upset who I was. Of course. This was the backlash.

"I'm going to say a few things." He glanced at me from under those dark, shaggy brows. If ever a man plucked, he was a candidate. He wasn't Neanderthal or anything – kinda cute really, in a disheveled muscly…way.

"Jazmine?"

I jerked my gaze to his face. "Go ahead. I'm not stopping you." Him saying my name made my stomach do evil flips. Names were possessions. He hadn't earned the right.

"I've seen a lot of victims in my previous line of work. You're demonizing me. I understand. You're still in shock and processing it all. You don't want me to touch you. Also understandable. But you need to try to work past that. If we're to get away. We have to trust each other. If you won't even let me look at your back…" He shook his head. "That's square one. For trust. Plus it's essential. You have to let me."

Then he waited.

I dug under my nails.

With my hands, I pinched the sensitive area around my forefinger nail. The pain helped. I breathed and took the pain from all the bruises into account. If I shifted, my back skin did too. The small lancing pains all helped to distract me from the prickling tension that took over my head whenever I thought of him coming near me.

"Don't you have something to say?"

Damn him for sounding so rational.

I dragged in a breath, released it. "I…" *God.* No emotion, remember? "I can see your points. Logically, you had to, uhhh, obey Gregor."

"Yes."

Ah, fuck. I needed to set boundaries. "You see, I've never liked people touching me. This is making it worse."

Pieter nodded. A reasonable man. What a contrast to…

The man with the whip circling, hitting me, eyes like stone on fire.

I gulped. "I don't think I will ever be able to let you touch me again."

Except for when Gregor made him. I shivered, cold. My nails were aching and I made myself stop digging at them before they bled.

Calm. Calm, calm, calm. Calmitty fuckitty calm. He was looking at me like I was turning into a psycho before his eyes. Be calm.

"So." I eyed the floor. "You're going to have to sleep there."

Just for a split second, his gaze went deep, like maybe he wanted to challenge that. I stared back and he shrugged.

"I don't know how long we'll be in here together. I'm checking out everything again." He rose.

"Why?"

His frown made as if he thought I'd just said the dumbest thing so far. "I never give up. You should remember it too. Never give up. Never give in."

"Uh-huh." It wasn't a bad idea, really.

I said it to myself. The words were ones I could cling to, and it was nice to have this man still trying to find a way out. I watched as he looked up at the dome of the showerhead that was bolted flush to the ceiling, as if he could unscrew it by staring. Then he leapt up, grabbed the window shelf, and did a chin-up to stare out my…our tiny window.

I realized I had given in. I had decided whatever Gregor wanted, he was going to get. No matter how much I had to hurt.

Never give up. Never give in. Pieter had given me something good.

"What's out there?"

"The courtyard. First a covered way right next to this room, then a courtyard." He let go and landed in a neat crouch. "It's where they had me staked out when I arrived. I was supposed to die until they decided I had a use."

A use? Torturing me. My mouth hung open.

"Do you still have no idea who this client is? Whoever it is only visits weekends, so far. I'm guessing they're from Australia. Someone you wronged, maybe?"

There were so many of those. I'd done a lot of stories, a lot of dirty laundry had been exposed over the years of my journalistic career, but no one special sprang to mind. "No. I can't think of anyone." I paused, remembered my fake career. "Librarians don't tend to annoy people that much. Overdue loans, I don't think anyone has ever been murdered over them."

Though journos had been, regularly, when people like the IRA got annoyed. I wracked my brains for a clue. Still none.

He nodded. "Okay. Can I sit there?" He indicated the bed.

Ice swept me. "No!"

His nod was too fast.

I'd goofed. "How about we play a game or something?"

"Game?" His eyebrows shot upward. "Like? Noughts and crosses? How about I do something useful like self-defense lessons?"

That sounded good until I figured out the flaw. "Only if," I said slowly, "you can do it without touching."

"Hmm."

Even that *hmm* reminded me. He'd said it once, before he finger fucked me. I didn't think I'd ever forget his words.

I want you. One day, I'll have you stand still, so I can look at you before I fuck you.

Such dirty words – ones that even now made me look at him and see the animalistic, dominating man who'd given me both more pain and more pleasure than anyone else, ever.

How could someone repulse me so much yet also make me want him to walk over here and grab me and do nasty things? Subtly, I squeezed my thighs together, feeling the tiny awakening throb.

We were going to have to shower and go to the toilet with the other person in the room. I prayed I could get him to turn away and not look…and that I could do the same.

His self-defense lessons were to the point and though maybe not as effective as doing them with a partner, I could practice eye jabbing on my pillow and shin sweeps and heel-of-hand to nose smashes. Things like breaking the hold when someone grabbed my throat from behind, they'd have to wait. I wasn't letting him near me. Even when he sighed at my obstinacy.

The more I did, the more my stiffness ebbed. I'd be sore later though.

"So." I straightened and kicked my pillow onto the bed, scoring a brilliant goal on the headboard. "Does this mean I stand a chance at taking out a guard?"

The hesitation said it all.

"No?"

"No. I wouldn't try it unless it was one on one and you were truly desperate. You'd lose against these guys, but it's worth knowing. We'll practice over and over. There might be a chance, one day."

"Sure." Gingerly I sat on the bed. "I figured as much." I sent him a wry smile.

"Now it's your turn. Game?"

"Uhh." I scrambled to think. Word games? I scuffed aside the tiny, thin rug next to the bed. "We could do hangman on the floor. Draw in…" I searched the room. "Water?"

"I doubt that'd be much use. About all we have is blood."

It was a joke, I reminded myself, but the space between us seemed to shrink.

"Fuck. Sorry. Bad choice."

I cleared my throat. "Yes. It was."

I could never completely escape the reminders of why I was here, locked up. Though I was getting good at shoving them away and carrying on. The pain, the beatings, would return when I was washing my hands, or just eating a meal, or in the boring times in between. They'd flash in and I'd freeze up then push them away. Life went on. I guess people always needed hope and some sort of normality, else they'd curl up and die.

I wasn't dying, not yet. *Never give up. Never give in.*

We ended up playing fast, with water. Speedy noughts and crosses. I beat him more often than not. It made me grin, even laugh once when he slapped his forehead and flopped backward, groaning at his mistake.

But I never forgot, even with him sprawled on the floor drawing *X*'s and *O*'s with his wet finger, like a small boy messing about with his sister. He wasn't a small boy. He was a big, powerful man and a sadist, who liked hurting me when given the chance.

There was blood between us. And sex.

With him this close, I wasn't sure which of the two bothered me the most.

When I took a shower that night, I couldn't tell if he looked away the whole time, and when he showered, I peeked. Impossible not to. My throat went dry for all the wrong reasons watching water pour down his hard body.

Chapter 11

Guess I'd gotten too used to a soft bed. The floor kept me awake. As it made various bits of me go numb, I'd shift and manage to numb somewhere new. At around three in the morning, I sat up. I ended up with my chin in hand, elbows on knees, studying her.

I was sure she had no comprehension of how guilty I felt.

For years, I'd lived with the mess I'd made of my life after my brother was killed. I'd thought I'd reined in the dark side of me. Ever since the murder, I'd run from one crazy thing to another, but I'd never abused a woman like this.

How did I reconcile this with my soul? Yes, I'd been forced to do it. But…

The room was rendered in dark sifted, tones of gray. Her toe twitched underneath the sheet and she mumbled something. Truly, she was sweet, and innocent, and I was the biggest, baddest wolf in creation.

Excluding Gregor.

I hung my head and grabbed the top of my head with my hands, staring down at the vaguely moonlit floor. If I'd been presented with a case like this in South Africa, I'd have been inclined to arrest myself and let the lawyers sort out who was guilty of what. Legally, I was probably clean, but morally I was fucked.

I let go and stared at her again, at the curvaceous length of her body. The tropical heat made sleeping under a sheet impossible most nights. She was lying on her side. Even asleep, I'd heard her whimper if she shifted onto her back. That was my present to her. I lay down and closed my eyes.

What was I going to do?

Keep obeying Gregor, that's what, because the alternative was worse and something I knew might be inevitable, considering where Gregor seemed to be heading. I might have to kill her – if she begged me. *Fok.* Not good. I wondered if she'd thought of it yet. Probably not. If she was like most people, she'd be subconsciously avoiding that thought pathway.

Though at times, when unawares, I'd caught her staring at nothing, with a haunted look on her face.

I hadn't seen the police officer she said had been tortured, but I'd heard him. My instincts, along with what had happened so far, told me Gregor and his client weren't going to be happy with simple beatings and sex. What if she never asked and it became too much even for me? Could I kill her?

I put my hand across where my heart must be. It actually hurt contemplating doing that. Maybe there was hope for me yet. Of course, if I did it, they'd kill me afterward.

The day's activities ran through my head. Games. We'd played eye spy even, and managed to find things we hadn't known were in the room. Like cracks in the wall. It had been ridiculous but fun. We'd both ended up laughing, for a while forgetting the circumstances of our imprisonment.

Yet another side to this woman.

I smiled in the dark. If the men I'd commanded had seen me doing that they would've poked fun. I recalled her hesitant giggle, the curve of her ear when she bent to stare at the cross I'd drawn with water, and the glimpse of what lay between her legs when she forgot to keep that skimpy dress pulled down and her thighs together. Not that I didn't have that etched into my memory already.

I glanced over. She'd wedged her arm under her pillow and was muttering into the pillow. I lifted my head to look at the quiet lines of her face. I doubted I could kill a woman. Not Jazmine. Already I knew her too well. She seemed so vulnerable in these empty hours of the night…and so passionate when she was tied up, whipped, and welted with my marks.

Jesus. I'd done some of the nastiest, kinkiest things I'd done to anyone, *ever*, to her. My cock swelled at the thought.

I sighed and rolled over. This was going to be a long night.

Morning came. Her eyelids rose, and she focused on me, peeking suspiciously, frowning, like she'd found a lion on her bedroom floor.

"Morning."

"Morning." Wincing, she levered herself onto her elbow then rubbed at her eyes. Her smirk seemed to take in more than just me as a person. There was a distinct sexual vibe to how she studied me. Interesting. "Have you drawn my bath and polished the Rolls Royce?"

Someone had decided I was safer than she'd thought I was yesterday. Good. I wasn't about to remind her of my bad side.

"The only bath I've ever drawn was probably with crayons when I was six, but if you want to lend me a Rolls, I promise I'll polish it."

"Hmm." She swung her legs down. "Not sure I'll trust you with my car yet."

There was a subtle psychological message in that. Trust. All my cop interrogation techniques came to the fore. Win their trust then get them to spill their guts.

Domkop. She's a fellow prisoner, not a criminal. Still. I did need to see her back.

I eyed her from under my brows, and decided not to take the bait. We could dance around a bit more with that idea before I'd push it.

I sat up and scrubbed my hands through my hair, stretching out some of the cricks in my back and limbs.

"*Blêrrie* hell. I'm going to suggest we swap tonight. You can have the floor."

Her flippant, "Wrestle you for it," as she stood, made me wonder why *she* was pushing this. It was almost like she was flirting.

I climbed to my feet too. "I doubt you're fit enough for that."

And I could beat you with my little finger, have you pinned to the floor, squirming under me.

Fok. The notions she gave me, almost every five seconds.

Looking down at her, did what it had a few times since they'd stuck me in this room with her – reminded me of her in that other room. But I wasn't some cave man governed by his dick. I could just say no and leave it in my imagination.

"Turn around, Pieter. I need to use the toilet."

"And after that, I want to look at your back."

"No."

I angled my head and she shrugged.

"I'll put some ointment on myself."

As if she could reach properly.

Soon. Soon I'd get her to let me. It was pretty essential.

I was pleased that she didn't look at all as if she doubted I'd look away. Except, when I went over to piss, I had the distinct feeling that she was staring at me. After years in the force and in the jungle fighting terrorists, my sixth sense was damn reliable.

For all that day, I didn't push that I was supposed to see her back, or not much. The woman was stubborn and scared of me touching her. Even so, I also knew Gregor would make sure to follow through if he had the glimmer of a doubt that she'd disobeyed him. And his punishments had a habit of getting worse.

I was close to grinding my teeth down in frustration by nightfall. Sleeping on the floor again while she lay a few feet away, unattainable, and tossing and turning as if in pain, only made me get up in the morning, grumpy, and determined to examine her back.

My one problem – this meant more to me than simply looking at the whip marks. It was why I was so conscious of keeping myself in check.

When she had a shower that night, I sat on the bed and stared in the direction of the door. To look or not to look? I was being stupid. Not pushing the issue because I had other motives was all very noble but it was still dumb.

Merely sitting opposite her, talking, had been enough to steam up my brain. With her flimsy dress on, she was tantalizing. Having fucked her twice, I could imagine a lot.

I steeled myself and I turned my head.

Hot woman alert.

She stood under the shower, facing away from me, with water streaming over her naked back. Jazmine left me in danger of swallowing my tongue. My dick shot up so fast and so hard I could've used it to shoot down planes. Her wet hair was plastered to her skin all the way down to her waist. The lower edge was like an arrow, slipping about in the water, and pointing straight at the tempting split of her ass.

With great effort, I ignored the memory of my hands on those gorgeous mounds. *Her back. Check that.*

Blue-black bruises but also one deep red area. *Shit.* Who knew if the whips and other implements here ever got cleaned? I needed a closer look. No ulterior motive, just common sense. If I asked her, she'd want to hide herself and I didn't fancy that soapy wrestle, not really. I'd do something I'd regret with her under my hands.

This could turn out so bad.

What man wouldn't get an erection looking at her nude? It was normal.

I stood quietly and stalked over, zeroing in on the dark red streak. If it was a bacterial problem, she'd be sore, wouldn't she? I wasn't certain but redness after this much time might mean infection.

Excuses, excuses.

Then I reached within an arm's length away from her and knew I would have to touch. With water cascading over the area, I still couldn't tell.

She was humming to herself, oblivious.

Shooting fucking terrorists was easier.

If I spoke, she'd jerk away, turn, cover herself, argue. *I'm an ex-fucking cop.* But...this was for her own good.

I nearly gave myself a brain hernia turning this over.

"Jazmine. Turn off the water so I can look."

Her gasp and screech were low volume. She froze. "Go *away*, Pieter."

I reached past her and turned the metal dial. The water slowed and stopped. The last clear stream trickled and died. I was so close I could see the fine hairs on her arm. The little silver angel, on the bracelet she never seemed to remove, swung in an arc from her wrist.

"Your hair's stuck across where I need to see. This won't take long."

"Fuck. Off." The trembling started and damn if that didn't make my hard-on harder.

"No. Ten seconds. Tops."

Getting there. Doing this. I counted downward from one hundred to stay focused. Naked woman, yes. Not mine. No.

I smoothed my fingers under her hair, shifting it aside, and just as I cleared the spot where the line of red swelled up, pursing her skin into an angry ridge, she tried to bolt.

I slammed my palm onto her, flattening her to the wall.

"Stay, girl. Fucking stay there!" My voice had roared into boss mode.

"Sorry."

God. That hitch in her voice. That spoke to my balls.

I pressed on her harder and squatted. With my free hand, I gently cleared away the last strands of her hair. My cock was making me uncomfortable with its need to get into her, between these legs. Even while I concentrated on her back, I was feeling myself sinking into her wet pussy.

There were memories that you remembered and *memories that held you hostage and threw you back into the moment, headfirst, cock first, scent, feel, and the slip of her cum on your fingers as you thrust them inside her.*

I cleared my throat.

The welt was a little red and puffy but nothing atrocious.

"This needs keeping an eye on."

Then I looked lower, saw the lips of her cunt. I'd been in there. I'd beat this ass, made these bruises. "You're going to let me check you every day, from now on."

Her swallow was audible. Her reply was as quiet as a drift of breeze. "I don't think –"

"Understand me?"

She didn't answer.

Water dribbled down the outside of her thighs. I'd strapped apart these legs. Been in this pussy. Made her scream. My mind was blown. I knew I'd never stop, not now. Need arrived, blasting in, blowing apart rational, civilized me.

Keeping that one hand on her back, holding her in place, I let my fingers glide down until they reached the top of a bruise a few inches below where her butt swelled outward. I wasn't using much force and she was staying still. Did she like it or did I scare the hell out of her?

Whatever.

Such temptation was never meant for any man to resist.

"Understand?"

"Yes." Feather quiet.

I looked up the length of her back. Her forehead was resting on the wall.

Then I leaned in, wrapped my hand around her thigh, and I bit right over that bruise.

Her gasp turned into a high-pitched "Fuck, fuck, fuck," before I let go.

While keeping careful contact with her skin with my hand, I climbed to my feet, marveling at the slopes of her warm body. Her submissiveness was intoxicating. She shuddered under my fingers and I detected the smallest nudge outward of her very female bottom. That signal, I could pick up from a hundred yards away.

I was sure lack of protest didn't hide unwillingness.

From no to yes in under thirty seconds.

"What are you keeping from me? Hmm?" I played with a wisp of hair at the side of her neck and began winding those few strands on one finger, around and around.

"Nothing. I want you to go away." As before, her words were so quiet, it seemed she barely wanted them heard.

"Do you?" My hold grew firmer as I gathered more hair. I tightened my grip until she had to bend back her neck. "I see a beautiful pair of eyes."

Jazmine blinked at me and, *fok*, she whimpered and parted her lips, sucked in a long breath – like she was about to run out of oxygen. Her eyelids lowered. Red rag to a bull.

If she wasn't turned on, I was a purple alien from Mars. I desperately wanted to push this. To see the truth beneath her wildly different body language.

I might not have played the dominant card with Elenor but with this one it came with the package. I tugged once on her hair. "You're going to turn around when I tell you to and stand there. Now."

I let go. My heart pounded away as if it too waited anxiously to see where this would go. If she ducked under my arm and ran…

Chapter 12

"...turn around when I tell you to and stand there. Now."

That command had me paralyzed. I was torn. I needed to get away from Pieter and I *craved* staying. I wanted him to make me do...things.

It was the stupidest desire ever.

Where he'd planted his palm on my back and where he'd bitten seemed hot as brands, reminding me of how easily he could handle me.

That was such a turn-on, but wasn't *me*. I was smart, independent. If a previous boyfriend had tried this, I'd have laughed, I'd have kicked their balls up into their teeth. Not that they would've dared try. Pieter...was different.

When he'd let my hair go, I'd bowed my head again. Now I was stuck here in limbo, knowing he wanted me to turn and face him and knowing if I did, it would be a huge mistake. Every other time, I'd been tied up. I had excuses. It had been forced.

I couldn't just obey him. Male dominance was ridiculous.

"If you don't move by the count of three, I'm going to turn you over my knee on that bed and spank you."

"Pieter..." I stalled, feeling like I was being strangled.

The worst part – I knew he'd do this and like it. That was so hot.

"Three."

I raised my head, teeth clamped on my bottom lip. Even thinking about deciding what to do was scrambling my brain.

Fuck.

And he'd be seeing my indecision. Probably thought it amusing.

"Two."

Crap. Spanked? He could do that if he wanted to even if I fought. I swung and found myself confronted by this huge man, who occupied more space then he should be allowed to. Air, I needed air.

My throat worked. I needed to tell him I wanted him out of my face. "I…"

"What?"

He whacked his hands onto the wall either side of my head then looked down at me. "Hmm?"

For a few seconds, his gaze moved lower, to my breasts. With his body so up close, my brain wasn't functioning. I was supposed to answer –

"Forgotten what you were going to say?" His mouth curved up, barely.

It was fearsome what I saw promised in that tiny gesture. Was that supposed to be a smile or was he about to pounce?

I blinked, not sure if I was breathing. I was the utter focus of his attention.

What he'd done in the other room was him. He liked hurting me, liked fucking me and tying me up. That knowledge riveted me to this wall. There was *fear* and there was fear.

He could hurt me, badly, if he wanted to. I didn't think he would, but he could.

A little bit of fear was a whole lot of thrill.

As he shifted infinitesimally nearer, I squirmed up the wall, trying to merge with the white tiles. A quarter inch, an inch? His body heat and his scent was a living force. This was the man who'd napalmed my ass. Any closer and I'd be lost.

"You didn't run."

I glanced to the side. "I um…" *Run?* Good idea.

With his whole hand, he gripped my jaw, as if he wanted to be sure I stayed put, then he dragged me back to the middle. Past a few dangling locks of hair lurked his clear brown eyes.

"Hello, there." That bear-growly voice of his should be illegal. "Place your *fucking* palms on the wall and keep them there until I say not to. Do you need more incentive?"

I'd flinched at the *fucking. Wimp.*

He pinched one of my nipples between finger and thumb and squeezed.

Gasping, and in increasing pain, I slumped as far as I could go with my nipple his hostage. That I'd become even wetter horrified me.

The pain dazzled. Like the cut of a scythe, it separated me from everything else that had happened before, from all the terrible things that might happen. All that mattered was him, concentrated. Distilled male.

Still unsure why, and what the hell I was doing, I crept my hands onto the wall. I felt the dips between the smooth square tiles. Water dribbled down my skin. His hand stayed on my jaw as did his crushing hold on my breast. And I loved it.

All those games we'd played meant nothing when he was like this. I saw him for what he truly was. I was dealing with the devil.

"Correct response. But slow. You will be punished for that."

Desire rippled into me, and I shivered for a full second. Visibly shivered. His threat had done that. Since when had I been into pain?

"You like that?" His eyebrow arched. "You like the threat of pain?"

"No." My denial was automatic, but I couldn't stop the tiny swallow that followed. He'd figured me out before I did.

His thumb swept across to my mouth then he curled out my lip as if checking the teeth of a bought creature.

Awareness blossomed in his eyes, a smug satisfaction that half made me want to wipe it away. But the other half of me wanted to do anything he asked.

"Liar," he murmured, stretching out my nipple, eliciting another gasp. "Pretty liars get hurt anyway. Say thank you."

My eyes widened. Then he shifted his hand, hooked two fingers into my mouth, and leaned that elbow on the wall behind my head. "Say thank you."

I wriggled in his grip.

"Say thank you."

"No, no –"

His fingers hooked deeper in, brushing my tongue. I was crushed, desire annihilating thought. My *thank you* tumbled out. Tears leaked and dribbled down my cheeks. This was insane.

He pulled his hand from my mouth and held my throat to the wall while he shoved his other hand between my legs, fingers curving along in my moisture and making me part my legs. Then he lifted me an inch or so. My back slid on tile, rekindling pain. I was pinned there, throat and pussy. A needy moan escaped my lips.

I wanted this, I did, but I was afraid. Who would stop him, this monster of a man, if he went too far? He could burn me down to the ground if he so chose. Want and sensible were at war.

"We can't have sex." I managed to gasp out, my throat moving against his hand. We couldn't because of Gregor. What a time to remember where we were. I did what was becoming a habit, I blanked it out.

"I can think of a hundred thousand other things I could do with you. All of them dirty. I own you, Miss Jazmine. Starting with this."

Own. The word stunned me. His predatory smile widened.

Then he kissed me.

I'd never been kissed before while someone held me down. This, *this* was what I'd been missing. Overwhelming mind-shaking passion. A desire so strong that it made someone want to hold you still while they used your mouth, abused your mouth, and ravaged you with teeth, tongue, and fingers.

Pieter was a storm not a man, a living, breathing, biting force of nature and I let him sweep me away.

"You know what?" he said at last, his words murmured beside my ear. I was trembling and only held up by his hands on my body.

I looked out through a tangle of his hair. Someone's hair was in my mouth. Whose, I didn't know or care, as I was too busy struggling to breathe. We were both sweating, our bodies sliding one on the other, his rock-hard chest squashing my breasts. At some point he'd ripped off his shirt and he'd done it so fast I'd barely registered the act.

"What?" I mumbled, and I gathered the strength to tongue out the stray twist of hair. "What did you say?" No sex allowed and here I was aching to get him inside me.

"One. You moved your hands. Two. I am going to enjoy this."

Shit. Panic galloped in. My hands were on his shoulders.

While I was still figuring out why his words had made me hornier, he took my wrist and towed me out from the wall. Then he strode to the bed, sat down, and patted beside it.

His erection was so obvious I could have taught penis anatomy with a picture of the gray pants he wore.

"Come here."

I actually had to mentally brake myself, so as not to twist my foot on the floor. I felt like a teenager about to get chastised. Only this wasn't going to be just a grounding.

"Come."

So assured, damn him, and his eyes devilish. The man was supremely confident I'd come when called and I… Truthfully, it made me want to go over there, kneel at his feet, and suck on that cock he displayed.

Hesitantly, I walked his way, only a little sideways, so that I might or might not be going there.

"Do you remember how hard I can hit, Jazmine?"

Duh. You fucker. I pressed my lips into a line and nodded. I think my eyes were on fire, I couldn't help staring at his lap.

"If I have to stand up and grab you, those bruises are going to be twice as big."

Bastard. "You're supposed to help me heal!"

He gave me an assessing look. "They will. Your hand." He reached out and stupidly I let him take mine and pull me to him. His palm massaged up and down my lower back. "Lie down over my lap, hands on the floor."

"This doesn't mean I'm yours or that I'm going to do this again. Experiment. Only." I was babbling.

For the first time he grinned.

Amusing, was I? "Fuck. I'm so confused." I was whining now. Shit. I was a wimp, a pussy, and a few other words I never wanted to be.

"Don't over think it. You like being made to do things. You like doing what I tell you. Nod."

What a trick. He'd made it easy for me and he knew it. Slowly, shifting my weight from foot to foot, I plucked up my courage, and I nodded, but I whispered, "Just this once."

"Lie down."

I was still naked.

I could see the headline – *female journalist is traitor to the feminist cause.* What did it matter? I'd already been tied up and tortured. I owned the *woman kidnapped and turned into sex slave* headline.

I sighed, looked once more at the erect present nearly poking a hole in his pants then lowered myself onto his lap until my hands were flat on the floor. Through the wet strands of my hair, I found myself looking at the silver angel on my wrist. I blinked at this pretty reminder of ugliness. Thankfully, Pieter began to wind my hair around his fingers, diverting me from thoughts of Gregor.

The tension and small pains as his fist gathered my hair were familiar, and as the pressure increased, I sighed with pleasure. This, I could grow to love.

"What an ass." He explored there while he held me in place. All I wanted was to lie on his lap with my head pulled back and my eyes closed, letting him do it, lost in the sensations as he smoothed his fingers over the mounds of my ass and into the divide. He teased me, swirling close to my nether hole, before tickling up my back and exploring elsewhere. Sometimes he brushed over old hurts and made me hiss. And repeat.

Mentally I was begging him to touch between my legs. My moans made him take another turn of my hair around his fist.

Nothing existed but this moment. Where we were, the past, *everything*, I let it drift away.

If I shifted on my hands, it was a distant thing, barely registered.

Every so often, he delivered a light smack. The frequency increased until I was both anticipating and dreading the next. The reverberations in my flesh and his gentle touches combined with lying naked across his lap, and trapped, was locking me into a mindset. What he did, I endured, because he was doing this to me. My normal logic died a fast death.

Once only, when I instinctively tried to escape, he locked his leg over mine until I ceased wriggling.

Damn, I liked that. I fucking loved being trapped like this.

Nothing he'd done before was as intense as this. This was his need, none others, to have me where I was and under his control.

I succumbed, writhing sometimes, crying out at the harder smacks. Under me, the pulse of his cock when I whimpered made me yearn to fuck him.

Then he stopped. He laid his hand over the hottest, most aching part of my ass. "You're loving this. This isn't punishment, is it?"

I sucked in some desperate air as I thought.

The question surely needed a no, because even if it meant more pain I wanted to see where this would take me. Crazy. I dug my toes into the floor then shook my head, feeling his grip reining in my moves.

Keep going.

"Your ass is going to be the end of me. I almost want to make you come more than make you hurt." He leaned down and added quietly, "And I never knew I'd want to hurt you so much."

I shuddered, reading a vicious guarantee in his words. My clit had been engorged for so long every pulse made it ache. I squeezed my thighs together.

His teeth bit my ear lobe simultaneous with the slide of his hand to my pussy entrance. He crammed slippery fingers inside. No preamble. I jerked and shot into extreme arousal so fast I choked. *More.* I coughed, swallowed, eyes shut. I tried to grind my clit on his thigh and heard him chuckle.

"Almost more, but not quite." Then he pulled out his fingers, and slammed his palm down on my butt, jarring me into his leg. "One."

I groaned.

"Two."

Pain flared.

"Three. Beg, girl. Beg to come and I stop. Four. Five." He kept going.

He wanted me to beg? Another smack hit me and I screeched. "Yes! Please. Please."

I sobbed. Tears leaked and dripped off my cheeks. These were far harder than before. Yet even this crueler pain somehow twisted in and made me ache.

"Please!"

"You want me to make you come? Say exactly that."

Fuck. Saying the exact words made it more humiliating. I jolted forward as he began again.

"Yes! I want to come."

"Incorrect."

What? I scrambled to figure it out. "Please," I blurted, still sobbing and hiccupping, and now I couldn't stop. "Please, I want you to make me come."

"Good. That's what I needed to hear."

I knew he was being smug again but I didn't care because he moved me up his lap until my mons rested on his thigh. My clit was on the dangerous verge of pressing on that nicely solid muscle. I squirmed, but not much, afraid this man would decide I needed more of his hurting.

Though that too enticed me.

My world was a little messed up.

"Stay still." His hand slid languorously, fingernails tickling and scratching, down the back of my upper thigh, then over the inner curve between my legs. He traced the seam of my pussy, nudging apart the lips, cruising the whole length of his fingers in my moisture until I was about to go cross-eyed imagining them going inside.

"What have I found? Don't ever tell me spanking doesn't get you horny." He slicked those fingers around and around in a little circle at my entrance. I was almost ready to beg again. "Hmm?"

What was the question? He'd stopped doing anything apart from resting his fingers *there*. So close to going in.

I wiggled, straining for more of his touch. "I won't."

"Good girl."

He slid them further under me, and searched for my clit, and found it. As he played with it, I arched, moaning quietly.

I was so turned on I'd have let him do anything to gain an orgasm. Spank me, tie me up. Anything. My body centered on what he was doing and the heat emanating from my newly hurt butt.

"Tsk. So wet. You're dripping all the way down here, girl."

Fuck.

Girl...again. I'd ignore that. He toggled my clit, slowly, squeezing it then teasing me by leaving it alone and venturing to my entrance, and dawdling there. My pussy walls clenched.

"Go in! Please?" I begged.

"Can't. You know that. Not now. I've already done too much. Though I'd love to fuck you."

Oh. Was finger-fucking sex? I didn't care as he'd fastened those fingers over my nub and was working at it properly now. Close, so close. I arched even more, grasping at the floor, shaking, my mind closing in, and then...and then, blown away. The climax ripped through me. I screamed once, panted convulsively.

"That's it," he murmured. "Come for me, Jazmine." His massaging kept on, around and around, wringing more from me.

"Oh fuck. No," I choked out.

"Yes." For just a second, his thumb slipped inside me, fucking me slowly.

No. No.

Another rippling orgasm shook me. Every strangled gasp hurt my neck and hair. His fist was still entangled.

At last he released my head and he turned me over in his lap, bringing my legs onto the bed, and cuddling me to his chest.

"There. Shh."

His pats seemed so at odds with what he'd just done but I needed them and I snuggled in, tired, with my lips on his chest. *Sweaty, salty man. Mmm.*

"See," he whispered, his face in my hair, inhaling. "I'm not all bad. Once upon a time I was a good man."

I answered automatically, barely able to think through what he meant. "Mm-hmm. You're not so bad. I think I like you even."

His quiet laugh made me smile and take another long breath. Funny how he made me feel safe.

Chapter 13

I dragged Jazmine over onto the bed to spoon with me. I left my pants on. If both of us got naked, right then, I'd think I'd have had an accident of lustful proportions and shoved inside her without thinking. I was happy just feeling her ass with my cock, through the cloth, if that was all I could get without endangering her.

After a while, I felt her slip into sleep. Her breathing slowed and she relaxed against me. We could shower tomorrow. Besides, I loved the scent of a woman who I'd just made to come. Being able to nestle into her, to lean over and watch her breasts rise and fall, to just be there beside her, was enough to make my chest ache, and it wasn't an oncoming heart attack. Touching, skin on skin, was an underestimated luxury.

We seemed to match, perfectly, in a way only the truly kinky could understand. I lay there, breathing in time with this warm, beautiful creature, wishing what was happening to her was some nightmare instead of real. It had been years since I'd had someone in my arms I connected with this well.

Hard to believe how this had fallen out. From my initial insane urge to help a gorgeous, sad woman I'd come across in Australia, to this. I guess, even back then, I'd fallen in lust with her, as well as a little in love with her bravery. She never gave up, despite all that happened. Not many could weather this sort of darkness and stay sane.

With her in my arms, hope arose. We had to make it out of here.

Her movements, as she turned over, woke me, though I'd only lightly touched sleep. Here, sleep was always shallow, like being in combat only worse. I had no one to trade watches with.

It was morning. Six AM, maybe. The sun was peeking in enough to see colors, like her pretty green eyes looking back at me.

"Hey, beautiful." Those eyes compelled me to kiss her nose. Then she smiled a full smile that made me sad inside. "I won't bite. Or not yet."

I had my arm draped over her and I stroked her hair, felt her curled fingers stir against my chest.

Her lips twitched. "I can't believe I let you do all that."

That little squirm she did with her butt reminded me of her squirms last night.

"Hmm?" I figured she needed some space to think.

"I mean, I know some people like pain but that's never been me." She shook her head and toyed with my chest hair.

I thumbed the frown lines between her eyes. "Did you like it?"

The red blush that swept onto her face was cute. Still embarrassed, after all we'd done?

It took her a few swallows and head shakes before she met my eyes. "I guess…yes. I even wanted more."

"So you wanted what I gave you?"

"It was…" She looked like she didn't believe her own words. "Incredible. But that wasn't…normal, was it?"

"Normal? My view – it's normal for you. Everyone, I've found, has some sort of weird kink inside them. Though not everyone lets their freak flag fly."

I shifted my arm down to gently smooth my palm across her ass. That squirm again. I must've touched somewhere sore. "If I can't fuck you, is it a crime to want to keep feeling you up?"

Jazmine studied me for a long while before answering. "No. I guess not."

An iffy reply if I ever heard one. Though I could see she'd been thinking about what had happened, I hadn't a clue as to what exactly those thoughts had been. "What are you thinking?"

"That..." She put her hands up and covered her face then breathed into them. "God. I don't know. This is such an insane situation. I guess, I don't even know if I'm going to be alive tomorrow and this is just crazy."

"Uh huh." Gently I pulled away her hands. There were tears beneath her eyes. "Keep going."

"Keep going?" She nodded, half to herself. "You're pretty scary, you know, though I hate admitting it, even if it's fucking obvious. I'm not a naive innocent, though. I know what BDSM is. And...I really have never wanted a man to..."

And there she stopped.

"Dominate you? Hurt you?" I raised my eyebrows and wiped away some of those quiet tears.

"Yes. It worries me that this is all because of what you did to me before, in front of...him. You know? This might be just some weird psychological thing?"

Talk about a difficult question.

"I don't know. What I do know is I want to get you out of this."

"Mmm. Yeah. That goes for both of us."

"Good." I pulled her close and kissed her, long and thoroughly until she was sighing. My leg ended up wrapped over her. Maybe if I tried I could make her part of me, make her so mine no one could separate us. I pressed my mouth against her forehead, thinking, hoping, trying not to despair.

"Pieter?"

I pulled back. "Yes?"

"You said you used to give your wife pain? So, she liked it? The same as..." Her lips twisted.

"You? Seems to me that talking about this is more painful than me beating your ass. Maybe we should go back to that?" A man could hope.

She snorted. "It's hard to get my head around. That I liked you going all cave man on me."

"I didn't go all cave man. That's just me. I let it out around you because you respond to it so fucking nicely. I enjoy it. So do you. Yes, my ex-wife liked being hurt and she's a masochist. No, I didn't go cave man on her if you're wondering because that wasn't something she liked. We were close to equals in the bedroom. You however, seem to love being my sub."

I grabbed her and rolled over so she was under me.

After one squeak, she lay there, staring up, her hands on my biceps like she was checking them out in a subtle way.

"Such little fingers you have." I pecked at her mouth but couldn't resist deepening the kiss. Then I wedged my leg between hers and leaned some weight on her there. Her eyelids fluttered down and she groaned softly. Magic. "See. This you love. Being mine. My submissive."

Her eyes flashed open and after a second she threw back, "That's still negotiable. If I say no, in the BDSM world that means you back away? Yes?"

Except when it came to what Gregor wanted, but I didn't think for a moment that she meant that. And he could get fucked. This was us.

"Yes. But I've seen a fair few people, men and women, explore their kinks over the years." I leaned on one elbow and swept some stray hairs from her face. "Once they find out their kinks most never go back to vanilla. It's like crack, cocaine, and a lottery ticket all rolled into one."

She blinked up at me, frowning. The woman was overthinking, again. There was no better way to prove she didn't want me to back away than to show her.

I shifted to straddle her hips then I took her wrists, ignoring her yanks to get free.

"Hey!"

I gathered them in one hand and pinned them to the pillow above her head then I pressed my fingers over her mouth, firm and a little rough. After a few wriggles, her breathing ceased, and she shut her eyes. A moment later, Jazmine sucked in some deeper breaths through her nose and past my fingers. Her tongue licked out, once, like she was checking it was me.

Cute. My balls liked that.

Arousal. For sure. On my part too. I shifted to get my dick more comfortable.

Damn, the things I longed to do to this woman. Guilt flickered in. What Gregor was getting me to do was like handing a plate of lobster and caviar to a starving food lover.

I loosened my fingers, lightly slapped her face, and grabbed a nice big hold of one breast, crushing in a little until it had to hurt. Though her eyes flew open, she said nothing except a muffled *fuck* in surprise. I felt her hips arch upward.

I know my own eyes were wide as hell right then.

I checked her out, hard smile on my face. Damn, this was sexy.

"Plenty of time for a *no* there, but you didn't say it, because you love me taking control." I waited. "Don't speak again while I look at you. If you do, I will punish you."

Ja, for sure I would, I might even go beyond what she liked, just because I could.

Her small shudder thrilled me. I was dead on target, clearly. Her nipples had peaked, small and tight. I took my time examining my girl and handling her like she was my little pet ready for a show.

We should think up a safeword but then again, if she ever really said no, I'd stop, wouldn't I? God, there was an extra added thrill to having no mechanism for her to stop me.

Exhilarating was the best description.

There was always that tendency to push. Dangerous, maybe. This situation begged me to go one better, harder, nastier. I *could* control it.

I could.

If there was one thing she stirred in me more than wanting to see her squeal and those red marks come into being on her skin, it was a desire to hide her away so that no one could harm her again. The difference between pain and harm had never been so clear to me. What I did to her, she wanted. What Gregor and his client wanted done to her could lead us god knew where. Sobering.

That night I convinced her to let me share the bed by simply telling her it was so. The satisfaction I got from that was immense. Ridiculous maybe, considering. Fuck though, I'd never had a woman react to me like this.

With Jazmine, now that I'd established who was boss, she was happier. Her smiles warmed me whenever I touched her, swatted her ass, kissed her, or grabbed her for a hug.

Elenor had been my only love after high school. We'd meshed like Ken and Barbie, discovered our love of the S and m dynamic together, ventured into the local Cape Town kinky scene and made some friends without being too involved. Being a cop had made me wary of outing myself, but I'd known all about Dominance and submission. Jazmine was submissive to me at least, maybe not to other men. One thing I'd learned from seeing my friends get their kink on was that everyone was a little different. No two relationships were the same.

If she responded submissively to me only, I didn't give a fuck. If anything, I liked it better that way.

This was the most tragic of times to find a woman who seemed my kinky soul mate.

The longer I stayed here and suffered, the more this place would grind me down if I didn't have a way to deflect. By helping her to survive, I was helping myself too. I wasn't invincible in body or mind. Neither of us were.

My life motto came in handy. I was never giving up on getting both of us out of here alive and intact.

Chapter 14

How Pieter was steering us frightened me sometimes. I was still wrestling with it in my head when he obviously thought he had it sorted. He'd work that alpha dominant routine on me and I'd melt at his feet. So bloody disconcerting. Was I schizoid? The terrible things we did outside this little room of mine…of ours, were impacting on me. Even when I tried not to remember, they'd enter my head like a rude explosion. My fingers would be like ice, my heart sped up, my mind would grind to a halt while I relived terror.

Small things, like someone leaning on the door would make me jerk around and squeak. I was like a mouse.

I hated that. The scars on my mind must go so deep. How would I ever recover? It seemed impossible.

There was one thing that no matter how I turned it around seemed to spell doom. I didn't want to ask Pieter for his opinion because if he agreed, it'd make it too real to bear. Besides, could I really trust him?

I fluffed the pillow into shape for the tenth time. The days in here forever see-sawed from boring to scary.

"You need a distraction. I have a good one. Bend over the bed and pull your dress up over your head so I can look at you."

"Not now, Pieter."

"*Ja*. Now."

I protested, but I'd barely said the *n* in *no* when he pulled my hands behind my back and forced me over the bed. His knee squashed the edge of the mattress down then the first swat landed. It was hard enough to echo off the walls. I gasped, but dropped like a stone into that mind state where I desperately wanted to obey.

I knew this reaction well. It still stunned me.

It was three more hits before I could catch my breath and choke out, "I'm sorry."

His grip on my wrists pressed in then he released me.

Without further prompting, I reached down and wriggled the dress up my body, baring myself.

"Spread your legs and tuck the dress over your head. I don't want to see you look out. Understand, my sweet little disobedient *meisie*?" He punctuated that statement with one last forceful slap.

"Yes!" I blinked at the sheet before me and shivered. *Meisie.* The Afrikaans for girl did something to my head. The accent maybe? Who knew?

When he laid his hand on my back and pushed me deeper into the mattress, I bit the sheet to stifle my groan. When he laughed at my noise, I dampened between my legs.

I was beginning to look forward to him making me do things. I was sick. No matter what he said. I loved it. I hated it. I shut my eyes and waited.

For ages he seemed to stand behind me, then I heard him step closer and he pulled aside my ass cheeks. The grip hurt. Knowing he stared at my pussy was indescribably hot.

"Put your hands at your back and hold your wrist."

I did so, drawing in an exultant breath when he growled approval. I was getting so wet he had to be seeing that too. As if to reinforce my thought, his finger drew a wavering line down my soaking wet seam then he thumbed apart my lips.

I shoved my mouth into the mattress and moaned quietly.

"*Fok.* Your hot *klein poesie...*"

Nothing more, but I could *feel* his stare and I trembled. What those words meant, I could guess. Arousal and submitting to him, they tumbled into one messy bewildering haze. I bit the sheet in frustration. I wanted, I needed, more of this. More of him making me. Just...making me.

When he'd had enough of looking and stroking, pinching and exposing me, like I was some pet project, he stripped off my dress and sat me on his lap. I curled up, my mind a little fuzzy. I sniffled and licked his chest. He said nothing, only touching me in a reassuring way, and I looked out at the twilight filtering through my window, wishing I could stay here with him surrounding me, forever.

He was so tender when like this, as if he needed the other before he could bring out his good side.

My question arrived and swirled around. Should I? With his chin resting on my head and his arms around me, I broke. My throat worked. Nothing came out then my question arrived almost before I knew I'd said it.

"What if I get pregnant?"

He stilled. "What?"

I guess he'd been off in his own thoughts.

"I'm afraid." *Say it.* "Why are they letting you have sex with me without condoms or anything?"

"I thought you must have told them you were on one of those long-acting drugs. You're not are you?"

"No," I whispered, ever more afraid. "No. Besides, there's STDs. This, to me, means they don't care. And to not care about your slave getting pregnant means you don't intend to sell her."

"The pregnancy thing..."

"They mean to kill me, don't they?"

"Shh. Don't go there. Besides, I've been tested for diseases and Gregor will know that."

That was good, I guessed. "But I can still get pregnant. Do you know how we can escape?" I lifted my head and looked into his troubled eyes.

"I said shh." He put his finger to my lips then he rocked back onto the bed, taking me with him. After holding me tight, he put his mouth to my ear. "I'm sure they at least have audio bugs in here."

My heart leapt into a terrified rhythm. Why hadn't he said? We'd done so many things. "What if they have video?" I whispered back.

His shrug said maybe he didn't know.

"Pieter?"

Did it matter? Apart from not letting them hear of our non-existent escape plans, we'd done nothing dirtier than what they'd seen before. Despair crept in. What was there about me that my captors hadn't seen? I was an open book to them. A slut to be catalogued, poked, and sneered at while wanking.

"Stop crying." He kissed my neck. "You know I'm not ever giving up. You need to enjoy what we have."

I trembled some more but his big friendly hug, the scent of him, and the heavy movement of his body next to mine slowly calmed me. My eyelids drifted down.

When the guard stepped in through the door, it startled me. Pieter stood and dumped me off his lap to stand between me and the guard. I grabbed my dress and tugged it on.

The man was young, with dark wavy hair and he looked like he'd be a local. A raskol, as Pieter said the gang members here were called. His eyes were wild but he shut the door behind him in a measured way. On a belt at his waist were a revolver and a knife. Neither was drawn.

God. I stared at his weapons, eager to act, to get out of here if this was our chance. Shit-scared but ready. Pieter, my big strong ex-cop and merc, could surely have those off him in seconds, if he decided to do it. But was this some sort of trap?

Pieter waited, hands at his sides, but balanced on his feet, ready to pounce.

The man held out his palms, waving them at us, as if that could stop Pieter. "Don't attack. I'm friend. I will help you. Yes?" He raised his brows, nodding. With his fresh face, I wondered if he was over eighteen. "I have key. This is end of my shift. You come out after five minutes. Okay?"

"Shh. You must be quiet." Pieter put his finger across his mouth then he pointed at the walls.

The guard stopped talking and looked puzzled. Then alarm hit him and his gaze flitted about the room.

"Why are you doing this?" Suspicion leaked from Pieter's whispered words. "Say it quiet. Say the truth."

Though his face had gone red, the man-boy subsided, took a breath and continued. "I tell you."

If anyone else was listening…

No video. Please not. I glanced around, as if I could suddenly see something that I hadn't found after all these days.

The guard pulled a few faces, staring at the floor, then at Pieter. "I see polisman hurt bad by Gregor. Women too. I'm no pussy but that is bad. Today I leave this work and not come back. I have a key, in my pocket."

Ohmigod. This was real. I wanted to leap up and dash through that door. I wanted to hug this boy for his goodness. I wanted to scream with joy. We wouldn't get another chance like this. Fast. We had to be fast. I jittered on the bed, toes bouncing off the floor.

For a moment, Pieter looked over at me, frowning like he wanted to slap me calm. I scowled. I could handle this. I stuck a finger in my mouth and bit it.

This is happening!

It'd be nightfall soon and if we could reach the jungle around this place, that Pieter had seen over the wall, we might be able to lose ourselves in it.

"Okay." Pieter stepped in and spoke an inch from this guy's ear so I could barely hear. "We're going to trust you. If you…"

Running footsteps had him raising his head. My heart lurched. The boots clattered to a halt at our door.

If the door had turned into a snake, it wouldn't have drawn us all to stare at it so. I bit my finger harder, tears starting. *This can't be right. Rewind.*

"Hey! We know you've got Ben in there. We know he's trying to help you."

No. Fuck no.

Ben. That was his name. His dark skin shone with sweat. His eyes looked ready to pop. While Pieter...he ran a hand over his head, like he was out on a job and someone had left the correct wrench in the wrong place. A little red and black tattoo of an octopus-like Cthulhu, that I'd never noticed before, rippled on the back of his shoulder.

"Hello in there."

That new voice was like a spear to my heart.

Gregor.

"We also know, my little performers, that he has weapons. Do not think we will let you use them without punishing you. If anyone shoots or tries to hurt my men, I promise you that everyone in there, Jazmine first, then Pieter, then Benoni, will be skinned slowly."

Cold prickled down my back. Gregor would do this.

"Fuck." The boy guard jiggled from foot to foot and played with the butt of his gun.

After a single hissed remark from Pieter, he released the butt.

"If you do not hand the weapons out through the hatch, when I say to, and then open this door, I will skin you all."

Pieter muttered and shot a ragged glance at me.

My finger was squashed so deep by my teeth, the dent bled at one corner.

"If, this is my last if, Pieter. This is just for you."

Why only Pieter? A ringing sound sang in my mind.

"If you don't want to be skinned, Mister Pieter, or your precious lady to be skinned while you watch, and trust me, I would enjoy this greatly..."

I shuddered.

"You must do this now. Kill Benoni."

I think my heart beat three times. We were a frozen room of human sculptures.

Pieter punched the boy guard in the throat, stepped in when the boy retched, ripped his knife from the sheath, and plunged it into his stomach in an upward direction. I saw the twist he put to the knife stab, heard the wet thud as the knife entered the body and the sigh from the boy.

I don't think he even managed to raise his hands. The knife must have punctured his heart.

If this was death, it was terrifying in its starkness. I blinked, and when I opened my eyes, Benoni was on the floor. He gasped twice, his body trembling. Blood leaked onto his pale blue shirt, staining it an almost innocent dark blue, before pooling on the floor where it miraculously turned red.

While I sat with my mouth open, gripping the bed to either side, as if that would stop me flying away, Pieter removed the gun from the belt holster. He went to the hatch, tapped to get them to open it, and pushed the knife and gun through.

The boy had stopped moving, not even his chest rose.

A thought wandered into my shattered mind. They had the room bugged for sound.

Jesus. What and who was this man I'd let kiss me?

Chapter 15

I'd never had children, but he was young and his blood stained my hands. I could still feel the drumming of his heart in my fingers. When I'd reached his heart, the beat had transmitted through the knife blade. This killing was a terrible thing, but it was done. Over. The past. I swallowed and dismissed my sorrow.

Looking at his body would do nothing. I tried to catch Jazmine's eye but she stared at the floor, or at the boy, her hands caught between her knees. So quiet and lost.

Not good. Though I wished I could comfort her, it wasn't possible.

"Step over here, Pieter, so we may restrain you. Then we can remove the young man's body and make your room clean again."

So many years of killing people and witnessing in-your-face violence had left me immune to wallowing in the emotion this sort of thing caused in others. I could wall it off. I backed up to the hatch. Once they'd manacled me, I followed orders and retreated to the shower area opposite. They hauled out his body then came in with a mop. Gregor did the last clean-up and wiped a towel over the wet area using his foot.

"There. Done." He beamed at me and at Jazmine on the bed. She'd sat there the whole time, stiff and pale of face.

When they all left and I was freed via the hatch, I went and sat beside her.

This was going to be bad. I waited.

"Why?" She shook her head, tears in her voice. "*Why?* He was alive! I mean, I know Gregor said…all that." She waved her hand vaguely, while choking up so that I could barely understand what she said. "But why? It was too quick. You could've talked! You could. How could you kill a boy like that?" She glanced at me then away. Afraid I'd see how blotchy red her face was? If she didn't burst into tears soon she'd crack.

Finally she stopped talking. I took her hand and she wrenched it away. Her fingers were cold and trembling. Emotional shock – it wouldn't kill her but I wasn't going to just leave her to suffer.

"I'm sorry."

"Do you even feel *anything*? God." She put her hand to her mouth and swallowed. "I think I might throw up."

I couldn't answer that. Not easily.

"Well?"

What I'd felt for a few seconds after his death, I'd locked it away. Opening myself up to feeling grief and remorse wasn't worth the fallout. Her, I felt for. Her distress was eating at me.

"I do." Truth.

"If you'd just *waited*. I'm too important to this client for Gregor to kill, yet. He wasn't going to do it." She nodded to herself. "He wasn't."

Could she be right? I didn't think so. "Gregor isn't a man who issues empty threats. This wasn't something small. He said he'd skin you alive." Imagining her being sliced up by Gregor sickened me. I reached across her back and pulled her close. Fuck her pushing me away. She needed a hug. I ignored how she stiffened.

"Listen to me. Look at me."

Though she hesitated before she turned to meet my eyes, she obeyed. Good.

"Someone has to be strong here. It's me. I can't afford to be weak. I can't afford to think I was wrong. I won't. Gregor is one of the coldest, most sadistic killers I've ever seen."

"One of?" She huffed.

I ran through my reasons. It hadn't been fear for myself. Yeah, she was right in one respect. I might've taken longer to kill the boy if she hadn't been in the room, though I was sure it would still have come to that. It was she who'd pushed my hand. Telling her that would be cruel.

I guess this was evidence I cared for her more than was healthy for a man who wanted to survive. Funny really. I searched within, trying to figure myself out. It wasn't likely to be love. It was the same intense feeling I'd get if I saw a dog shivering by the roadside.

With the hand I'd wrapped around her shoulders, I touched her neck, marveling at her softness.

The light bulb came on. Who was I kidding? It was far more than what I'd feel for an abandoned pet. When it came to women, I was a fool. I sighed, wanting to kiss the top of her head but sure it was too early.

"Listen, *meisie*, I'm not ever going to risk you dying because I hesitated at the wrong time."

"Fuck." She ducked her head into her open hands. "I'm still shaking. Don't know if I'll ever stop."

"You will. It will pass. Lie down with me for a while. Please."

She let me pull her over so we could lie together on the bed and slowly the tension ebbed from her muscles and her shaking did stop. I played with her cold fingers until they warmed, stroked the curls of hair at her nape.

"I won't ever compromise on keeping you safe."

Her silence stretched awhile. "I don't know if I will ever get over what you did."

My stomach seemed full of cement. She hated me right now, or at least the part of me that had killed the boy. Though *ever,* like never, was a silly word. People could get over a shitload more than they gave themselves credit for, if they tried.

"Killing a boy in front of me, a boy who was helping us, will never seem right. Even if there is some horrible logic to it."

There was the never word too. How did I fix this? A boy? He was a guard first of all and a young man, an adult. She was ignoring that. A criminal who'd likely maimed a few in his rise to becoming a guard here.

That he'd baulked at women being tortured, or men being skinned, was a point in his favor but he was no angel.

"You'd have died, if I'd done anything else."

This time she remained silent.

A few times during the night I felt her tug to get loose but I woke and held her to me.

Nevertheless, when I woke at the approach of boots outside the door, she was huddled in the corner of the room, her head hung low, as if she tried to sleep sitting up.

"C'mon!" yelled a guard. "Gregor wants you chained up again, Pieter. To the door, if you please, sir." He laughed at his aping of Gregor's voice.

Kak. Jazmine was awake too and staring at me.

I went to the door, turned, and shoved my wrists at the hatch. Once I was manacled, Gregor himself entered with three of his guards. Overkill, as always, but I guess being sure of men like me was how he stayed alive. It wouldn't help him in the end. I would kill this man one day, unless he killed me first.

"Good morning, you two!" His booming voice brought Jazmine to her feet, wary.

She was right. The more cheerful Gregor was, the nastier his surprises. From the neatness of his scalp, he'd recently shaved it. His blue eyes fastened on me while his men added more leather to my bonds and shook out the bag they used on my head.

Fok. What was up?

"You are wondering, sir? Hmm. Today is Saturday!" He swept his arm about to include Jazmine. "Tomorrow the client arrives for a show. And, after I told them of your little ruckus last night, they were most happy to try something I suggested. You." He prodded my chest with his leather-gripped cane. "Are going to do something special. Hmm?"

What the fuck did special mean? If there was one man who could scare me, if I relaxed an inch, it was this one. The client probably just nodded a yes to all his ideas.

Though she was trying to look calm, I could see the fright in Jazmine's eyes. They were taking me away from her so she'd be terrified when next she saw me. I hadn't even managed to explain the killing to her yet.

I dared a comment to her. "Don't worry."

"The bag, please." Gregor whacked his cane across my chest. "Quiet, Pieter, or I shall do something to her now."

I seethed inside but I smiled as they bagged me again.

This bastard deserved death like no one else. I'd never before spent so much time imagining so many ways to kill another human.

Chapter 16

It was Sunday.

They didn't bring me breakfast, though the cleaning lady came in and quietly left a paper plate with a pile of bandages, gauze swabs and iodine over against the wall. I didn't go closer but I thought I glimpsed a needle and thread too. She'd smiled sadly before leaving.

No breakfast? To make me hungry? Or were they afraid I'd throw up when they did whatever they were going to do to me?

The boy's death never left me, but it receded before this new threat.

My headache vied with the nausea and the trembles. I was a big ball of cheerful healthiness.

Obviously, the bandages weren't needed, yet. They were to make me nervous. Despite resolving not to look at it, the plate drew my eye. Gregor was capable of anything, both deliberately scaring me for no reason, and getting Pieter to do something that would hurt me terribly.

What was it to be? Iodine could mean wounds. Cutting. Piercing.

If they had brought food I doubt I'd have eaten it. Such a small innocuous pile of things. Most people carried all that in their medicine cabinet.

If I'd had paper and pen, a book to read, or a laptop, I'd have diverted myself, and fuck me how likely was that? I craved reading and writing. The other thing I craved was him. Pitiful.

I still hadn't wrapped my head around the fact that he'd killed, *exterminated*, another human being so easily. It wasn't simply the quickness or the efficiency; they were expected considering his training. It was the lack of effect on him. He'd done it, dusted his hands, and moved on. Mister Cold-blooded Robot-killer.

Cliché alert.

I sighed.

I still wanted him here so I could wrap my arms around him. So abnormal for me – I'd never been one for excessive hugs and had never even kept a teddy bear when I was a kid. Pieter was my teddy bear cross killer. A little hard to accommodate those two together.

When you make yourself not look at something, the mind has a way of seeing it. The plate pulsed like some black creature hiding in a corner. I could've pointed to it without turning around.

Don't look.

My stomach growled but I ignored it. I smoothed out the sheets, plonked myself down on the bed, and covered my face with my hands. *Imagine you're about to write an article on all that has happened, plan that out, Jaz.*

It worked. I sank into the mind space where words were my playthings, my slaves, my pieces of a big literary jigsaw. Damn this would make an amazing story, if only I could survive. Pulitzer Prize, here I come.

There was always hope.

When the key turned in my door, my heart flip-flopped and I nearly swallowed my tongue.

Being led, blind, along the corridors, off to become Gregor's screaming plaything had never been so terrifying. Every time I went there it was worse.

The opening door into the Room, the echoes of their boots and *pat pat pat* of my bare feet on the cool concrete, the tinkle of the chains and the laughter of the men – these were as familiar to me as the decoration of a Christmas tree in that season of joy.

Chapter 17

A splash of water across my floor reminded me of playing noughts and crosses with her. The flutter of bird wings up high, outside my pillbox-style slit window, reminded me of looking up at her window while lying on her bed, with my arm under her shoulders. When I sat and regarded my open hands, I recalled spanking her, holding her throat, and the wet warm lick of her tongue on my skin.

I'd doomed myself in her eyes. I'd come to see that within a few hours. Maybe I could still make her understand. I'd try.

For a man trying to become better than I was, I was good at fucking up. What to me had seemed the only solution had made her see me as evil. If I'd had time to think more... My naive librarian angel had seen me murder someone. Even if it was a kill or be killed situation, what else would she be but shocked?

I paced up and down then saw sense and went through an exercise routine. Chin-ups on the window edge. Star jumps. Push-ups. All the while, I thought through the routine in this House, looking for flaws. The place was built so soundly I'd need locksmith skills, explosives, or some free time with a jackhammer to break down the walls or door. Concrete and steel, that was it.

There was only one weakness I could see so far – the cleaning lady. She never spoke to me, hadn't answered my few trial questions, but this last time, after the boy's death, she'd given me this determined look, with her lips pressed together. There'd been a nod. A nod could mean anything, but in that second, I'd seen sympathy. Had she perhaps known the guard?

If that was so, possibilities opened up.

I'd keep trying. I couldn't talk to her anyway. My room would be bugged but maybe I could pass a note? I just had to figure out how to do it secretly.

Sometime late morning, they came for me, locked me up, bagged me, and marched me away.

If only I was Bruce Lee and able to defeat armed men with my kung fu skills while blind and restrained. I'd loved those old movies but I knew when not to push, when to cooperate. Rebelling might get me injured and I needed to be fit.

The guard had been stupid to take a job here, and stupid to blurt out his plans to us like he had. When a cop, I'd reserved my sympathy for the victims, not the criminals. Always.

It occurred to me that I'd not have thought much of myself for falling into my current predicament. I'd have shrugged, muttered *poes* and moved on. Those who live by the gun die by the gun. Only in Gregor's case, it was often the knife.

When they took off my bag in the Room, I saw that today the knife wasn't being featured. Under the center lights, they had a roll of single-stranded barbed wire, pliers, and a pair of heavy gloves.

And…

I swallowed.

Jazmine, naked, hands tied above her head to the chains, with her head still bagged. Seeing her like that always shot a jolt of lust into me.

I'd have bet a million dollars they hadn't told her what was at her feet. They wanted me to show her the surprise. My mouth was dry and my hands were sweating as the last guard unlocked them.

Be good, man. Be good.

"She's waiting for you," he said, chuckling. "Give us a fucking good show, man. I wanked ten times a night all week after the last show."

Driving my fist through his chest would have to wait, but I made a rare exception to my rule of disengagement and mouthed *you bastard* in the direction of the dark window.

Gregor started up. "Go to her and take off the bag, please, Pieter. We want her to see what is coming."

Her feet shifted on the floor, toes clenching. As I approached, her head swung my way and I could hear rasping breaths. Getting enough oxygen in those bags was often dicey.

Looking wasn't a crime if she didn't know, surely?

The peekaboo secrets of her sex where the beginning of her slit showed and the cute round targets of her nipples were blatant advertisements of her femaleness. I lingered, willing my cock to behave.

She was the definition of alluring.

"It's me, Jazmine. Ignore him. Just listen to me. What you'll see isn't good, but it's not that bad either. Think of it as creative wrapping." I whispered the last. "I will be as gentle as I can."

Their no talking rules may or may not have been in effect. I didn't care.

Then I undid the neck cord and took off the bag. Her gasp and facial flinch made me want to hug her. *Fuck no.* I needed to make this look worse than it was, not better.

"Is that barbed wire?" Her question was so quiet I had to strain to hear it.

"Yes."

"Oh." She sucked in her bottom lip and looked to me.

"Keep watching me. Don't look down."

The speaker clicked on. "You are going to wrap the little miss here in the wire. It should be most interesting when you make her orgasm. Hmm? All those nasty fucking sharp wires. Digging in? Hmm?"

Where was a rocket-propelled grenade when you needed one?

"Answer me, Pieter."

I nodded slowly, while I looked at her small feet and the remnants of red toenail polish. That reminder of normality disturbed me. "Yes. It will be interesting."

Then I found a blindfold and fastened it over her eyes.

"Why'd you do that," she asked.

"I think it'll be better for you if you can't see the wire."

Her breasts rose and fell. The overhead lighting painted her nipples glossy and luscious and shone on the upper slopes of her breasts and her long thighs. I resisted touching. *Pretend she's made of thorns.*

"Answer me this," she added quietly, her voice wobbling. "Are you afraid I'll see you enjoying this? Have you got a hard-on, Pieter?"

You clever girl.

I said nothing, afraid the thickness in my throat would mess up my words. She'd hear my excitement. I couldn't afford that. I'd lose her.

"Shhh." I put my palm over her mouth. If she continued, I'd gag her.

I hadn't expected my reaction to be this extreme. It didn't matter. I'd be careful, like I'd told her. This was happening whether I enjoyed it or not.

How could I not? She was female and I was a sadist given carte blanche with a roll of barbed wire and her naked body.

But with the roll of wire at my feet, glinting like the silver angel on her wrist, with the gloves in one hand, and the heavy pliers in the other, I made myself stop and think. What was tumbling around in my head was making me feel like a schizoid evil clown.

I'd vowed to help her, not feast off her defilement.

I sauntered over to pretend I needed something at the rack of implements, but all I was doing was staring at the wall. Dirty red-brown rust marks meandered across the cracks.

Victim. She's a victim. I care for those, remember? I'd never have done anything like this to Elenor, or not and enjoyed it. Why was this different?

It shouldn't be. Where had my resolution to be good gone?

Perhaps because, deep down, I'd convinced myself that I could make her like this?

Yay for me, and what a good convenient excuse. I'd beat the most hard-core alcoholic at this game – how to get your fix without breaking the rules.

I *didn't* need to be a switched-on sadist to make this particular scene work. They'd left me an electric vibe to make her come. The white lead trailed across the floor to where it lay near her feet. Wrapping her in wire wasn't a delicate composition of pain and pleasure like before. This was construction work.

Pretend you're wrapping a cake in wire. Where was the pleasure in that?

If I got off on this, I'd be one step closer to the gutter.

"Are you doing fine, Pieter?" Even through the crackles I could hear Gregor's amusement. "We are getting just a little bored here."

I clenched my hand on the pliers then shuffled on the gloves. I turned and made for the wire.

"Good man!"

Fok jou.

I picked up the coil and played with the wire – bent it, got the feel of it and its springiness, tested the points on my skin. At least it seemed super clean. I looked her over, ambling in a circle while trailing my fingertips at her waist.

"Just me," or "good girl," I murmured now and then. Most of the bruises had faded. A new canvas for pain. Already I could imagine her squeals.

Thank god she couldn't hear my nasty thoughts.

What was the name for a man like me? Pain-oholic sounded right though fucked-up would do too.

I started checking her body again, turning her a little this way and that with my hands at her waist, bending to kiss her back, her nape, while wondering where it would be too dangerous for those sharp points to rest. Bad was anywhere that blood would spill badly if punctured, or that would choke her, or maim her permanently. Not her throat, not her face. *God, no.*

Her mouth was in mid-pout, her feet flat on the floor, muscles quiet. She seemed…at rest, calm. My handling and talking had relaxed her.

I inhaled. *Damn.* She trusted me.

"I'm starting now."

I began to wind on the wire, beginning with her legs. Sometimes I'd be brought up short by a glimpse of a particularly fascinating part of her body or by the leak of blood where a wire scratched her pale skin. Or, worst of all, by a restrained whimper. Those quiet female noises grabbed me every time. They were like the scent of prey to a hound on a trail. Fresh meat. Something to devour.

I'd catch myself looking or listening, shake myself, and move on. I lessened the cruelty by stroking her as I went. With the lick of my tongue and nips of teeth, I laid the ground for the course of the wire. I found ways to help her feel more than pain. I sucked on her nipples, ran my hands over her mound and all the while I desperately tried to stay disengaged.

Impossible…but I kept trying.

The wire was starting to restrict her responses to pleasure. Her body would undulate then she'd hiss or whimper, catch herself, and stiffen.

Once only, I kissed her. The softness of her lips contrasted with the hardness of the metal across her belly. I held my bare hand against the wire as I moved her lips aside with my tongue.

Her moans then that gorgeous flinch from the metal while I breathed into her mouth, kissed her hard, and penetrated her mouth with my tongue…it was so addictive.

My heart did away with blood and pumped obsession.

Where the barbs dug in just under her nipples and below her breasts, or where they pressed on her mons above her clit, I had problems. Some things were too mouthwatering to avoid *seeing.* My inner sadist was being bad.

Sharp and deadly versus soft and vulnerable. Like fire to an arsonist, searing me, searing her.

Move on.

But the urge, *ohmigod,* the fucking urge took me in its vice, ground me up, spat me out all delirious. Those glittering shards embedded in my mind.

I retreated, backed away, breathing hard, stood there with my hands at my sides, overwhelmed.

I could look at this forever, my siren in wire.

"Pieter?" She searched blindly for me, carefully, so as not to rub on wire. "Where are you? Please?"

My cock was begging me so much I'd have fucked her in an instant.

Didn't *matter*, none of it. The alternative was Gregor. I could help her still.

I understood now. A man faced with a beautiful naked woman parading on a beach could look away, but gift him with that woman to touch and play with and he'd have no hope of staying calm. Neither did I, when handed this.

She couldn't see the state I was in.

I wiped my mouth and stepped closer. "I'm here."

When it came to switch on the vibe, I flicked the cord out of the way then I took one look at my wire-wrapped beauty.

There were gaps, there was looseness, but I had no idea what would happen when she came.

"We are ready, Mister Pieter! Make it good."

I stepped up and squashed the rounded head of the vibe to her clit, nestled it in so the lips of her pussy bulged out around it.

"Ready, *meisie*?"

Her mouth opened and I paused a moment to admire the swell of those ripened curves. Even there, she mesmerized me. I pressed the switch.

The hum made her hiss and arch instantly then jerk back as the wire's points dug in.

My heart thumped but I held the vibe in position.

Her little whines built in intensity as the climax came over her. She screamed then rocked and juddered into the vibe, her thighs tensing, but little else of her moving. Surprising to me, how fast that had arrived. Thirty seconds?

"More, Mister Pieter!"

I didn't need prompting. I'd left her nipples bare of wire so I pulled and pinched them as I revolved the vibe's head in small circles.

She shook her head, begging. "Not…more. Not yet."

"Shh."

"No!"

I undid the blindfold. Eye contact might help her.

Then I put my whole hand on her mouth, listening to the hiss of air through her nose to make sure she could breathe. She looked at me, then down, focusing on my hand, as if fascinated by my hold on her. As I worked at her clit, her eyes hazed and her hips arched out, until the wires must be hurting. The tips dented her skin. This time, her screams and whole body shudders lasted for ages. Small droplets of blood trickled down her upper thighs. Sweat stood out on her brow.

Her gasps and screams through my fingers had been…enthralling. Watching her come while in pain…like this. *Fok.*

I stepped back, still holding the vibe, to wipe my forearm across my face. My breathing was a little chaotic. The vibe hummed on while I counted. It was thirty-five before she recovered and relaxed and her hands uncurled from the chains above.

But there was blood. I frowned and dragged myself out of my sadistic study.

I'd failed a little by enjoying this, but I'd succeeded too. She wasn't injured, just scratched.

"More, Mister Pieter!"

Shit.

"Last time," I yelled back at them. No reply. I took a deep breath and approached her.

My relief when she came again and no one screamed *more* at me was immense.

There was some fresh bleeding on her stomach. I'd check that when the wires came off.

Before I could unwrap her, they ordered me to back away and be restrained. I bowed my head a moment before obeying.

The lock of the cuffs on my wrists brought Gregor into the room.

"You were a little too gentle and look." He went to one knee and picked up the silver bracelet with the angel. "She has to wear this or I punish her. You know this angel, hey?" He nodded at Jasmine.

Her lips trembled. Above her head, her fingers tightened on the chains making them sway and clink.

"Answer me."

"Yes, sir," she whispered.

"It was my fault!"

But he ignored me, tugged on the gloves I'd dropped, and began to roughly remove the wire.

"My fault! Not hers." I seethed.

"Never mind. Next time you will know. Be silent or this will be worse for her."

I lost count of the new scratches he created and the slaps he gave her face and breasts. Jazmine was sobbing uncontrollably by the end, streaked with red like a cake iced entirely the wrong way.

Yet another point on the list of reasons to kill him.

When I ground my teeth, the guards near me laughed. So many people to kill, so little time. I gave myself some gold stars for caring. They almost cancelled out the black marks I'd gained for wallowing in her pain.

By the time they delivered me to her room, she was there, waiting, naked except for the blood. Exhaustion blurred my mind, but I went to her.

The distress and her choked out noes drove me away for all of half a minute before I growled, advanced again, and tucked her into my arms.

"I'm sorry. I'm sorry." I rocked her a while, aghast at how much I'd done to her. Not all of it had been Gregor's fault.

Now that I had her, she didn't move at all. That scared me most of all. She hadn't forgiven me for the boy. What was going on in her thoughts?

Chapter 18

"Come. You have to clean off the blood. Don't stay too long. It'll keep the wounds from clotting if you do." A voice like the tide coming in, soft and persuasive. With his big hands on my back, he herded me to the shower then turned it on, held me there a second, as if afraid I'd fall, or wander off…

Mute, blank, nothing happening in my head, I stood there with the cold water pouring down me, stirring up the pains. I hissed but with time the pain dulled. *Cold.* I shivered.

At least some of the bad seemed to wash away in the flow.

The things they'd done to me.

Maybe I deserved it. Maybe. My tears mingled with the water. I'd done bad things in life. Maybe this was karma. My eyelids drifted down.

I stood there, being washed away, being hurt.

But it wasn't Pieter. It was him, Gregor. The dismissive, casual violence he did to me, as if I were nothing. Absolutely fucking nothing in this awful world. I was a piece of dirt to him, a piece of temporary enjoyment. Gregor would kill me as easily as he'd crack an egg.

I opened my eyes and put my palms on the white wall, leaned in.

As each blow of his had bruised me, the pain had hammered me down inside. Why did what Gregor did or thought matter? I despised him. I gave him power by letting anything he did to me hurt.

Pieter was different. Even when he'd killed that boy, he'd said it was his only option, that he did it for me. I hated the boy dying. Yet the *why* of it…it made Pieter more in my eyes. Even if he hurt me and did what Gregor asked with no protest at all, he was my warped hero.

Everything that happened in this place was dirtied.

The water was helping. Under it, with the roar in my ears, I felt protected in some weird way. Here was safety.

Of course, Pieter didn't protest because that might make things worse for me. Everything he did here seemed aimed at me. He liked hurting me but the difference between his type of pain and Gregor's was vast and puzzling. I didn't really understand why he helped me. I didn't understand why he liked hurting me. Worst of all, I didn't understand how he made me like it.

When my shivering started again, I stirred.

Don't stay long. It'd been ages, hadn't it? My mind wasn't functioning well.

Where had he gone?

I shut off the water and dripped dry, watching the droplets dribble down the strands of my hair, down my legs, then into the drain. Still, he didn't come to me.

The towel was a gray-white but by the time I'd dried myself it'd become a mess of pink, red, and gray. My belly leaked blood. My legs too. Watery blood. My breasts were patched with blue and dark red bruises. Those were from Gregor. I stuffed my face in the towel and breathed there shaking. Everything about me might fall apart if I moved. I shouldn't have turned off the water.

"Give me that." From behind, he took the towel from me and wrapped me up. Warmth. His body gave me something solid to lean into.

All my head seemed to register was that here was security. Safe again. Though he said something to me, I'd lost the ability to concentrate.

We were moving and at some point, somehow, we reached the bed. Once I hit the sheets, my thinking shut down and I was gone.

When I woke it was light still. Or was it morning? From the pallid color of the wall next to the bed, it was early morning. I'd slept and now I hurt. So stiff. Places unstuck as I rolled over, my head ending up half off the bed. The sheet slipped away. I was still without clothes.

Last night in the Room had really happened. I shut away a sudden vision of Gregor hitting me.

Was Pieter here? Had they taken him away? I panicked, stupidly, focusing through sleep-glued eyes. There he was.

He sat on the floor, back against the wall near the door, head shaded by his hands. This glowering man, who scared me as much as attracted me, was lost in some reverie.

None of my lovers, few in number that they were, had ever seen me exposed as rawly as he had. If they had, I doubted they'd have cared for me. I'd become so dirty. Sullied was the word. If only I could get home again and curl up in bed. If no one saw me, it wouldn't matter.

A dream but a good one.

I wanted to be alone as much as I wanted to be with someone. Just look at what had happened here – people had messed up my beautifully organized life. Fuck them all.

I pried myself from bed, set my feet on the floor.

I limped to him, hesitated when I reached his side. When had I ever hugged anyone voluntarily? Over-effusive boyfriends never stayed with me long. Family gatherings were a nightmare.

But I longed to touch him, this man who had wrapped me in barbed wire.

Yes? No? Touching him by myself made my stomach twist. I stretched out my arm, my forefinger an inch from his shoulder. He was unaware.

I lowered my arm, willing him to turn and see me, because that would be so much better.

A strand of my hair grazed his cheek.

Then he did turn, and he looked at me and nodded, then hauled himself to his feet. He raised his hands as if to draw me close, only to lower them.

A pang of disappointment saddened me.

"How are you? I'm sorry, I was thinking."

About what? A score of possibilities reared their heads.

The darkness I'd glimpsed in his expression daunted me. The man had demons. With his past, I expected that. Asking what he'd been thinking might give me more than I wanted right then.

I shrugged then winced. Tiredness dulled my reply. My jaw ached when I opened my mouth. "I'm sore."

"Mmm." His gaze travelled over me. I could see him stopping at each wound, a frown would touch his brow then he'd move on. "I wish we could do more than wash these down."

"There are bandages and some sort of antiseptic." I pointed at the plate bearing Gregor's gifts. "They brought it yesterday."

"They left it before they took you to the Room?"

I nodded, remembering how it had bothered me.

"*Fok* them. *Fok* them all to hell and back, but I can use it. Come to the middle so I can play doctors and nurses." He flashed me a smile then waited, maybe to see if I had it in me to smile back.

Wrapped up in misery but grateful, I walked to the middle and pretended to be tough when he dabbed iodine on the cuts.

"Doesn't look like you need stitches. These will hurt for days, you poor baby."

Baby? How weird being called that and by this man who'd made some of these holes in me. Then he came in close. I dropped into flight or fight mode and stiffened.

He whispered into my ear, "I'm getting us out. You need hope. Here it is. I've figured a way."

So soft. Had I imagined those words?

I stared at the wall like a robot then cautiously turned my head. He gave the slightest nod.

Last time I'd had hope it'd been the boy guard and look what had happened there.

A nightmare I'd never forget, while that boy would be silent forever, wherever they'd buried him. If they had. He could be lying out there somewhere in the jungle.

I blinked.

Pieter wasn't a man for casual promises. Like Gregor, he reserved words for when he meant them.

The next burn of the iodine seemed to add fire to my mind. *Getting out. If only.*

My vengeful daydream surfaced.

Run to the police. Fuck them over. God, I prayed they'd all die horribly. Then dig to find out who organized this shithole torture palace. Someone could rip this enterprise open to the world with the right article. I could do it. I fucking could.

Please let it happen.

The pain from a dab zapped me back to earth. "Owie." I ducked away, tried to shift my feet, only to be brought up short by his hand wrapped around my knee.

"Stay, girl."

"I never thought I'd see you kneeling for me."

Pieter grunted.

I might be a prisoner still, but I had hope now, because of him.

He rose from where he'd been painting my thigh. Back in my real life, I'd have been horrified at a man doing this while I was naked.

"Better?" His question was loaded with extra significance.

"Yes."

"Good."

My thoughts tracked sideways. I needed hope but, *oh my*, if I wrote an exposé about this place, *if* we escaped, would it bring him down too?

I shook myself. Of all the things to worry about.

What a beautifully constructed man he was.

Even as I trailed my way along, from those biceps you could bounce a bullet off, to the thickness of his shoulders, to his small smile, I knew a truth. He wasn't for me. I wasn't for him. Some people were as opposite as the arctic and the middle of the sun. Sure, he could make me come a zillion times while he worked his magic with pain, and that had been such a revelation. But in my life? Mr. Let me hold you still while I fuck you and beat you? He adored pain. He killed without looking back.

Me, I could barely squash a cockroach.

I'd be more likely to invite a serial murderer to my bed. Ice trickled in my veins. For all I knew, he was one.

How many women had been through here and sold off as slaves? Too many. There was no doubt in me – given the chance for revenge by my usual means, the power of the word, I'd do it. Whether it hurt him or not.

Escape. Please let it be so.

He nestled his hands at my waist.

Accompanied by the bone-deep throb of bruises and the sting, that touch seemed to affirm some connection between us. *Wrong.* My pussy clenched. Stupid female reaction. I held my breath, resisting.

The intensity in his gaze added to his hold, as if he claimed me. *What big brown eyes you have, sir.* I shivered. The familiar pull and push. Running backwards until I hit the wall wrestled with staying in his hands.

I took a controlled yet ragged breath. Time to reclaim some me. "Let go. Please."

When he did so I felt lighter, relieved, and bereft.

Chapter 19

If she wanted distance right now, I would give it to her even though every instinct in me said to give her a big hug. I wasn't sure how she was even standing. She swayed as I looked at her. For a little librarian, she had strength in her, down deep, where it counted. Some of the men I'd worked and fought with could've learned from her. She bounced when others would shatter.

Me…I'd left bruises on Elenor but she'd wanted them. Disgust was too good a word for me, except when I remembered how I'd felt *then*, in the moment.

It wasn't surprising she was confused since I'd totally fucked over my own head.

I'd never had a high like yesterday and I'd never before felt so destroyed after an S and m session, or whatever you called what we'd done. Abuse, probably. Guess this was karma's retribution.

"Think they'll bring us breakfast soon?" She fiddled with her fingers as if nervous. "It's crazy, but I'm starving."

"I hope so. You need it. They left you a dress." I fetched the little blue scrap of cloth from the bottom of the bed. The sheets were spotted with her blood. "I suppose you think you can get this on without help? It's going to hurt you."

"Yes. I'll do it." She put out her hand.

Ja. Stubborn, but it was her call.

With the iodine on the scratches, she was a spotty patchwork of orange-brown, red, blue, and pale skin, as well as the darker triangle reappearing at the juncture of her thighs.

Of course, if they'd given her a razor, I'd have fashioned a weapon from it.

I saw more than bruises.

The curl of her ear enticed me, as did the delicate pout of her lip, the sadness in her eye and the sensual curve of her breasts. I was getting a little lost in admiring her and I realized that I wanted her to want me to touch her and in more than a purely sexual way. More than a "let's have a comforting hug" way. I wanted to find out who she really was.

She shook out the dress and turned away from me, as if uncomfortable with me watching.

Before I could be some creepy admirer, I needed to fix what was wrong and get us out. I didn't look away. That quirky inclination to see her as mine tainted things. What did it matter when next time in the Room I could do what I liked?

It matters because it's the decent thing to do.

For all of a second, I looked away.

Watching her put the dress on when she was obviously hurting from bending this way and that, was an exercise in agony. My hands itched to do something. When the hem fell in place, it only grazed the back of her thighs, revealing a hint of butt, same as the previous dresses. Damn she was pretty. I'd never get tired of looking at her, whether perfect or blemished. Besides, some of those marks were mine. Some of them when she'd screamed through those orgasms.

No man could forget that. It had left an imprint on my mind.

The door rattled.

Jaz flinched enough that even her face twitched. She backed away and crawled onto the bed, then curled up near the wall.

"Breakfast! Here, Pieter, boy."

Mocking me seemed to have become a sport. They thought me safe, but I went obediently to be manacled. Getting angry was pointless. I needed to be good. The manacles clicked on.

Jaz had perched on the bed and was absentmindedly swinging her long legs. A nonchalant act, perhaps. I was beginning to know her. Like anyone, she got scared. She just hid it well.

I went over to the far wall, as they let the cleaning lady in. Same woman, plumpish, with dark curly hair at neck length. She never did more than glance at me though with Jaz she sometimes smiled or exchanged a word.

Three guards out there covering the door. Breakfast had arrived with the lady. She bustled about doing a perfunctory clean and changing the sheets. Jaz helped her with that as if this was some family place and an aunt was fixing the bed linen in our room.

The paper plates held a fried mix of meat, tomatoes, and potatoes, and an apple for us each. They fed us, though not enough. I'd lost muscle mass.

After eating, with me sitting on the floor and her on the bed, I washed off my plate and dried it. This one was a keeper. I needed it.

I'd boiled my strategies down to me rampaging through this place killing people after somehow, miraculously, getting out of the room, and then of course I'd die.

Or there was me and her somehow escaping the room and then reaching the jungle, or a vehicle. Or, last and best, getting word out to my friends who were ex-military and here in PNG for the same reason as I was – looser country borders and policing, less chance of being arrested for past crimes. Some of the cops here were bought. My friends were not.

"Let's play spin the bottle."

Jaz lowered her head and peeked at me. "What? There's only two of us."

"It'll be fun, and I get to probe you for all your dirty secrets."

The cogs were turning. I'd bothered her. "We...don't have a bottle."

"We have this." I twisted the plate into a long curled mess. "It'll do as a pointer."

Sitting down in front of her on the floor annoyed her. Her mouth twisted and there was evil in her glare, but she shrugged.

"Fine. No kissing though, or anything, as prizes." She drew her legs up and crossed them. "Not sure I have any dirty secrets."

"No? We just have to answer a question." I lifted my brows. "We all have dirty secrets."

Some of mine were so dark I'd not tell her in a million years, but some of the others, I was strangely looking forward to spilling. A fact landed *ker-thud* in my head. It wasn't likely we would ever leave here. Bleak but true. I wasn't giving up but I knew the odds and they were poor.

She snorted lightly. "I guess."

At the least, I wanted to get to know my pretty roommate. More of her than I did now. I might know the color of her nipples, but I wanted more, before we came to whatever end Gregor planned for us.

"Mm-hmm. Scared?" I grinned.

Jaz had this little blank expression that flitted across sometimes, like now. What did a librarian have to conceal? I flipped that. Maybe she *was* just scared. As if that was new.

Watching her making the bed and exchanging little smiles with the lady had brought back memories of me and Elenor, back when I had a home…back when I had a wife who would smile at me or, when I got too silly, throw pillows at me.

I missed that so much.

Life has a way of giving you stuff you barely knew you appreciated, snatching it away and then going *see* that was what it was all about.

"Let's do this. This squidgy end is the pointer." I spun the squashed plate.

"It's you! Good! Tell me something funny."

I pulled a face. "About?"

"Hmm." She wriggled her feet, with her hands on her ankles, looking every bit like an excited teenager. "Your childhood?"

"Okay. Let me see. One morning, when I woke up baboons were in our kitchen. Somehow they'd gotten in through an unlocked door. My mother had to shoo them out with a broom."

Jaz giggled. "Baboons?"

"Yes." I nodded, trying to look wise. "The mess in the kitchen was so smelly our dogs went crazy."

"Baboon shit. I'll never beat that." Her grin was big and infectious and I could've watched her forever.

Being creepy again. Even if it was in a good cause.

I spun. "Your turn to cough up a secret."

"Jeez. Rigged. I get to spin next time." She peered down.

Good. If she did that she'd be halfway on the floor. At the least I'd get to look down her cleavage, and why that was appealing when I'd just seen all of her was a baffling secret of female attractiveness.

"Rule. When you get a question it has to be connected to the last one. So tell me something from your childhood."

"Ugh. No baboons there. I got lost on the way to school. My mum sent me off on my bike in Grade five. New school in an outback town, middle of Australia."

How old was she in Grade five? Eleven? "Where'd you end up?"

"The library. I was playing hookie. I hated new schools."

When they came to get the breakfast leftovers, we'd likely get to keep this plate, and maybe the paper cup of coffee dregs. I needed that too. Writing in the dark was going to be hard to do, but I'd manage.

I'd thought a long while last night and this morning. It all depended on the cleaning lady. What I planned could save us or it could bring Gregor's anger down on us.

Giving Jazmine hope had been my first gift. Even if I did have a plan, it was by no means as sure as I'd told her. It had been worth the lie to see the brightness transform her face. Lies to me were like payments to the devil. Hated them. A lie had killed my brother.

My second gift to her was to do everything to keep her well. I wanted to earn some gold stars for my poor battered soul. I was so fucking tired of hating myself. I'd told her that I could forget things but it wasn't true. Short term, yes. Later, no. The past came back and chewed me over, made me feel like every part of me was so wrong, so bad, and that I'd never be a good person again.

Enjoying what I'd done in the Room had guaranteed a year of guilt.

We went through more questions and I slowly gave her more of me and began to doubt how much of her I was really getting.

It was unfair but…if she was lying, I guess I understood. I still hated it. I wanted her, not lies.

"Tell me something that you regret."

Ah. Now that was a nasty one. I felt compelled to tell a truth, if not the whole truth. "When I shot a man in the face, and killed him."

"Oh."

She looked as if her stomach was as sickened as mine.

I'd said a stupid answer, but I'd have done it again. Killing the boy guard was more recent. Funny how that made me numb more than sad.

The pointer was on her again. "Tell me something about being a librarian. Something cute, funny, amazing."

"About being a librarian? Amazing? Seriously? Okay. The day I managed to pull a whole bookshelf over on my head. Talk about embarrassing."

The flatness in the telling made me wonder if that was true. How many questions had she answered that had made me go, was that really the truth?

Who was this woman?

I hated lying, but the more she did it, the more intense my curiosity.

"You might want to stop crossing your legs. You're flashing me every so often."

"Oh." She brought her legs together. That bright red blush was part of why I wanted to know who she really was. That she could still blush after all that had happened, it spoke of a naivety around men and that just…appealed. Might be my kinky imagination but I could roll with it.

That night I sat down on the bed, in the faint moonlight, and attempted to write a message with coffee on a paper plate. If she just threw this away we were fucked. I had no idea where else to go from here.

Gregor ran this place like a clock. A nasty, malevolent fucked-up clock.

Chapter 20

There were days I wanted to be so close with Pieter that our skin would merge. He was big, powerful, a rock of serenity in the middle of this mad place. Then there were days I'd look at him and remember what he'd done, how good he was at killing, and I'd recognize my previous foolishness.

He didn't understand how most every little thing he told me about himself was reinforcing my fear of him.

I didn't understand why he could nevertheless make me catch my breath when he stripped off for a shower. Or like now, when he'd looked at me through those dangling untidy dark locks while doing push-ups. With his... *fucking* shirt off. *Swallow thy tongue.* The little octopus on the back of his shoulder gleamed and writhed as his muscles slid.

Yep. He affected me *not* at all. Trying not to look hot and flushed, I shifted my legs and stared at the paintwork instead.

Pieter was my own private tiger and I was locked in the cage with him.

Drooling at men wasn't new. Having a thrill run through me at the potential for a man to grab me and do something unexpected to me – that was new.

Yet even when he told me about his ex-wife my throat closed in. Why? Who the fuck knew. Perhaps because all these details made him real, like someone I could date, and that was terrifying. *Not* in a million years would

I ever date him. Silly reaction, though. My mind needed to catch up on the news. I might die tomorrow.

My teensy window up high was acting all cheerful again, letting in an actual visible shaft of late sun along with golden, whirling particles of dust.

"Wish I was Tinkerbell so I could fly on a sunbeam."

He grunted, pausing at the top of a push-up. "Yeah?"

"Must be windy out there." A breeze was getting in past the seals. The glass rattled. My sunlight faded, vanished.

Despite doing more push-ups, Pieter replied. "The weather is pretty dirty. A storm might be coming."

There were places out there where people were free. "Last night, I heard a woman crying. The poor thing."

"*Ja.* It was bad. You have a kind heart, Jaz."

"I do?" Guess I was soft at times.

"You think of others. Even when you are worse off."

Funny but I'd always thought myself self-centered. Anyone could empathize though. I was bad at really doing anything that changed things. Maybe thoughts counted?

I put my hand on my heart and wished us all home, every single one of us captives. *Zoe.* I remembered her. I prayed she'd escaped.

Even those many lonely nights when I'd eaten takeaway in my apartment by myself or walked past restaurants and cafés and looked in at loving couples, I'd pay almost anything to have those in my reach. I wanted to be ordinary again.

Please, please, *if there's a god up there. One of us deserves to have our lives back.*

Tears filled my eyes and threatened to spill. I wiped them away with my forefinger.

What was there left for Him to do to me? What came after barbed wire? My mind went straight to the bleeding wreck of a man that Gregor had created with his knife.

If it was that next, could I kill myself? I had no clue how anyone suicided without drugs or a weapon. I might manage shooting myself in the head but anything else seemed unlikely.

How bad had things become that I contemplated this?

How many people would have done it already?

I dropped my gaze to the bed. The guard had poked these sheets through the hatch and they'd come back with dark spots. Their laundry methods hadn't washed out my blood.

Yesterday, after three days without seeing her, the cleaning lady had returned. My opportunity, or so Pieter had whispered. I gave her the plate with an apologetic smile and a *here's some rubbish you missed.* What were the chances she would read it? She'd looked at the writing, frozen, and then I'd crumpled it again and tossed it into her bag of rubbish.

Please help us. They killed a young boy here. They torture me. Go here. Say Pieter sent you. Say where we are.

Below that was Pieter's signature, an address, and a note that said to give her a large amount of money – a coffee-flavored message. It was weird. Like hiding a hacksaw in a cake.

She'd gone and now I could only wonder. What if? I'd had a nightmare last night where Gregor burned us alive. If he found out what we'd done, he would punish me. I'd seen that possibility from the moment Pieter suggested this.

"Are you okay?" Pieter was at my side, panting, looking all sweaty and male.

I shrugged. "Just thinking."

"I'll have a shower then and join you in that thinking."

"Mmm." We shared a bed at night but I'd made clear to him that he wasn't to touch me sexually anymore. That he obeyed was amazing. I eyed him sideways as if dubious. "I guess thinking with me is fine."

He shot me one of those inscrutable frowns that had the potential to stop my heart. I'd figured out I could either act daunted or flippant when he did this. Acting frightened was stupid, like blood on the ground to my tiger. Besides, I found I liked living on the edge and teasing him.

So I grinned.

"*Ja*, it sure is bloody fine. Don't go away."

That he now said the Aussie *bloody* instead of the South African *blêrrie* was cute.

I counted days. Was it Saturday? "Gregor's back soon." Breathing became a forgotten thing.

That I'd said it aloud registered a second later.

In mid-stride to the shower, Pieter turned back, his lips compressed. "Yes."

Even if the cleaning lady went to his soldier friends, it might be too late. Dread arose from the ashes of my thoughts.

They'd do something awful to me tomorrow. It was always worse.

The shower came on. I blinked then rearranged myself on the bed and looked the other way so I wouldn't have to see Pieter's toned butt or any of his other interesting bits.

A guard banged on the door. "There's a cyclone coming! Should be here tomorrow. If it doesn't knock the place down, you should be fine. Don't expect food for a couple of days. Fill these up with water."

He shoved a few plastic containers through the hatch, old milk bottles from the looks of them, and then a bag of apples, a few packets of cheese, and some bread. They thumped and scattered onto the floor.

A cyclone. That was why the high winds. *Fuck.*

As if on cue, rain speckled against my window and a super-big gust shook the glass again.

We might drown or…or *anything.*

And if the building fell over, I didn't give a shit. Maybe we could escape even. I flopped back onto the bed and grinned at the ceiling.

No Gregor. Yes!

Chapter 21

"This place is concrete above," I pointed at the ceiling, "and there. Concrete walls, steel door – not a hope it'll blow down." At Jaz's crestfallen expression I rummaged for something heartening. "If a tree fell on us, maybe, just maybe, a wall might crumble."

But I doubted it. More likely we'd drown if this place was near a river or the guards would forget to come back and feed us. There were two locking mechanisms on the door and one of them was a bar they lowered on the outside. The hatch was an inch thick, slid to one side, and had some fastening on the outside that I couldn't get to. I'd looked at shifting that on a few nights.

"I didn't really think it was likely." Jaz went to our little collection of bottles and food and picked up two of the bottles.

To pick even the pickable lock I needed metal. The only metal in the room was wiring and it was screwed away behind thick plastic plates. I needed metal to pry off the plates to get the metal. I'd have risked getting electrocuted if it was possible.

I needed a fairy godmother, or a greedy cleaning lady with a conscience. My friends were true friends. We'd do anything for each other, including coming in guns blazing if they knew I was here. No one fucked with Randall, Glass, Jurgen, or me. Even if Jurgen was only a few years shy of fifty. Except they *were* fucking with me.

I heaved out a sigh and went to help filling up bottles. Five bottles, so ten liters. If the taps stopped working, we might last a few days before we were desperate enough to drink the toilet water.

I watched her struggle to press the stiff button to keep the water flowing while still holding the bottle in place.

"Give me that." I took the bottle from her and stuck it under the tap.

At least she was healing well. After a week of treatment, I had no reason to paint her nude body with iodine anymore. Such a pity. Though handling her was torture for my dick and gave me blue balls for ages. Her newborn reluctance to let me kiss her, sit her on my lap, or spank her cute little ass…

An ass that was partly on display what with her kneeling to get some stray apples off the floor. I wrenched my gaze away. Yeah, not being allowed to touch her seemed a suitable penance as well as a test of willpower.

I wanted to be a good man. This was it. Even if I only lived another day or another week, it was worth it.

I'd be convinced of this, until the next time she gave me cheek. Equality just seemed wrong with Jazmine. Whenever she started up the shower, I remembered her behavior when I went all alpha male on her.

But I didn't have the right to do that. *Or the right excuse.*

The cyclone hit early the next morning. I'd been through two of these big storms before, what the Americans would call hurricanes, but Jazmine hadn't. She'd lived too far south in Australia to see them. From her wide eyes and the way she cowered at the far end of the bed when the bigger wind gusts made the building shudder, when the air was filled with so much noise we had to shout, it made me offer to take her in my arms. The relief when she swarmed up the bed to accept was immense.

First time in days. I held her so tightly she squeaked.

"Let go a little, Pieter."

I chuckled and loosened my grip, but I smelled her skin, I felt those curves that were Jazmine, and I breathed out a slow, happy breath, then I smiled into her hair. That old saying – my heart lightened – had never seemed so real or so right as now.

Mine.

I almost didn't care how dark it got when I had her with me.

For hours the rain and wind blasted against the wall. If the window shattered we might get showered by glass. I did the best I could while standing on tiptoe on the bottom rail of the bed. With my fingertips, I wedged one of our two pillows up against the glass in the little concrete alcove. Only a sliver, at either end of the window, wasn't blocked. If the ceiling light failed, it'd be dark.

I jumped down.

"Will that work?" Jaz said loudly. She eyed the window, then me, while hugging herself. The constant extreme weather beating at this building had dropped the temperature to winter levels.

"It'll do. If I could shift the bed into the middle I would." It was bolted down. Though if the worst happened and the wall did get damaged, she could hide under there.

The rain intensified, the hard taps sounding like bullets hitting the glass. There'd been bright green leaves stuck to the outside of the window and the sky was so dark it seemed as if the apocalypse was arriving. Outside something scraped across concrete, smacked into our wall, then slapped rhythmically.

"What's that?" She sidled closer and I took the opportunity to put my hands on her hips and nestle her into me.

"A palm tree leaf maybe. Or a deck chair. The guards probably laze about sipping piña coladas in the quadrangle on their lunch hour."

"Hmph. Probably. This is fucking scary."

"We just need to wait. This is probably the strongest building I've ever waited out one of these in."

"Oh?"

"Come back to bed." I ushered her to it then climbed over her to spoon. The best benefit ever. I should've been praying for a cyclone all along.

"You make that sound dirty."

"True."

I coughed as if her hair had annoyed me then smoothed it away from my face, exposing her nape with all those sweet little spirals of hair. When she snuggled back into me, I considered nibbling her there. My cock pulsed in agreement.

Don't push. She's coming around to letting me touch her again.

"Where else have you been during a cyclone?"

"An apartment in Port Moresby, and on an island, that was the worst. The big seas ripped up the beach. A friend who's a pilot uses one as a waypoint for his seaplane on the way to Australia." Illegally. I'd been stuck there for days. There were the remnants of an old ramshackle resort on the island from almost World War Two days.

"Trust me, this is far better than huddling in a decrepit hut praying that I wouldn't get sliced up by the next bit of corrugated iron whirling past."

At that, something slammed into the other side of the wall the bed rested against. I reached back and placed my palm on the ice-cold concrete. The winds rose in tone to a shrill whistle and a hum that vibrated the wall.

"What. The fuck. Was that?"

Gregor's dead body, I hoped. "No idea. Maybe you should try to sleep?"

The power failed and she shivered.

"It's okay. We don't need it."

Hours later, the serene eye of the storm arrived over us. The wind dropped to nothing. It was cold but all was quiet. Midday by now? We had no watch and the sun wasn't easy to see. Blue sky showed beyond the pillow's edges. In here was dark.

"Wow. That's it?"

"We're in the eye of the storm. Depending on whether we're on the edge or in the middle it could last ten minutes or ages."

She glanced over her shoulder at me and wriggled into a sitting position. "Then the cyclone comes back?"

"Yes." Fascinated, I smoothed my hand up the back of her dress over her spine.

As if I'd poked her with a pin, she jumped up and went to the tap, turned it on. "It's still working!"

"Good."

"I'll just get a drink."

I sat on the mattresses' edge. With my elbows on my knees, I watched her potter about drinking, going on tiptoes as if to look out the window, then at last she walked over and sat at the other end of the bed.

My frown arrived after a small struggle. Was she so fickle? "You're avoiding me."

Her eyes squeezed shut. "I just don't want to give you the wrong idea."

My next words would be setting a trap for myself, but I said them anyway. "Which is? You've been in my arms for the last two or three hours. The idea I'd gotten was that you'd figured I was safe after all. A friend."

Her sigh lasted ages and seemed to deflate her like a balloon. She covered her face with her hands. I waited, impatient, but I waited.

Being impatient was a revolutionary emotion for me but damn if this woman wasn't frustrating.

"What you are to me is so warped I don't know where to begin. Friend seems wrong. Don't you see? I don't want you to think that I like you…that way."

That way? What the fuck did it matter? When we'd possibly die tomorrow? When we could comfort each other? "You hate me that much? As soon as the scary storm dies down you can't stand me?"

Her green eyes looked over the top of her hands. "I…no. You've been kind to me. It's me. I'm not into close contact that much anyway. It's just *me*."

My hands, where I'd wrapped them together between my knees, were a safer study than her. I hung my head, but I was no coward. I looked at her, even if it was the bleakest stare I'd summoned for her, ever.

"Kind?" I'd been more than kind. My restraint had been phenomenal. "I've seen how you respond to me." From what she'd once said, I was the only man who'd ever made her come.

She scoffed, but wriggled as if uncomfortable under my stare. *Good.*

"That's purely physical. You don't jump on every woman who stares at you, surely? Do you?" Her words were mocking and steeped in challenge.

I should back away. I should. And in half an hour, she'd use me as a safety blanket when the storm came back.

"No. I don't."

But you, girl, you're different. Couldn't she see the possibilities? I said a string of curses in my head. Anger was foreign to me, most days. I was seething and I wasn't sure why she brought this out.

Being scared of me wasn't all of it. She seemed scared of people in general, up close. Of what might happen with that next step, where she'd have to give away a piece of herself. Every step of the way she pulled backward, until forced.

I got that.

It was the possibilities that terrified her. She'd made a little safe cocoon and left to herself, she'd stay there.

I tapped my fingers on my leg.

Smirking, she shrugged at me. "See. We agree. We should do another game."

"A game?"

"Mm." Her movements were stiff. The girl looked brittle as glass but maybe that was me glowering.

Another place, another time, I'd have backed off. But here, now? I could let her keep doing this, keep pretending we were a pair of *poeslekker* aunties having a tea party, or I could do what every part of me was itching to do. What I was damn sure she needed, let alone wanted.

It almost seemed negligent to let her go on without seeing who she could be. She must have been so fucking lonely from what she'd revealed. The submissives I'd known, back in Cape Town, had often seemed to have the best of love.

And then, there were my needs...

They crawled across my skin, tugging at me, reminding me of how I'd had her, of what I'd done to her in here, not in Gregor's dungeon, *here*, in this room, where she so primly sat pretending that nothing had ever happened.

"Noughts and crosses?" she asked brightly.

"Noughts and crosses." I turned down my lip and pretended to calmly consider it. "You want a game? Do you remember the one where you kneeled for me and loved it? Have you forgotten? Me, I remember." I nodded. "I remember your sounds when I played with your body. Your cries when I gave you pleasure. I remember, not just in my head, but in here."

I whacked one hand on my chest. A little over dramatic but I felt like thumping something.

The flush hit her face in a rush.

"I never… I never really liked that."

"Never?" Talk about denial. I snapped out a command. "Give me your wrist."

The slightest sign of obedience would be enough.

As if I had her on a string, her hand came up. The stunned expression when she caught herself, halted the movement of her hand, and stared at me, unleashed a torrent of satisfaction.

I grinned at her malevolently.

"I wasn't going to –" she began, her eyes flashing, her tone so damn indignant.

"You were." This woman begged to be dominated.

Some things just needed doing.

I lunged sideways, grabbed her hair, and hauled her over despite her screech, pulling her onto my lap and ignoring squeals and flailing arms. I released her hair, ducking back as she swiped at me, and captured those scratching hands at the wrists. Then I held her down by pressing those wrists to her back and with my leg wrapped over her thighs.

"You are such a brat."

She stilled, spluttering into the mattress. "Pieter! Fucking let me go."

I ignored her. Her next attempts at squirming free were even crazier but I hung on. There wasn't much she could do, though it took five minutes before she decided that and collapsed panting. Her dress was so short it took the smallest flick to bare her ass.

"Nice." I murmured, cupping the lower curve in my hand. Then I smacked her once, sharply. Her angry gasp and the clench of her pussy made me smile.

"Let me go!"

"Uh-uh. The more you say that, the worse this is going to be."

A red handprint showed a few seconds later. This ass never failed to get a rise from my cock. Spanking was not going to do it for me. Not enough. Not anywhere near enough. I wanted her to know I could do anything. I shifted her along my lap and leaned in to place a deep bite on her ass, right in the middle of one cheek. She didn't squeal, or demand I let her go, only gasped once and whimpered. Better, I figured. I hung on. Her breathing became a whine then a rapid, coughing pant and her feet tried to drum the floor.

Eventually she went limp, only shuddering out gasps, and one pleading word. "Pleeease?"

I sat up and drew my finger around the already bluing mark. Her fingers that had been wound in tight fists relaxed.

My teeth would show there for days.

My good inner man seemed to have run away and hid, and I didn't give one solitary fuck.

Since I seemed to have her subdued, I took the pillow with my free hand and stripped off the pillowcase with the help of my teeth. Looping it around her wrists and knotting the cloth made her squirm about then raise her head.

"No." With a fist crunched into her hair so tight it hurt me, I took control of her head, bending back her neck. Her eyes were closed, the lines there showing the effort she put into keeping them that way.

"Look at me." I jiggled her head. She inched them open, a tiny crease forming above. "You're going to do what you're told, until the storm returns, because right now you're fucking mine."

The tremor that shook her body lit up my eyes.

I was tempted to kiss those petulant lips but it was too nice, too intimate and she didn't deserve it. I had a craving, now I'd let this side of me loose. I wanted to mess with her so badly.

"Ten each side. Say a word and I double it." Then I shoved her head into the mattress and went at spanking her properly. The smacks ripped through the room. After twelve her cries began. By twenty the redness was a mixture of burgundy and pretty pink. My handprints showed on top of the bite. When I slipped my fingers down her seam I found her cunt wet and swollen.

"*Ja*." I chuckled. "You like this, Miss Jazmine. Next time you want to tell me to piss off try not to get so excited when I spank you."

Her little growl made me smirk.

"Still got fire in you? Hey?"

So I added another ten. By the end, she had the side of her face resting on the bed and her eyelids were at half-mast. The pain got to this one just like Elenor, so long as I mixed it up with dominance, I was ninety percent sure of it.

"Off and on your knees."

When she slid off my lap at my small push, and only looked at the floor, the room shuddered and dislocated. Everything collapsed down to this instant. I had Jazmine kneeling in that rough bondage that she could have wriggled out of if she'd wanted to, and I was right. She was submitting to me.

I didn't give a damn about tomorrow or the storm. Only her. Only me.

I could've drawn her in ink with my eyes shut, not because she was pretty but because I saw every line and every contour of her bowed head, every shadow of her body. Yet her mind could be so much more addictive. There, I'd not yet understood. Whatever flaws in her made her go back and forth like a bloody seesaw, I could dig them out and fix them, bind her to me…

If.

And I sucked in a breath.

I could. I could make her mine truly, make her submit for more than a temporary window of time. If only there was more of that precious thing – time and life.

Where to begin? I stood and walked around her. I dared break the spell. “What are you thinking? Hmm?”

She swallowed but only gave her head a miniscule shake. I lifted her head with a hold on her jaw and made her shuffle around on her knees. “I’m remembering how you smiled when you obeyed me.”

She shut her eyes.

“Look at me.” Those green-gray irises had me in an instant. There were traces of tears but I traced slowly around her lips, refusing to soften my decision. “Do you like being where you are?”

Chapter 22

The question he was asking went straight to the heart of my problem. He wanted me to admit I liked being here, at his feet? I was on my knees, stinging from his blows, reminded of how easily he could overwhelm me, both terrified and turned on. I welcomed the pain because it was his pain.

So fucked up.

I'd fought off this weird influence he had on me. Being made to face it again was wrong. He was *nothing* like the paragon of virtue I'd long ago imagined my shining knight would be or the man I'd fall in love with.

I'd said yes before, to almost the same question, and he'd used it as an excuse for this. It'd be stupid to fall into the same trap.

"Answer me. With the truth. Or do I have to spank it out of you?"

I widened my eyes. "No!"

"The truth. I will know if you lie."

He couldn't, but with his hand under my chin, my hands tied behind me, and with him pinning me with his dark eyes, I accepted that I liked this. And I would never tell him that again. The only knight he could ever be was one in dirty armor.

He wasn't for me. Ever.

"Answer."

I pressed my lips together and shook my head very deliberately.

His fingers crushed in until my skin hurt where he pressed it onto my jaw and I winced.

"You're a stubborn bitch." Pieter straightened but brought his forefinger to the center of my forehead. "I'm not Gregor. I won't torture you to get results."

I dared to let a smile creep onto my lips.

"Oh, I *would* torture you but just because I want to see you wriggle more when you come."

Pieter torturing me…the many ways he might do that flowed into my head. A thrill washed through me and I felt myself dampen between my legs.

"I'm getting to know you, *meisie*. That turned you on, hmm?"

Shocked, I mouthed a *no*, and tried to crawl backward. His hand raked into my hair and halted me.

"You are lying. I bet I could slip inside you and fuck you like a jackhammer right now and you'd love it. You'd squirt all over the floor because, even if you won't say it, you love being on your knees and you are a pain slut, *my* pain slut."

All through his little speech, I was increasingly trying to shake my head.

"I don't know why you're so fucking stubborn but lying earns punishment. When the storm comes back, I will hold you if you want me to, but nothing more. You tell me the fucking truth. We're here." He swept out his other arm. "In the middle of Hell and you want to lie over something that you enjoy? And all I can think is that I'm not worthy of you. Well *fok jou*, to the end of bloody time. I will be your protector and make you submit to me when I want to, but do not expect friendship."

Tears were flowing by then and my chest seemed to have cracked right down the very middle. It was me who was unworthy. I knew it. I hurt and I was confused and I felt so bad about deceiving him that my head was a whirling muddle. But I would not let go. This was *me* we were talking about and he had no *right* to do this.

He reached and yanked at the zip of his pants, then shoved the pants down until his cock swung free.

Damn.

I knew what he intended and couldn't help staring. For ages I didn't blink or breathe. An erection always intimidated me because once I saw it, there was only one thing the man wanted to do to me.

In the past, I'd dithered, debated, found other things to do. Sex was like a haunted playground, but this man *made* me. That was the beautiful difference. That he wanted me so much he would make me do it. I'd always seen my boyfriends as wimps when they backed away.

"Punishment. I have a hard-on that needs your mouth and you're going to suck it like a whore because you like me forcing you."

The man was apparently an encyclopedia of me. How did he see me so clearly when I never knew it until *now*?

He took a fistful of hair either side of my head in a grip of stone. The small pains from my pulled hair sent delicious bites of fire swimming into me.

I gasped. Stupid mistake, as it gave him room to push the soft head of his cock into my mouth. He scrunched in his fingers, awakening more pain, and his dominance strengthened until a giant of a man seemed to have me in his grip. Nothing existed but him, as if he was the god of my mind. All powerful, all seeing. I hadn't a fraction of freedom, and his eyes were fierce enough to cut.

"This is skull fucking, *klein poes.*"

With my hands tied, I could do nothing except be his receptacle. My eyes locked to his as he rocked himself in and out of my mouth. Saliva leaked, built in my mouth, dribbled past my lips. I'd never mastered deep throating because no man ever got a blow job for more than twenty seconds. I found out how determined he was to fuck my mouth. My retching and coughing when he slid too deep only made him halt for a few seconds. Then he plowed back in.

A thrust went almost in to nearly balls depth and I burst into splutters.

He fucked my mouth hard, ramming the head into the softness inside my mouth, scraping my teeth. My ears filled with the strange sounds of my gagging and humming, the soft slurping noises of his wet cock sliding on tongue, and his grunts.

Tears streamed down my face and he paused a moment, most of the way in, to study me, my mouth full, my lips stretched wide.

"You're learning."

Lost in a world where I was only his thing to fuck, I blinked hazily up at him.

I pulled at the tie on my wrists, reassured to find myself still bound. His thrusts became more determined. Then he stiffened and jammed himself in. A thrill vibrated along my tongue from his cock as his cum filled my mouth.

The taste was as riveting as a drink made of warm blended mussels and snot. I retched. Pieter slid his cock from my mouth.

The winds were lifting in noise, louder, more shrill. The cyclone. I swallowed reflexively though the taste left me grimacing.

"Good girl. Say thank you."

Now we had a problem.

I frowned and stared at the floor

"Still not talking?" He observed me before turning to walk to the basin. As he washed himself, he added, "You can stay tied up then. If I have to hug you, you can be my little fuck toy for as long as I wish you to be.

"What?"

This time I began to really try, quietly, to get loose. The pillow slip shifted. One wrist slipped.

"If you get that off," he said, deadpan. "I will put ten more bites on you like the last one. And not just on your butt."

I subsided onto my heels. My gulp may have been small but he smiled.

"Good little fuck toy."

"I am not –"

"If you say anything else before I say you're allowed to, I will put five bites on you…for every word."

Insufferable. And, and…

He came to me and helped me climb onto the bed to lie on my side. "At least you don't need food now I fed you some cum."

My first suck of air to angrily reply was met with such a pregnant silence that I caught myself. I couldn't speak. If he bit me like he'd threatened to it would hurt, but worse than that, I didn't want to disobey. I was down the rabbit hole again, in no man's land where up was down.

I let him pull me into his body then push my head down so my spine bowed and he could poke at the wrist tie.

"It's good," he murmured. "Nothing blue. Except your butt."

The sudden pinch down there had me stiffening and a single whimper passed my lips.

"I almost feel sorry for you." His lips pressed on the back of my neck. "But I don't, and you know why?"

I waited.

"Because I find I like having you quiet and tied up, as my fuck toy. I like," he added, "saying you're mine. Even Gregor can't take that away. Maybe I will like making you come while you're here in bed too."

I was barely hearing what he said.

Outside, the rain had started roaring; now it was rattling down like bullets on the roof far overhead. With the storm howling like this, he hadn't a hope of making me orgasm. I shivered. We might be drowning in a few hours.

Little did I know.

Screaming as I came, with his hand planted on my back, my head stuffed into the mattress, and his fingers up inside me, definitely beat shaking in fear. Was it four times, or five?

Being made to display my pussy while he studied me, my legs spread wide on the bed, made all the other craziness fade to the background. There was method in his madness. Or he just liked looking at my body and making me obey.

I found out, I didn't care which it was.

The cyclone passed over us. Pieter untied me, though by then the pillowcase bonds were only symbolic. If I was inclined to, I could have shaken them loose. I sat quietly, tired, my arms wrapped over my knees, unsure what would happen next. Pieter seemed content to let me stew.

When the power came back on, late that night, the guards arrived through the slush and torn vegetation. I could hear the water outside as they trod on the sodden pathways. They came and they took him away. We'd said nothing more. Now, I was truly alone.

For a dénouement to our relationship, it was a destructive way to go out. Typical Pieter.

Somehow I both knew I was his forever, and knew I'd never let him near me again, voluntarily. I felt used, abused, overwhelmed, and on the edge of a precipice, at the bottom of which might be paradise or oblivion.

Chapter 23

The bag was dragged off, revealing the outdoors, and flopping my hair across my face. I shook it aside. This was where they'd staked me out when I first arrived. Wet leaves and pieces of branches were underfoot and sticking to my soles. The cyclone had been two days ago and the ground was as mushy as porridge and strewn with rubbish and vegetation. It squished as the guard backed away.

Since they'd left my wrists manacled at my back, and attached me with a chain from my neck to a tall, steel pole cemented into the ground, I wasn't going far. Pity. But Jaz was here too, and I couldn't run without her, or with all the guards around me.

After adjusting to the glare, I checked in a circle, counting. Eight guards. Some were loading gear into two trucks that were parked on the one road out. The quadrangle was an open square between the four joined parts of the House and every door I could see was open. Were they evacuating?

I looked up, squinting into the pale, cloud-wreathed sun. The hills overlooking us were that startling New Guinea green. It'd been too long since I'd breathed outside or sun had warmed my skin. Maybe we'd die here. Maybe this was our chance?

I flexed my muscles, discreetly. If they freed me, would I be game to try something? With one weapon in my hand, an automatic, I might. None of the guards near me were armed with more than batons.

My bones told me we weren't out here to pick daisies.

Jazmine...I had to take her too. She kneeled six yards away, still with a bag on her head. Before her, Gregor sat in a chair and beside him was an elderly man – precisely cut grayed hair, a buttoned light gray shirt, and black pants that looked ready to match the jacket thrown over the back of his chair. Sweat darkened his shirt yet he kept it on? Executive persona, from the attitude. He focused on Jazmine like she was the last woman left on Earth, and the steel in his gaze was more than the appreciation of a good fuck or a victim for his fetishes.

This was the Client. It was a fact delivered to me by smoking meteor.

She had no idea, poor girl. As I tried to move my arms and was brought up short, the chains clinked. I ached to grab her and run.

This day would not end well.

Never give in.

"Glad you could join us, Pieter," Gregor declared in a joyous tone. He'd say it the same way if announcing we were to be raped by wild pigs. "You are here to witness Miss Jazmine meeting her client. Perhaps we will let you join in the festivities too? Hmm?"

The client shifted on his seat but barely glanced at me. His lips stretched as he looked at Jazmine. "Let her see me now."

At a click of Gregor's fingers, a guard strode up and removed the bag. Her black hair tumbled in glossy waves down her back.

Her head came up and I thought she stared at the client. If she recognized him, I couldn't tell, but her fingers laced into each other as if she needed to shore herself up. Like me she was bound, only her wrists were cuffed in red leather not metal.

My ache intensified until I wanted to grind my teeth. I went forward as much as my chain allowed me.

"Impatient to get going, Pieter?" Gregor tsked. "You will get your turn."

A guard behind me laughed.

Whatever he meant by that I really did not want to find out.

"I want to talk to her first." The Client leaned forward. "Do you know who I am?"

Jazmine shook her head.

"Say it." Underlying all his words was this menacing tone.

Her head must be so messed up with, in front of her, Gregor the man who skinned cops for fun, and this mystery man who had ordered her defiled and tortured.

He'd asked if she knew him. Which meant there was some connection.

She ducked her head, then looked up and said, "No," in a strained voice. "I don't."

"Aren't you going to beg me to free you?"

As if he would. Loaded question.

Her chest expanded then she breathed out roughly. "I know you won't."

"Smart woman, but you always were too smart, as well as vicious. My name…" He rose to his feet, walked to her side, and bent to whisper.

All she did was shake her head then stop.

"Ahh. Have you remembered? Do you know why you have to pay?"

"I… I'm sorry. I don't understand. Why are you doing this?"

"You think it was nothing? He's dead, and his wife and kid. Maybe you missed that little bit of news?"

"No. Is that tru –" She swung her head and looked up at him. "No, I didn't know, but I had nothing to –"

The crack as he slapped her, then her fall to the side, seemed as lethal as a bullet. My head filled with anger that buzzed into my forehead. My teeth ached. It took a moment before I figured out why, and made myself relax my jaw.

He helped her back to a sitting position then released her upper arm and wiped his palm on his pants. "You will pay for the rest of your life. I find I like seeing you fucked over day by day. At first I meant to have you killed, but no. I'm going to have a finger cut off so I can watch you scream, I'm going to fuck your pretty face, then I'm taking you with me."

What they'd made me do to her had been insane but this chilled me. I could take men dying horribly but not this.

She panted loud enough for me to hear and shook her head crazily, before spitting near his feet. "Why?"

Bloody hell. I smiled even as I dreaded his response. She was *fokken* angry.

"You'll understand eventually. I'll make sure of it. For that, I may take two fingers. If you think you can bite me, think again. Gregor!" He gestured.

Gregor rose with some device in his hand. A spider gag. I thought I recognized it. The metal spokes would open her mouth widely and keep it open.

I never said please, never begged, with men like this. I fucked them over and killed them.

They pushed the gag into her mouth, despite her screams and violent attempts to evade them, and strapped it on.

I couldn't take this. As a guard came forward with a pair of bolt cutters, I growled, surprising even myself at the animalistic sound. Gregor brought over a small solid stool, undid her cuffs, and wrenched one of her hands over, pinning it flat.

"Wait!" I lunged forward, jerking as my collar chain snapped taut. "Please. Let it be me. Take my finger."

"Really?" The client angled his head, assessing me. "You're that enamored of her? I was going to have you fuck her ass while I fucked her mouth, but I like this idea. Of course, if you can't get it up, I'll have you shot after."

This man was Gregor's equal. I stared at him. If it wasn't me, he'd get a guard to ass fuck her. "Do it."

Though she couldn't speak, Jazmine pleaded with me with her eyes and made whining sounds. I figured she was saying no. I ignored her.

He nodded. "Take the stool over there. I'm not having him near me with his hands free."

Now this had possibilities. The bolt cutters were big, mean looking, and heavy. A lethal thing if you hit someone with it. I could kill with it. But eight, no ten men? If I killed Gregor and him, would the others scatter? They'd get me, but maybe I could free Jazmine and she could run? So dangerous a situation, so iffy, but it might be her last chance at freedom.

Never ever give in.

Only Gregor had ideas too. They hauled over the stool, strapped one arm to my body, thoroughly, and forced me to my knees. There were guns on me. No one gave me an inch. They strapped my knees together, before freeing my other hand with a chain attached. Then they chained it down to the stool. I had nowhere to go.

Fok them.

I was going to lose a finger, at least.

A guard wearing a baseball cap came forward and took the bolt cutters. "Which one?"

"The little finger." The client unzipped and took out his cock, began to roll on a condom.

Grinning at me, the guard anchored down the stool with his boot on the rung underneath the seat, and fitted the blades over and under my finger. "Say cheese."

Then he closed it with a crunch.

The pain was immense, burning my hand, burning up my arm, exploding in my head. I screamed once then tensed up, shuddering.

Blood squirted from the stump. Least he'd missed the one next to it, my logical mind informed me.

I bowed my head and muttered curses. My finger lay in the mud inches away, blood staining the ground. More blood dripped from the edge of the stool. Grunting in air like I'd run a race, or had a digit *bloody well severed*, I raised myself up. They wouldn't see me grovel.

The client had his cock an inch away from Jazmine's mouth with Gregor holding her head in place. He studied me. "Take another finger. The one next to it."

"Sure. Man, you're fucked." The guard wriggled the blades through the blood and under my next digit.

I stared at my hand, said a goodbye to my finger, and had a mental block. Why was I doing this again?

Because of her. I looked at Jazmine, waiting there, gasping and wriggling to avoid the cock he was presenting to her mouth, waiting to be defiled yet again. If I could've killed them all with my eyes, it was done, then, in that very second.

When it was me hurting her, it was better, because I cared for her. My sight blurred and I blinked to clear it. I could have wept but not for me. For her. I'd give a whole hand to have her for my own.

I met the guard's eyes, took in that stupid grin. "*Fok jou.*"

"You too." His chuckle ended in blood as his head ruptured. Pieces of flesh splattered into the air and pattered like rain onto my face.

What the *fok*?

It took me all of three seconds to figure it out, with the rapid *thwap* of rounds coming in. Some harder, with more boom. These were sniper rounds. An attack.

I ducked, spent all of a millionth of a second on the asshole next to me twitching and bleeding out through a hole in his brain.

Were these good guys or bad? They couldn't be worse than Gregor?

Bullets cracked through the air. Strapped in place, though trying to keep my head low, I watched the guards spin and fall. The Client was down. Gregor sprinted toward the nearest covered way. He tripped, tumbled, and slid, with blood spray decorating his vicinity, like a ragdoll through the slush. When his body stopped sliding, he moved not at all.

Gone. Possibly dead. Badly wounded at least. *Fuck yeah.*

I was sorry they weren't mine to kill. These ambushers shot straight and fast.

A straggly line of men, likely to be raskols, ran in, weaving past the trucks. As they passed downed guards, they shot them again.

By the time I was freed, Jurgen, Glass, and Randall had arrived toting scoped rifles. Now I knew who the first shooters had been. Rescuers, not worse. My heart slowed as relief washed in.

There were none still alive, except a moaning and crawling Gregor. The client lay silent and twisted with his cock still out and limp and half his chest blown away. My finger hurt but a man had tied it off with a cloth tourniquet before releasing me.

Sounds were muted. My head rang from a round that'd spun past my ear.

Jazmine clutched at my leg, wiping her face. "Show me your hand."

"It's fine. I'll fix it after."

"God, I'm sorry. I wish… Do you know these people?" The last was whispered after she climbed up and stood, and she stared up at me, desperately hoping.

"Yes. They're friends. Wait. I'll be back. Sit down on the chair. Okay?" I led her to it and made her sit.

A grim job waited for me.

After a quick hug, I went to Gregor, collecting the chunky stool on the way.

Glass followed me over, asking distant questions in his ridiculous Brit accent that I'd never been so happy to hear.

I watched Gregor claw at the ground whimpering, his face in the mud. Gloating wasn't my thing…normally.

"Hello, you fucker." I spat on him then kicked his side, drawing a small, coughing moan.

Disappointing, that I hadn't boots on.

"You know, Gregor," I croaked out, past the rage clogging my throat. "Evil bastards like you die because you make too many enemies. One day, the hate spills over, and you drown in it."

I kicked him again, harder, and hefted the stool by one leg, considering my options. Heavy timber. The things he'd done to me and Jaz. A hundred times over, I'd killed him in my imagination. Beating him to a pulp with the stool would leave me satisfied but disgusted. Just standing over him, breathing in some of the putrid air he'd breathed out, and watching his wormlike movements, made me want to vomit.

"Your Ruger." I held out my hand to Glass, giving him a bare smile. We went way back and didn't need fancy hellos.

"Yeah?" He drew it from his holster and gave it to me. His bright white blond mohawk and aviator sunglasses stood out like a model ad billboard in a swamp. The man had perfected rugged male chic and his girlfriends knew it. "Who's he?"

"The bad guy."

Shooting him in the dick might be justice but I didn't want to see his face while he still lived. I put a round into the back of Gregor's head and he stilled instantly. Blood puddled under him. Then I emptied the rest of the clip until the back of his head was mush. The front? I flipped him over with my foot. Worse. Grass and dirt stuck to him, but he didn't have a face anymore, just blood, meat, bone chips, and frothy redness.

Glass whistled. "Guess he wasn't a nice man?"

"*Fokken* understatement of the year."

Blood had spattered all over my legs and I prayed reincarnation was real because if he came back I could kill him again.

But it was done. Jazmine? I turned and saw her wide eyes fastened on Gregor, her mouth half open in shock. Then she shifted her gaze to me and her expression didn't change.

My stomach flopped. Had I done bad again?

"Who is she?" Glass holstered the gun. "And man, we need to get that finger fixed."

"A…friend."

Holy crap. We were free. Damn finger was leaking again. I held the base of the stump, grimacing as I scanned the surroundings again for enemy and found nothing. Though the raskols were a worry. "Are they safe?"

"Yes. As safe as we can get."

Jazmine was looking lost and everything in me was yelling go to her but there were things I had to say.

"Pretty thing. She looks like she needs someone to lean on." Glass rubbed his chin with the back of his hand, while checking her out.

"Yes, and that's going to be me." In other words, *fok* off. "Wait."

As I jogged to her, already I could see her withdrawing. I had to stop killing people around her. Or maybe I should just do it quieter – like without the ten shots to the back of the head. She hated Gregor and would've wanted him deader than dead, same as me, but doing it messily must've reminded her of my nastier tendencies. I'd definitely fucked up and hell if she didn't owe me a finger.

I went to one knee beside the chair, looked her in the eye. "Hi."

Her mouth quirked to the side. "Hi."

"There's a lot of bad stuff happening and I'm sorry you had to see it. But I can also see you need a hug."

When I put up my uninjured hand to cradle the back of her head, she flinched but I carried on. This was one time she definitely wasn't avoiding human contact…*me* contact.

"Come here." I pulled her closer and into the angle of my shoulder and neck, pleased, after a few seconds, at her little *mmm* and wriggle.

"You're free."

She heaved out a long sigh then choked up. "I know."

"*Fok* you're strong, girl. Anyone else would be bawling their eyes out."

"Hah." Her hand came up, and she wiped at her face. "You aren't."

"I took my tough pills this morning. Though my finger hurts like hell still."

"Tough pills? So that's the trick. You should get some painkillers."

"I will. Shut your eyes. You need to."

"I…guess. Okay. Wait." Then she went to sit up, except I kept her down. "The others! Are they looking to see if there are other women?"

"They will. I'll ask soon. *Shh.* You close yours, I'll close mine."

Not that I did, but I felt her relax.

For a while we breathed together until Glass signaled to me. I kissed her head and rose. "Be back soon as I can."

"'Kay."

Glass waited, head angled. "We have to leave soon. You had questions?"

Where to start? "How the hell did you find us? Did the cleaning lady here send out a message?"

His perplexed look gave me the answer. "No. The police found out one of their own was killed and that you were here, and of course you're one of us. Jurgen pays them enough. If you have possessions to grab, say so. We have to be out of here in an hour, before the cops officially arrive."

So…" I figured it. "You're doing their dirty work?"

"Exactly."

Pieces were missing.

"How'd they know *I* was here?" I frowned. "The dead cop?"

"I heard a little girl knew your name and a messed-up version of my address and she told her mother. It went from there."

"What? A little girl?"

"Yeah. The day they brought you here. You spoke to her after you saved her from a dog."

"I can't remember that, at all." I shook my head. "Doesn't matter." I ran through the problems that might pop up. "If they have an office, can you grab records? Hard drives? I don't want anything there pointing to me or to Jazmine. Plus…" Did I want to do this? Yes, I did. I needed the truth and I had a feeling she wasn't going to supply it. "I'd like to see her records. Especially."

He nodded. "We're torching it anyway. The dirty cop has interests to be protected too. His friend died here. I'll grab what I can – just it'll be our secret. Okay?"

"Yeah. You know me. Mouth is zipped. Are you checking for other captives?"

Glass tapped his earpiece. "They've found three women in cells. All are going to be left alone for the cops to find. They're well enough to wait. We can't afford for more people to see our faces."

"Casualties?"

"Just your finger and one bullet wound through an arm. We can fly you out. The rest will be taking trucks on a long drive back down to Moresby."

"Okay." I turned to Jaz. "Her too. She comes with me on the plane, or I stay."

"Shit. I guess the little Cessna can take you all. The climb out of the airstrip is a fucking tight one. We'll have to jettison a few things. I don't want to side-swipe a mountain."

If I left her here, even with my friends, to drive out on miles and miles of roads, I'd be the worst man ever.

“We have to decide what to do with her, Pieter.” With the hand carrying his rifle, he gestured toward her. “She’s seen us all, knows you, and our rogue cop won’t be happy with a witness on the loose. Can we trust her?”

Good question. I did and I didn’t. “I think so.”

“We have to be sure. She can stay in the compound under lock and key until I talk to you some more.”

Under lock and key? After this? But he was right. No matter how bad Gregor had been, a ton of illegal acts had just been committed. I understood his problem.

“Now, go back to her.” He slapped my good arm. “We’ve been waiting days to get in here and if what I saw through the scope is any indication of what went on here, she’s going to need you.”

She did. If only I was sure she would agree with that, because now we were free I had to get used to normal etiquette with a woman. Whatever the fuck that was. She’d want to go back to Australia, where I couldn’t go, and the thought of losing her was combining with the finger pain to give me a big fat headache, as well as making me want to hit someone.

Chapter 24

His arm rested across my shoulders and with every bump, as the plane hit turbulence, I was rocked against his body, his muscles. I loved it, I wanted to wrap myself around him and let loose all my sorrow by weeping on him, knowing he'd understand that need. What I would soon have to do made me feel ill. When he spoke, his soft words seemed to grind their way to my heart leaving bits of me in their wake.

I was lost.

No collar, no wrist cuffs, no angel bracelet – they'd all been removed. Who was I now?

Having Pieter being so gentle after everything that had happened – the violence, the killing, the sense of freedom that had blasted its way inside me – it was too much. I could barely cope. One minute, a victim without any say in my degradation by that man…

My name is Andrew Gavoche. I am the father of David Gavoche.

That statement had embedded in my head. I'd never forget it, accompanied as it was by a barrage of confusion, then recognition, then terror.

The man who'd been orchestrating my torture wasn't just having some terrifyingly illegal fun or exploring a deviant perversion, he wanted to destroy me.

The jump between that second and my old life as a freelance journalist had been too abrupt. At first I'd scrambled to recall the old me. I hadn't known why David had died but it was clear I was being blamed.

Then the Client died, and Gregor too, after Pieter had spat on him, kicked him, and shot him so many times I'd been stunned by the callous ferocity.

He's dead, you can stop, please stop, I'd wanted to scream. I'd seen enough of people killing each other. The sound, the blood, the stench of bowels from men shot through the guts – I could taste it on my tongue, the viciousness was so thick in the air. And after all that Pieter had come to me and held me, and made me accept his hug.

Fuck.

I'd done a 180-degree turn and just for that moment, I think I loved him more than a little. Which was making me have to hold back tears to the point of my head almost exploding from the ache in the middle of my forehead, chest, and stomach.

I was going to leave him and I was certain he had other ideas. No man was this this…what was the word? *Nice* would do…unless he wanted you in his bed.

Well, I'd been there and he was the best as well as the most insane lover I'd ever had.

And he scared me so much at times that my heart nearly stopped beating.

When he'd shot Gregor…and the knifing of the boy…those acts bounced around in my memory.

I would never be able to see him and not see them. I would never be free of the thought that he might do something like that again. I didn't need this in my life. Safety, comfort, boredom – I needed those again, desperately.

I needed to get away, and yet I wanted to stay in his arms. He was something unique in my life. Why did he also have to be so wrong for me?

"We should be there in fifteen minutes." He squeezed me. His finger stump with its gory bandage dangled against the seat rest, bouncing as the plane's movement bounced his arm.

My mind went off on a tangent. A good one. I could repay some of his kindness.

"Time to loosen the tourniquet?" It had to be done, regularly, his friend and fellow ex-soldier Jurgen had told me, or risk killing off the rest of the finger.

"Sure. Can you do it again?" Pieter rested his hand on my lap.

Carefully I untied the little knot and released the pressure for a few minutes. At least it wasn't gushing blood anymore. The end of the finger was gruesome. A sliver of bone wriggled. *Ugh.*

I glanced at Pieter. The man was made of rock. His face might be tense, but apart from a twitch at his wrist, he barely moved as I reapplied the tourniquet then arranged the bandage.

"Want a lollipop?" I grinned at him.

"For what?" His tone was incredulous.

"For being good. All the kids get one."

"Your jokes will never win awards."

"*Mmm.*" I snuggled back in and resumed worrying.

A few minutes later, he told me something that put ice back in my veins.

"We're going to land at an airfield outside the main airport and drive into the city. Glass has a problem with trust." He stroked my cheek with his finger. "You're safe. I'm going to make sure a doctor examines you, *meisie*, but he wants you to stay inside his house until we figure out how to get you back to Australia. Okay?"

They were locking me up again. *Okay*, he asks?

I didn't look up from my lap.

"Why can't I fly back?"

"Because, there's legal problems. These friends of mine who rescued us, like Glass…" He pointed with one finger forward, at the pilot.

Despite the drone of the engine, Glass heard and waved back lazily, without turning.

"If you arrive and people find out how you got here, bells will ring. The law will find out you were back there. That people rescued you. There's a cop involved who helped organize this and he has to stay totally unseen. You would get questioned. People who are friends of friends would be implicated in murder, extortion, bribery."

I swallowed. "So how do I get back home?"

"To Australia?" Big pause – like he was wondering about asking me to stay here? I could read him like a book. "The best way to avoid you being questioned, fingers being pointed, is for us to fly you back into Australia illegally. We have to smuggle you back in."

Then what? Pretend I'd been wandering around Australia for weeks, unable to find my way home? I guess that was their plan. I could imagine the questions that would stir up. I would've been a huge news item for ages after I vanished. Not easy to explain away. But maybe they never meant to free me?

Pieter wouldn't allow that, though, would he? I sent him a fleeting look. This man, I knew him like no other. How could I not, after all we'd been through? We'd survived the furnace together.

But I didn't know this about him, because I'd seen how ruthless he could be. I'd also seen what he was willing to do to me in the name of just plain...showing me what I liked. Just because he thought I needed to know. He didn't always ask before he did. It seemed I needed to escape, again.

I had this big Rottweiler of a man hugging me, like he'd turned puppy overnight. I wanted to soak this up, because it spoke to some new part of me that I never thought I had. And I wanted him far, far away. The correct answer always was the safe one, right?

I turned my face into his chest and inhaled. He smelled so good.

Tears arrived and I let them leak onto my face silently.

Chapter 25

After the doctor left, I took a minute to check out the neat bandage on my finger stump. Having him chewing away bits of the sticking-out bone while I watched had been a little too personal. He hadn't been keen on doing his surgery here, in Glass's dining room, but the young doctor had adapted, laid out instruments like the big bone crunchers he'd used, injected the base of my finger with local anesthetic, then he'd gone to town cleaning up the debris and stitching me. Even without the X-ray he'd muttered about needing, he'd done a great job.

So now I had nine and a bit fingers and the woman upstairs I'd sacrificed it for was unhappy with us…with me, for keeping her locked in her room.

I went up the stairs two at a time, knocked after yelling, *it's me, Pieter*, then unlocked the door. No protests were sung at me so I walked in. She was standing at the tall window, breeze blowing the lace curtains around her, looking out at the distant sea, over the tops of the houses. At least Glass had taste and had put in antique-style bars on his house.

Her little yellow-and-blue summer dress clung to her in all the right sexy places. I imagined one of Glass's girlfriends was supposed to get it as a present. No shoes, but I liked her feet bare, and her calves too. I remembered running my hands up those while studying her body higher up, and her looking down at me, eyes bright, lips parted.

Damn. My hard-on had appeared as if to say, get to it. I wished.

"Hi." I kicked shut the door.

There were six houses in this secured compound, and all of them belonged to Glass and people working for him and Jurgen. I knew some of the ways they earned money but had never dug too deeply. It wasn't legal, that part I knew. I'd done some jobs for him, but I had a feeling he shifted drugs into Australia, as well as people circumventing the immigration laws.

"How did it go?" Jaz grimaced as she caught sight of the bandage then her brow furrowed as if she was wondering what lay underneath.

"He did a good job." I shrugged. "It's fine. I have antibiotics. I thought you might like to ask me questions?"

I had ones for her. Though we were still waiting on the IT expert to decrypt the hard drive from Gregor's computer, I needed to hear it from her. I needed to know, firsthand, she was being honest with me, or why she wasn't.

"I do have some, but I need the right answers."

"The right answers? If you're lucky, I might have those. Lie on the bed with me. After all the hacking at my flesh and the drugs he injected, I'm feeling a bit woozy."

"Really?"

"Yes." I half-climbed on the bed then flipped myself down on the mattress, full length. "Here." I shifted over and patted beside myself.

When she looked dubious, I grinned and patted the bed again. "I won't bite. Promise I won't touch you unless you say so."

One eyebrow arched in skepticism but she sat on the edge of the bed.

"That's it?" I was tempted to drag her down.

"Best you'll get."

I propped myself up on an elbow, hissing as the finger tangled in the quilt for a second. The anesthetic didn't stop the pain that throbbed into my hand. "My head is on a level with your ass if you sit like that. Which…I'm okay with."

Her sigh was exasperated.

"I bet you are. Fine! You win." She slid down and ended up lying next to me, grumpy yet amused, while I was still up on my elbow. Her hair fell over my hand.

The view was even better with the top of the dress askew but I pretended I didn't see that.

"The doctor. What did he say?" He'd checked her out first, when I insisted.

For a second, Jaz turned down her mouth. "Nothing. I have scratches, abrasions. He told me to get some blood tests done, as soon as I can, just to be certain of things like hepatitis and so on."

"That's it?" Her summary struck me as too fast.

"Yes."

When I studied her for a while, she only looked annoyed. I smiled. "Good. Next. Remember what I said about a lot of people potentially getting hurt if anyone finds out you're in Papua New Guinea?"

"Yes."

"Okay. Some of these questions may be hard for you but you need to answer them." At her nod, I continued. "Glass wants to know why that man wanted you tortured."

She answered slowly but without a single tremor in her words. "I told you, I'm only a librarian in Sydney."

"But the man? How does he connect to you?"

"I know his son. He was a doctor, that's all. I went to him about some plastic surgery but chickened out. I know he was arrested for fraud and was going to go to jail over it, as well as paying back millions to the government."

Her shrug was dismissive.

"That's all?"

"Yes."

Such wide eyes, and too steady, like she was afraid if she looked away I'd see it as a lie.

"His name?"

"The son was David Gavoche. That man said he was Andrew, the father. I had nothing to do with the son's death." She was shaking and her eyes shone. "*Nothing.*"

I went to reach across to her but she glared, her eyes sharpening.

"You said you wouldn't touch me."

Silence.

Yes, I had, but the vehemence in that was shocking. I searched her face. "I'm not your enemy, Jazmine. You know that."

Her sniff was followed by a deep breath, and she squirmed her nose about.

"If you want to cry, there's no shame."

Her answer came out through teeth. "I don't want to fucking cry. I want to go home. I want out of here!"

How had we gotten to this? Her yelling at me with hate? Her determined to go home without even passing go and talking about us?

Us. I'd thought, hoped, there was a chance for something to happen. I'd really hoped. After all these years, I was tired of being alone, but all she wanted to do was leave. All I wanted to do was turn her over my knee and spank some sense into her.

Except I couldn't. Or was that *shouldn't*?

Definitely shouldn't. She'd been through enough to break anyone, but at the back of my head all I could hear was, *if she leaves, you will never see her again.*

And wasn't that a happy piece of news.

"Okay, so you don't know why. Next question. We need to know if you are going to be okay with lying to the authorities in Australia about where you've been. It's best if you just say you've been travelling with someone and you don't want to get them in trouble, so you won't identify them. Can you do that? Even if you're pressured? If there's been a lot of news coverage of your disappearance, and police investigation, the cops will be really interested in you."

"Yes. I can do it."

I watched her, raised my eyebrows but she didn't twitch at all. The girl was stonewalling me.

Last question and the one I'd thought she'd say no to. If she didn't trust me. This one, I almost didn't want to say because if she refused, I wasn't sure where to go from here.

"We also need to know your full name and address so we can check it's all valid. So we know without doubt, that you exist as who you say you are."

The *nothing* blank look on her face was quickly replaced by a puzzled one, with her shaking her head. "What? You're joking. Your friends are the murdering criminals, not that I'm not abso-fucking-lutely grateful, but I seriously do not want them to know who I really am."

"And me, what about me?" My heart sped up. This was like putting my soul out for her to knife. *Do you trust me?* "If you tell me only, I swear I won't pass it on. I'll do all the checking."

Then she ran on, blurting out something that I couldn't understand, but from the rush and the little movements of her face, it upset her greatly.

"What? Say it slower, *meisie.*"

"The doctor...he said I had a drug implant in my arm. Under here." She touched just below her armpit on the side near me. "It means I can't get pregnant. Works for ages. Did you know?" Her look was imploring, hurt, uncertain. "Did you know they'd done this to me?"

"No, I didn't." I frowned. It was invasive, but what did it have to do with what I'd just said? "This bothers you?"

"Yes." Her toes seemed to fascinate her. "Even here, I'm not rid of *there*, of what they did to me. What you did. I need you to go, Pieter."

I shifted higher. "Hey. I'm your friend. You know that."

"I need you to leave." She sat up then slipped off the bed, wiping at her eyes. "Please."

Fok this. "I need your name. Your address. You have to say."

"No. I don't. Go."

"If you don't tell us. We can't let you go."

But she only folded her arms and glared.

Shit. Stubborn bitch, alright. She was having some sort of emotional upheaval and it seemed I hadn't a clue how to fix it. Forced hugs wouldn't work this time.

"Dinner is in an hour. I'll come get you."

"Send it up. I can't face eating with anyone."

What the hell? She was going to hide up here, totally? Like we were lepers?

"Please?" Her tone was so wobbly that I switched from wanting to chastise her to wanting to help her in a second flat.

"Okay."

I closed the door and stood there for several minutes staring at nothing. How was I going to make everything right again?

Dinner was strained without her, though that was more my effort than Glass's. Within seconds of my return downstairs, after I delivered her meal, he sat down at the table and tucked into his plate of takeaway.

"Tomorrow I'll know anyway," he told me, around a mouthful of fried rice.

"How?" I poked my plate with the fork. Eating should be a high priority after the crap I'd had for a month. "How will you know?"

"My IT guy is running the hard drive through his algorithms, or something. He says it should pop sometime tomorrow. Then we'll know who the bloody hell she is anyway."

"Uh-huh." I took a swig from the bottle of Aussie beer he'd served, then read the label. *Eumundi lager*? It had a weird Australian tree on it, which actually…looked South African. But it was ice cold and delicious, and I was pretty sure my finger felt better already. Maybe I'd stick to beer for dinner.

"She's stupid. Thinking we can let her go without knowing who she is."

"Stupid?" I leaned back at a steep angle onto the chair, crossed my legs. She wasn't that. "No. She's just hurting, doesn't trust us…me." It was the *me* that pained me. "I sort of understand."

Tomorrow I would know who she was and… *Surprise, surprise.* That knowledge had sent not dread, but a thrill of anticipation into my balls.

With my thumb, I smeared the cold droplets on the glass of the bottle. If I knew who she was, maybe I could find a strategy to keep her here?

Weaknesses might yet be found in this woman. In the past, her weaknesses had been engrossing.

"How are you taking it?" He pointed with his fork at my finger. "This and all the rest, it wasn't standard operating procedure for combat. I know you can handle that, but what I saw up there...crazy shit." He shook his head and waited.

I chugged down some more beer.

"I don't know. It has fucked with my head. Given my priorities a shakeup. I'm not seeing everything the same way."

"Yeah?" He drank from his own bottle. "If there's anything I can do? More work? I know you need money? That job for Vetrov led to this? Right?"

"It did. It was exactly what you saw back there. Women being caught and sold...tortured. Only Gregor got out of hand over here. I can't imagine his boss expected torture like he was doing it."

"The other women were fine according to what I saw. Just traumatized. I'm sure they were raped but not tortured."

Maybe it was just her and the cop that Gregor got carried away with? Screaming wasn't exclusive to people being tortured. The women would perhaps have been worth tens or even hundreds of thousands to the right buyer. They had this huge set-up. Implanted them with contraceptives. So for them to make an exception for Jazmine, the Client must have been paying a lot of money. Why?

I jerked forward and sat up. "If you have a job or two, I'd consider it."

"More than that. You know if you want to commit, I can let you in for regular work that pays very well. I need reliable men for shotgun duty. You can share a house in the compound with Jurgen and his lady? Or even bed down here?"

"Okay." I nodded. It was either this or I could try construction work. I had some possibilities there too. It paid less, but it was legal. "Tomorrow, as soon as you find out, tell me who she is."

"I will. Though the way you said that, you don't think you know who she is." Flat statement, but he'd hit the nail on the head.

"No. I don't."

"That's…not comforting."

"Yeah. So true."

I drank the last of the beer, rested it back in the circle of condensation on the polished timber table. That gap in my facts was scary and frustrating but finding out the truth, now that was exciting.

Confronting her might make my day.

Chapter 26

The strip of plastic I'd found was from a clothing label, from the looks of it. When wriggled into the door latch, it'd let me, eventually, after hours of fucking around with it, open the damn thing.

My one advantage – this house wasn't made to be a prison, just secure against criminal gangs like the raskols. From memory, most of the foreigners in Papua New Guinea lived in these secured compounds.

The house was dark. Early still. Too early and the darkness would terrify me. I just knew it would. The crime rate here was high and a foreigner on the streets in the early hours after midnight, especially a woman, would be robbed, assaulted, and raped. As a journalist I'd heard all the stories coming out of Port Moresby.

I needed money, maybe a phone.

In the early dawn, I sneaked downstairs with a small purse, empty, but it made a good prop, and to my desperate relief, found a wallet in a bowl in the side room near the front door. Being in a secure compound had obviously left Glass certain no one could rob him.

But no phone. *Shit.* I was going to have to take a chance.

What was I going to do? If this place was alarmed, I was up the creek with no paddle. I opened the front door and tensed, waiting for the blare…nothing. I shut it behind me quietly, and set off down the short road toward the obvious entry, my little tan sandals *clip-clopping.*

A guard stood there in a khaki uniform. Sparrows pecked at and swooped across a stretch of mowed lawn to the side. The sky…was so blue. I smiled and felt buoyed up by this unexpected dose of beauty.

"Excuse me ma'am. Where would you be going?"

Be bold. "I'm a…lady friend of Glass and I need to get to the nearest corner shop. Is there anywhere open yet?" I smiled and flipped my hair off my shoulder, trying to act like a pretty girlfriend and not an escaped prisoner.

"I think so, yes. Can I call you a taxi? I have a friend. He's honest and a good driver."

Oh god, oh god. Yes!

I broadened my smile. 'Yes. Please do that."

"Did you know you didn't turn off the alarm before you opened the door?"

Fuck. Think!

Did he suspect me? If he did I was screwed. I made myself *not* look past him. That might be a red flag that I was thinking about escaping into the street. If I ran, if the guard didn't catch me, Glass and Pieter would. Or if not, I'd still be lost in the streets.

"Damn. No I didn't. Can you fix that? I wanted to surprise him with a proper cooked breakfast and all the man has is canned stuff."

Sweat prickled my forehead and I clutched my purse like it was a lifeline. *Believe me, please.*

"*Ahhh.* Lucky man. I can do that yes."

"Thanks." I attached another smile to my face.

Five minutes had never taken so long.

When the taxi pulled up, I slid into it as sedately as the queen on an outing, arranged my dress, and waved to the guard. We drove off. Thirty seconds later, I leaned forward. "Do you know where the Australian embassy is?"

"You mean the high commission? Yes, I do."

He spoke English, and he was right about it not being an embassy. A smart taxi driver. My luck was turning.

"Take me there, please."

"Sure. Though I don't think they open this early. It's way across the city."

Fuck. "It'll do."

I could wait.

And so, I left Pieter, my fellow captive, my rock, and maybe the only love of my life, behind me. But you couldn't really love a killer, could you? It was just a phase. Had to be.

It was Stockholm syndrome. The realization jarred me. The taxi, the surge of the engine, the bumps as he drove, the smell that said used-by-a-hundred people, it all faded. I was a fool. How had I missed that? Years of journalism under my feet and stories filed about kidnap victims, I knew Stockholm syndrome back to front. I'd missed it.

Why? Because he'd gotten deep under my skin, into me, and so logic made as much difference as a grain of sand in the ocean. *Pieter.* I'd never forget him.

I cleared my throat of the sudden thickness then sat up straighter, staring out the window and seeing little through my blurred vision.

My life was moving on. My Pulitzer Prize was waiting.

He was back there. I wondered if he would understand.

Chapter 27

The door banged open and I jerked my head off the pillow.

"Get your ass in gear. Your lady friend has escaped."

I blinked away sleep crud. It was Glass, dressed, grumpy, and as determined as a bloodhound on a trail.

Ma se poes. Escaped? "Where the hell is she going?" I flung back sheets and rolled to my feet. That she'd run from me, rather than trusted me, was the cruelest part of this. And damn if I didn't want her back. The need had never hit me so hard.

How dare she slip away without talking? I yanked on shorts and a T-shirt.

"Where? The high commission. Hang onto my mobile phone." He tossed it to me. "Tell me what the guard sends us. Luckily he thought to double-check her story. He's down as *Security two*."

The high commission. Now that was serious shit. If she spoke to anyone there, we were in deep *kak*. I ran with him to the door that led into the garage. The big outer door was trundling up already. We slid into his jeep and rumbled out onto the road.

Once through the guard's checkpoint, Glass threw a querying look my way. "News?"

"The guard says he's talking to the taxi driver via text. The driver's pulled over and he's telling her he has a problem from base to sort out."

"I told him to get the driver to pretend he was going to the high commission. He'll be going to a different address." He spun the wheel and headed out along a straight stretch between suburban houses. "You need to be ready." He glanced across. "I know you like her but this isn't good and I have an email about who she is too. Read it. Top one in my Gmail account. Her name is..." He stopped at traffic lights. "Jazmine Foulkes, and she's a journalist. Known for breaking some big stories. My guy did a shallow search for info on the net."

I'd found the email. She wasn't a librarian. I sagged back into my seat. "Well, this is just *fokken* dandy, hey?"

"Surprised?"

"*Ja.*" I'd known, really, all along. In my gut. It still hurt. We surged forward. "I want to sit her down and lecture her and then..." Do something nastier that I should really be ashamed of thinking, outside of Gregor's little dungeon. I wiped at my mouth.

"What? You sound as pissed as me. Lecture her?" He chuckled. "Sure. We're going to have to think hard about what to do with her."

I checked his expression. I'd never thought Glass would kill to protect business interests, but there was so much riding on this. "You can't kill her."

We drove to the next intersection and zoomed along a quiet street behind some warehouses, then up behind a tall office building, where there was an entry to a deserted car park. Glass cruised past that, stopping alongside a section where there was only sidewalk and the flat walls of the office buildings rising up to both sides. At around seven in the morning, no one was at work.

"No CCTV here," he murmured. "And no, we won't kill her, as long as you have an alternative, because there's no way I'd trust her enough to let her go, not after this." He regarded me steadily, like I was a magician about to pull a rabbit out of my ass.

The way he said that made the possibilities obvious and after we'd just rescued her from Gregor it was ironic. I drawled out, "No killing. Which doesn't leave a lot of options. You keep her somewhere. Someone else keeps her, or I do. Which are you thinking?"

"That you're a kinky devious bastard with the hots for her. That you want her. Wrong?" He cocked his eyebrow.

I shook my head. "I never thought I'd ever think of doing this."

"Sometimes fate takes a hand in our lives and we have to do what she asks us to."

"Philosophy à la Glass?"

"Yep."

"She won't like my plan. But I will." I nodded to myself. "Are you still having trouble with petty thieves taking fuel and supplies on Rakenest Island?"

"I am."

"Let me be your solution for a month. Me, her, whatever I need for a month out there. I'll make them rue the day they stole from you. I'll make her wish she hadn't run." I ran through things in my head: pluses, minuses, how she might react. "You need to follow my lead when I talk to her."

In the mirror I spotted a white taxi overtaking us and it came to a stop just ahead.

"Sure."

I hadn't been quite the model citizen for years, but with my hand on the door handle, I said the words that severed my connection to the good, the sane, and the law-abiding world forever. "Let's do this."

I flung open the door, jumped down and strode to the taxi, then opened her door. About the same time, Glass arrived on the opposite side. She was sitting forward, saying something to the driver. The moment she recognized me, the exact second those pretty green eyes focused, I registered it like a hit from a missile.

Baby, you've done bad, bad things. Seemed like Jazmine discipline was my number one addiction. I was looking forward to this so much I could've jerked off to it. My choice of words gave me pause.

Not hunting, discipline, because she was mine, by rights.

Her loud intake of breath warned me. When she didn't actually scream, I guessed she wasn't sure of our intentions.

If I could avoid panicking her, I would. Play it by ear.

I spoke quietly, ducking my head to address the driver. "Could you step out for a minute, please, I need to talk to her."

"Yes, sir." The man looked nervous but Glass had said he was a relative of the guard.

As he exited, I slipped in and sat beside her.

As long as I wasn't arrested, I was making this happen.

"Don't scream, Jaz. We're not here to grab you." Except we were. "Just to talk. You know what you're doing is going to hurt me. Why are you doing this?"

"I..."

Her hands fidgeted in her lap and she looked from me to Glass, who'd slid in on the other side. So I put my hand over her small one and squeezed. Her perfume teased me, reminding me of her sexuality, her femaleness. As if I needed more reminding than the upper curves of her breasts where her bra pushed them above the dress's neckline.

My new possession. My submissive girl, only she didn't know that yet. What could I do to a woman who was utterly mine? For a dirty creepy sadist like me, the world was wide open. It was unsettling, in a way, yet such a fucking jolt to the system.

Chapter 28

I had Pieter on one side and Glass on the other. Screaming and trying to get out was on the agenda, only I knew I'd never make it. My one hope, if I struggled, was that a passerby would hear me, or the driver would grow a conscience. The latter seemed unlikely.

That Pieter seemed reasonable and not angry meant I could salvage this, didn't it? Fuck, I hoped so. I wasn't going to escalate this situation. If anyone got hurt it would likely be me.

He'd asked me why. For a last second, I tussled with what to do. A big man to either side, and Pieter's disappointed gaze on me. The man could play the hurt puppy so well.

I actually felt guilty. What if they did plan to only help me? They'd staged a full-scale assault to get me out. A man had been shot. Maybe I was stupid? And plain ungrateful.

"I'm sorry. I had a brain spasm. I panicked. I thought you weren't going to get me home."

The crease between his eyes made me feel even worse. "You did?"

"Um. Yes. I did."

"She doesn't know me," Glass murmured. "It's understandable."

The sad look on Pieter's face shamed me.

I felt as small as a pebble between these guys. My thoughts of running shrank to nothing.

"What can we do to make it up to you? You want to get home faster? Glass?" He put his arm on the backrest and toyed with some strands of my hair where they'd draped across the upholstery then looked across me at his friend.

What was I supposed to do in the face of this? I'd betrayed the man who'd been my one reason for staying alive for the most terrifying time in my life. On the other hand, if they were prepared to drop their quest for my name and address, I should grasp this opportunity with both hands before they changed their minds again.

"I'm sorry, Pieter. But…yes. I do want to go home." Hope stirred.

Glass cleared his throat. "I guess I could do a flight tomorrow? I have got a job I need to do. A delivery. We'd have to stop at Rakenest Island though. I've had some islanders stealing fuel and equipment there. You cool with that, Pieter? You were coming on this flight to take her back?"

"Yeah, I was." The low rumble of his voice settled into me, as comfortable and familiar as a rainstorm sweeping in on a day when you were snuggled in bed.

I hated myself in that moment. The least I could do was to let them do this the way that was safe, for them.

My memory jogged. I'd heard Glass mention that he'd salvaged a hard drive from the office at the House. My name might be on that. They mightn't know who I was yet, but it was possible they'd find out soon. "Is there any chance of this happening today? Or do you have to lodge flight plans?"

Glass guffawed. "Flight plans are the least of my worries. I don't know. Maybe?"

"Tell you what." Pieter opened the door at his back. "Give us some time to run around getting everything Glass needs prepared and I'll see if I can get this expedited." He slipped out and put a hand out to help me from the taxi. "How's that?"

"Expedited?" I grinned. "That would be wonderful." Glass slammed his door and came around to us. "Is it really do-able?"

He grimaced. "For Pieter, and for you, I'll do my damn best. Main thing I have to do is make sure there's someone to take you farther once you're back on the coast of Australia. So it'd be best if you're there anyway, Pieter, to keep her safe, get her to the nearest town. Once we land there, I can give you money, for food, a bus maybe, but you'll be on your own. Okay?"

It was happening. *Ohmigod.* "Yes!" I squealed, just a little.

Pieter smiled. "I can't stay in Australia. Wish I could. How do I get back here, Glass?"

He wished. Once again I was torn by that attraction to this hunk of a man, but I could see a strange glitter in his eyes, as if something disturbed him. He'd been a little obsessed with me. I heaved in a breath. For the best. Maybe I could contact him again one day. Make things friendly but not too close. Yeah, I could do that. I just needed to be a safe distance from him.

"I can pick you up on the coast, a day later. I'll show you on a map."

My guilt swung back, full force, and I swallowed, finding I'd teared up a little. "Thank you, guys."

"No problem." Glass nodded. "Let's get back to my house and do this."

Which was how I ended up squeezed into a seaplane with Pieter, Glass and some supplies only a few hours later. Whatever checklist they'd run through had been finalized in what seemed superhuman time, but Glass had been planning this for days, just not with me in mind. Whatever he was smuggling in the boxes he'd loaded, I did not want to know.

After my stupid debacle of trying to go to the high commission, I'd decided to be good, for once. I'd write up what had happened as best as I could, in a way that didn't implicate anyone…or I wouldn't do it at all. Likely, that meant a no. I'd wear it. I'd get therapy. I'd get over this, somehow. Criminals or not, Glass and Pieter had hearts. I owed them.

We flew for over half an hour before the little island he was aiming for appeared on the horizon and slowly grew. It was late afternoon and it seemed he meant to arrive on the Australian coast around sunset. That meant instrument flying on the way back, I figured.

I'd told them over and over that I'd pay them back for fuel and other costs but Glass had only smiled and refused. I'd do it still, I vowed to myself. Somehow.

From the sounds of it, I'd be on the far north tip of the country. Catching a bus south would be the best idea. All the way to Brisbane, if I could, to make it less likely people would wonder how I'd ended up in far north Queensland.

Landing on the ocean in this plane must need low seas surely. Despite Pieter taking my hand, and running through some spiel about safety, I worried. The palm trees on the island grew in size as did a small jetty on one side, and a collection of low dwellings. The island was crescent shaped and we were heading for the more sheltered concave part of the crescent. The plane tilted, angling in, the engine lowering then roaring in tone when Glass adjusted the throttle. I clung to Pieter's biceps.

"Here we go. Don't worry. Glass has done this a hundred times. As long as the weather's this good, with quiet seas, he can land without fuss. Years ago, a foolish entrepreneur tried making this a resort and failed. No one else lives here."

"Why?"

"Why'd it fail? In storms, the place isn't good. No water supply. A tsunami would sweep straight across it."

Ugh. Thank god we weren't staying long.

The plane shushed along in the water then purred its way to the jetty.

"Out we get." He unlocked the door and swung it open before stepping down into the sea.

Smiling, I followed, jumping into a couple of feet of water and feeling the sand squish under my toes. This was a deserted island in the middle of the most amazing environment. Open space all around, sky, sea, and me…deep rolling ocean farther out. I needed a camera so badly.

The water was clear as the sky, like blue glass, and small fish, colorful as china ornaments, shot away when my legs pushed through the coolness. "This is paradise. Like serious holiday material."

"Let's get all the stuff unloaded that Glass wants to leave here."

The small pile seemed to be most of his cargo. What the hell was left to take to Australia? It had to be drugs.

But before we left, I ran over to do a pirouette on the beach with my dress swirling out in what must be a revealing way. Who cared if they saw my panties? On the last turn Pieter stepped up and caught my hands, sliding down to hold my wrists. Odd. I frowned as his hold tightened.

"I'm glad you like this place, because you're staying here with me, *meisie*, until I say we leave."

What. The fuck. I blinked at him but before I could process that or say a word, he spun me around. Metal clicked on my wrists, circling them. Cold metal. Handcuffs.

"Pieter!" My mind batted back and forth for all of a second. What was going on? He couldn't be… Not him. Heat and cold flashed and buzzed inside my head, running down my body in a paralyzing wash. "Why are you doing this?" My throat caught on the last word.

I'd been betrayed. By Pieter. And Glass. The men I'd thought had hearts. The breeze blowing across this little beach made me shiver. I tried to turn but he held my elbows, his grip so rock hard it hurt. Then he pulled me into his body.

I panted, still trying to squirm loose.

"Hello, Jazmine Foulkes."

I stiffened.

"I know who you are. And that you've lied to me all along, and now I get to teach you why that was wrong. When I release you, you're to kneel in the sand."

His fingers, encircling my elbows, pulsed on my skin.

Then he let go. I stood there breathing hard, deprived of oxygen and dizzy. *He knows who I am. He knows. Even if I escape, he will find me.* Then

I turned and sprinted for the sea. I'd rather drown than be his thing to play with. I couldn't face more of this darkness.

He caught me in the shallow waves, and dragged me, sobbing, back to the beach.

"No. Fuck no. Let me go!" I whispered the words in a squeak. My tears and the seawater wet my face. My nose ran with snot and sand stuck to my face.

With his hand screwed in my wet hair he towed me forward and made me go to my knees, and he held me there.

I trembled, eyes puffy, heart pumping so hard it might burst from my chest.

A seashell decorated the sand at my knee. Perfect and delicate. And a monster had me, again. I waited for my sentence. I'd been so close to going home. *So close!* Home. My bed. My neighbor's cat who came to visit. My garden. The café down the road. Almost, nearly, *real*, if only the plane had kept going. I jammed my eyes shut. But it was not to be.

"I'm not Gregor, *meisie*, but I will not be lied to. You're going to learn and I'm going to enjoy teaching." His hand turned my face so I had to stare into his eyes. With a cloth, he wiped away some of the sand, some of the tears. "You may not believe me yet, but I think you're going to be happier by the end. You're mine now and you're precious to me. I'll never hurt you terribly like him. Never. Understand?"

Understand. As if his words helped.

Though maybe they did. Even in my misery I began to think. He wasn't Gregor.

"I won't be gentle all the time," he continued, in that horribly reasonable tone, like a man aiming to convince his pet that it couldn't go out through the cat flap today.

Choking in breaths in an attempt not to cry, I frowned, looking downward.

"But sometimes, I will be. It's the punishments you should fear, and I need to punish you now because you've been bad."

"No." I shook my head, in a determined way. If I wished it enough, it might come true. "You can still let me go." I met his gaze, though I cringed. "Please? Let me go, Pieter. I wasn't going to write about you, or Glass, or the others. I swear."

"Shh. You can bear it."

"I won't do it. I won't tell. Doesn't that mean anything?"

But he only snorted, and picked me up, then he toted me up the beach to a bench under a roof at the jetty. He dragged me across the bench with my bottom up, sat beside me and pushed up my dress. Then he edged my panties down to the top of my thighs and spanked me. My knees were jarred into the sandy concrete. Every finger mark he left seemed an insult. When I attempted to rise, in spite of still being handcuffed, he tsked and pushed me back then hit me harder. With Glass somewhere nearby, I bit back my noises, clenched my jaw. Only a gasp or two escaped me. Damned if I would show how this affected me.

Another slap landed on my ass, cramming me forward onto the metal slats, then another, and another, until the pain seemed to balloon out from my skin with each pulse of blood. My humiliation, anger, and misery, tangled up and shattered my self-control, and I cried.

From then on each blow drew more loud cries or words of protest from me until I was barely conscious of what came from my mouth.

By the time he was done, Glass was preparing to leave, and the props on the plane were turning. Through my tears, I saw this, before I turned away, embarrassed that he too saw my degradation.

This was far beyond what I could have imagined Pieter was capable of and I was trapped here with him, with no one to see what acts he perpetrated on me.

I *had* to get away. From the corner of my eye, I could see the endless surface of the sea. This was so far from civilization, from other people and he could overpower me with one hand. There'd been a rifle unloaded with the boxes. I didn't even know where this island *was.* Despair wrenched another sob from me.

Then he laid his big palm over one cheek of my ass. The burn from the spanking seemed to intensify where his skin met mine.

"Poor Jazmine. I guess I should feel sorry for you. Do you think you've been punished enough?"

What a dumb question.

If I was good, subtle, sneaky, maybe I could slowly win him over and convince him to free me?" "Yes," I squeaked out past a sniffle. "I do."

"Hmmm."

Chapter 29

The ache in my finger stump on my left hand reminded me of what I'd lost to Gregor, but having Jazmine ass up before me, over this bench, what did that mean to me? The feel of her softness under my palm, and knowing I could stop or I could keep going until every bit of her was equally red…

Crazy.

Such a gorgeous ass too, attached to a woman I should really have naked right now. The breeze played with the blue-and-yellow cloth of her dress where it lay shoved above her waist. Where I had left it. Me. Her owner.

I could do what I liked with her.

The headiness of this situation was getting to me.

All my careful thoughts had been obliterated by the reality.

The roar of the plane's engine faded into the noise of the surf crumpling onto the beach on the other side of the island. The sun would be going down in a few hours. I should be thinking of organizing all the gear, but I had a woman here, trembling at my touch. I squeezed her butt then scraped my calloused thumb across her skin, brushing a mark I'd just made. Nothing. No reaction. I dug my nail in harder, still harder, scratched it along. And she whimpered and tried to shift away.

Fok. Scintillatingly good.

There was no one to see what I did to her. Not for a hundred miles or more of bare ocean. Only the fish, the birds, the crabs, and me, the big dirty-minded sadist.

"You think I'm done, do you?"

She watched from the corner of her eyes, face damp from tears, sucking on her lip. If I hit her right now she'd bite herself. Those tears were so attractive, as were her little sounds when I hurt her, and that wriggling she did would win awards for seductiveness. My cock was telling me more bad things I could do.

I reached down and traced the path of her tears over her cheek then I freed her lip from her teeth. As slowly as a snake traversing steps, I bumped my finger along her front teeth, nudging past her moist little tongue tip. That she didn't dare to try to bite was telling.

I could, theoretically, fuck her mouth right now. My cock hardened and I reached down and grasped myself through my surf shorts.

No one to stop me putting it there, or anywhere else. No watch dogs, no police, no neighbors, and no limits whatsoever.

What the hell was I doing?

I wrenched my attention away from her, stood, and walked off the concrete to the beach. I let the wind buffet me. Sure there was only me, but I'd been used to putting my trust in myself all my life. I liked making a woman scream when I whipped her but that wasn't new. The only novelty was that this one, Jazmine, had no say in what I did or when I stopped.

Being her judge and executioner was totally doable. *I* trusted me.

I took my dose of antibiotics from the packet in my shorts and swallowed them. Then I looked at her, noting she'd moved back into a kneeling position. There was a good reason for chastising her. I hadn't told her to do that. Having logical reasons for my sadistic impulses seemed important.

I went to the box full of toys and goodies I'd bought in a rush this morning from the local kinky shop – my first essentials for this desert island holiday, along with food, torches, sleeping bags and so on.

Gags, whip, rope, straps, bars, more rope, clamps, etcetera, and so on and, of course, the cane. I fished that out along with a pair of padlockable ankle and wrist cuffs, her new red collar, and a leash that had come from the pet store. I'd found a good metal tag that had *Kitty* engraved on it. Damn, I hoped she'd spit when I attached it to her neck.

I'd even packed some needles. Elenor would've run screaming from those.

When I turned up in front of her with the collar in hand, her eyes grew round.

"No. You took off the collar from the House. Please, those are evil." Her shudder rocked her breasts, reminding me of my idea.

When I laid my finger across my lips, she fell silent.

"This is a collar from me, no one else. It says you're mine. You're to leave it on, unless I say to remove it. Sit still."

As I adjusted and buckled the collar, her lips firmed and I sensed a new determination to resist me. So be it. Game on. I had plans to make her mind come around. I didn't intend to have to monitor her every day, every second. The tag swung and I flicked it.

"Says Kitty. I could call you that but *meisie* will do unless I'm in a kitty cat mood."

Now the fire was lit. "I'm not a cat!"

"You are whatever I say you are, and from now on I don't intend to call you Jaz or Jazmine. You will answer to *meisie* or maybe Kitty. You will be given daily punishment, whatever I choose, as well as any extra punishment you may have earned." I grinned. An explosion seemed imminent. I put my forefinger on her forehead. "If you talk without my permission, you earn punishment. You will call me Sir when you address me. If you have a question you can ask permission to talk by saying, 'please Sir, may I ask a question?' Clear?"

Her bodice was heaving dramatically. "Fuck! No, I will not!" At the slide of my fingers up into her hair and the levering backward of her head, she clammed up.

Bingo. Caught you. I leaned in, with a nasty twist to my mouth. I was trying so hard not to smile. I made my voice low, so low earthquakes were a distinct possibility. I wanted to scare the crap out of her now, today, early. To nip rebellion in the bud. To make her know I was her master. Her eyes went wide and still. Her mouth gaped as if she had more words but she'd decided to swallow them.

"I have noted that *fokken* outburst. If there's another one, I'll punish you now. Got that? Say, yes, Sir."

I almost hoped she'd be bad again, but she whispered a *yes, sir,* then waited.

"Good." I went behind her and released her wrists, tucked the handcuffs in my pocket then attached ankle cuffs and linked them. Now she was hobbled. "We're moving the boxes into that first cabin up there. It's the only one with an intact roof and Glass has the generator and the fuel drums nearby. You're helping. So you don't do anything stupid, this island is too small to hide on and the nearest piece of land is hundreds of miles away. Try swimming somewhere and I guarantee you'll get eaten by sharks."

The fuel drums were far enough from the hut that we wouldn't go up with a bang if the fuel erupted, close enough that I could watch for thieves of that or any equipment like the bolted-down generator.

The little cabin had no paint left on the weathered timber walls. The windows were long gone but we had shutters. No lights unless I ran the gen and I wasn't doing that. We had some gas lanterns, some torches. The satellite phone would go in the waterproof safe bolted above the floor. Cooking was going to be limited to driftwood fires and gas. Once a week, Glass would return with supplies. Once a day I would check in with him on the sat phone.

At least we seemed to be missing any mosquitoes.

As we tromped to and fro transporting the stuff, I was pleased at her behavior. So far so good. The rainwater tank was filled to the brim from the cyclone.

After a quick swim to wash off sweat, while she waited on the beach, I carried one of the chairs from the hut out onto the little patio. I dumped a sleeping bag on the concrete at the foot of the chair, and sat down to watch the stars come out. The vanishing sun was turning the few clouds pink and orange. Another three quarters of an hour of light perhaps. I'd grabbed a cane from the gear and had balanced it across my legs.

"Sit there. On the bag."

Her elegance as she sat and folded her legs under her was the natural movement of a young woman. I approved wholeheartedly, especially when she winced as her derriere touched her legs.

"Now, before we eat our gourmet canned soup and bread." Tomorrow we could sort out more complicated food. There were long-life milk sachets packed away some bloody where. "You are going to strip off that dress and say I am sorry, sir, for being bad today. Then I am going to cane you for that mistake."

The whine in her throat and her pleading eyes wound up the tension in me. The thought of doing this to her had kept me hard most of the afternoon.

"Now."

"Pieter –" she blurted.

"An extra two strikes for that."

"May I –" She swallowed and shut her eyes. "Ask a question, Sir."

"No. Undress now and say the words, or I will add more strikes."

Her head bowed then with it still low, she pulled off her dress over her head then dropped it to one side. She rattled out the words. "I'm sorry sir, for being bad."

Not terribly heartfelt, but a start. *I'm getting into your head, girl.*

Oh yes. At last. Pretty woman with a bright blue bra and panties set. I reached down and took first one breast then the other in hand, weighing them. Jaz had nice full breasts and there was nothing I would change about her, nothing. Her dark hair swayed across her face.

"Put your head up. I want to see you."

I used the cane to make her raise her head. There were the tears again, lining her eyelids. Would she ever run out of those? I hoped not. A woman crying was one of the sexiest things in creation.

"Scoop your tits out of your bra and hold them up to me."

She did it without hesitation, even if her expression seemed set in stone. I made sure to keep eye contact as I took both nipples in finger and thumb and squeezed them. The abrupt flutter of her eyes and the parting of her lips could hardly be missed except by a blind man. I let go and pulled her up by her upper arms, then treated each nipple to a good long suck. She may have stayed silent but her hips swayed toward me.

Enough with her pleasure.

"Go to your knees facing away then bend over and put your head to the floor. Though her hands clenched into fists and she did a funny little stomp with one foot, she turned and did as I asked. "Tell me, how many strikes do you think you've earned?"

Her reply was muffled yet distinct. "None."

I laughed silently. "I can see you've not played this game before. That means I add extra. Especially for that foot stomp."

I had a try at shifting her panties down with the cane but it wasn't made for this work. Besides, hands-on was far better. I stood then wriggled her panties down to that exquisite spot where her ass ended and her thighs began – a sweet and cute woman's bottom with a few small red and blue spots from earlier but nothing much in the way of marks, yet.

I couldn't cane her every day, but today was number one on the calendar of the training of Jazmine. Though, really, I'd begun at the house. She'd taken to being my submissive from the day I first fucked her.

The rattan cane was nice and whippy. I set out a warning. "Move from your place and I add more."

The first whack was the beginning of a concerto in cane major. This wasn't for her, this was for me and the warm-up was near nonexistent. A few taps and I began. Each strike left a welt, and some of the welts would leave bruises. Her little cries and squirms only drove me onward. I counted to fifteen and she hadn't moved her knees. Impressive.

Jazmine was a smart woman. She was either in subspace from a few hits in or very determined not to earn more blows from the cane.

I went to the front and lowered myself to one knee. "*Meisie?*"

Her subdued "*Mmm*," with her head turned to the side and her lowered eyelids, said subspace.

By her hair, I pulled her up off her knees then I shoved down my shorts. "Open your mouth." Sliding into her mouth along her tongue then feeling the soft bump at the back, *god damn.* I half-closed my eyes and shunted in and out accompanied by her hums and gasps as she sucked in more air past my cock.

After making her ass red, I was close, fast. "Stay there." Having pulled out and released her hair, I walked to her other end and assessed her. *Red, red butt up in the air, perfect, and a beautiful wet cunt.* This was going to hurt her when I thrust in all the way. *Good.*

If there was one thing I'd yearned to do today, apart from punish her, it was fuck her properly. I kneeled and probed for her entrance, hearing a small moan when I hit the spot between her pussy lips and entered her to the depth of an inch or two. My next thrust cruised in all the way. Caught in that amazing moment, sunk balls deep inside her, and revved up by her high-pitched squeak, I pushed to seat myself in her pussy. Her moisture slicked my balls. She let out a little grunt and I bent over and kissed her neck.

"You're as well-lubricated as any whore, girl. Caning gets you horny quickly, doesn't it?"

I wasn't sure, but I may have heard a soft curse, so I pulled out and slammed in again, even harder.

Her cry was almost a sigh. Guess she liked it.

"*Ja. Fok.* Amazing." I groaned myself, at the same time as her then sank my teeth in her neck muscle and fucked her hard and fast, with the sleeping bag moving back and forth under her clutching hands. As the force of my thrusts escalated into pile driver status, her moans turned into yelps and she reached back to stop me.

"Not happening. Stay the fuck still." I slapped her ass once and watched her flail around and twist.

Impatience drove me to put her into a headlock with my arm wedged across her throat. That worked, she couldn't move without me strangling her. That and growling in her ear as I banged her. When I shot my load of cum into her, I could watch her reddened face from an inch away, feel her muscles straining to get loose, and hear her whimpering gasps right up close.

"Seeing you like this. Beautiful." I licked the side of her face. "Beautiful end to the best fuck ever."

Best because I'd claimed her with it. I pulled out, keeping her flattened to the floor with my hand planted on her back. I grabbed a wet palm of her juices and my cum from between her legs then smeared it down her back. "Wear that tonight. Tomorrow you can wash it off."

Chapter 30

I wasn't sure moving was possible...or allowed.

He'd wrapped me up again in his arms. My underwear were partway up but askew, his cum was on my back and squished between him and me. One of his arms I lay on, the one with the hurt finger, while his top arm was barred across my neck again – like he was scared I'd run.

Which I would, if I had anywhere to go, just on principal, even though the pain left me lazy as a cat on a window sill in the sun.

My butt and between my legs throbbed where he pressed into me and where his thigh pushed mine apart. Sleepily, I eyed the arm beneath my chin. Licking his biceps was a craving I had to suppress. The taste alone would get me off.

Men. So dirty. So primal. I could smell us both. With every inhalation, the tang in my nostrils reminded me of the sex he'd just forced on me. My apartment was kept so clean I refused to let my friend, Lani, bring her new puppy inside for fear it would pee on the carpet.

I could ask to get clean. Say *please Sir may I.* The very notion was demeaning and I had no way around it without getting my ass turned even sorer than it was now. Plus he'd say no. So how was it that I felt so right here, with him closer than even my gynecologist had been?

Stockholm syndrome, I reminded myself, like a scratched disc on a repeating loop.

I frowned. Inside his arms was an awesome place to be. I was such a slut. Every time he did mean things to me, made me take what he did, even if it hurt, I loved it, maybe more so if it hurt.

Okay, I accepted that. Didn't mean I wanted to stay his little damn slave.

Where and how could I get away? Was it possible?

Fly? Sure, I'd magic up a plane. Swim? Haha. Sharks and, yeah, I was a super woman. A boat? Maybe. If there was one here. The best possibility was that sat phone he'd mentioned. I'd need to get into that safe and to have it to myself long enough to contact someone.

"Let's get some food."

He removed his arm and I rolled onto my back then tried to rise. His broad foot came down on my neck, just resting there. I swallowed, worried about what he intended.

"Decided you can stay there." In the fading light, his eyes were dark behind that curtain of his salt-thickened hair. From his shorts, he fished a chain link leash and he knelt to click it onto my collar then stuck the other end, the loop, under the chair leg. As if I were too stupid to get it out from under there.

I didn't dare say anything, only lay on my back waiting permission to rise.

"Good."

I sucked in a breath, feeling my bared breasts press into the rolled-down cups.

His gaze cruised down me. "Stay there until I say to move."

I could have fought but like him at the House, I needed to conserve my energy. He'd once told me he hadn't fought back because it was clearly useless, a waste of energy, and likely to get him hurt when he needed to be healthy. Two could play at that.

I could play a waiting game.

The haze from the caning was fading, though it left me prone to despair.

The last possibility for escape, the one I tried not to think about, was to wait until we left the island, even if it meant being his *kitty*, his bed toy, and his precious piñata. But this last option for escape scared me, because already I could see the break between the old me and the one here, now, on this island. I'd changed.

"Mmm. I like seeing you down there. You are showing me stuff about myself I never knew was there. I don't think I could *fokken* well ever go back after having you. There's something pure about owning someone…or you, at least."

His words seemed to echo my own thoughts and I lay there a little shocked. He sat down and put his feet on my side and smiled, as if to say, *you are worthy of being my footrest.*

Confusion – that was the summation of my thoughts.

Resisting wasn't worth it? The problem was I could see the allure of being his toy taking me over if I left it unchecked. Kneeling, not speaking, obeying, it dulled the mind. I had to keep myself thinking. What was his motto? I'd have my own.

No giving in. Yes.

No giving in could sustain me until I found my way out. I'd be meek, pliable, his, I'd kneel and be his footrest but I'd still remember to be me. I'd lull him into a state of vulnerability.

Another option came to me. The rifle I'd seen him carry into the hut. I could kill him if I got hold of it. Could I kill? Maybe. But did I want to?

"What are you thinking?" He peered down at me.

"Nothing, Sir." I blinked innocently.

"*Ja.* That's good then. I believe the sun rises in the west too. Sit up and kneel. I'm getting our dinner."

Wary, I did so. When he returned with two bowls of soup and some bread then put a bowl down before me, and the other on an upturned box next to his chair, I wasn't sure what he intended.

"Eat."

No spoon? I looked from the bowl to his hand and the bread he carried.

The chair creaked as he sat. Then he leaned sideways to tip up the chair and free my leash from the leg.

"Go on. I want to see you lick it up. Be good. When you want bread, nudge my hand." He smiled but there was a dark glitter in his eyes, as if he expected a challenge.

Fuck you, Pieter. Another demeaning task. *I see what you're doing, sir.*

No giving in.

I counted to ten. I could do this.

Then I crept forward and began to lap. I was hungry and my resources needed to be kept in reserve, plus my butt hurt, he was big, and I had zero chance of winning a level fight. Licking up soup took time and he finished before I did. To get him to give me the bread I found I had to butt his hand with my nose, but then I got a smile and a pat on my head, and once a kiss. It was so humiliating that it made my toes curl, but in my affection-starved universe, where once upon a time the best I'd had was a peck on the cheek or hug from an aunt or my friend, this was alluring in a weird way.

I could feel the effects inside me, warming me, and it was so scary.

I didn't like this, just like I didn't like pain. I stared at my empty bowl and called BS on my logic.

While I was wrestling with my weirdness, he traipsed inside and returned with a stapled-together sheaf of pages then sat down and leafed through them.

Reading the words on the flipped back front page wasn't easy.

"Time for your lesson."

I whipped my gaze to his face. *Lesson* sounded bad.

"Jazmine Foulkes. Freelance journalist. As you can see, I printed out some information before I left. Very interesting. You are a clever girl. Want to tell me how you really got into this mess you're in? You can talk."

Then he turned it around and showed me page one where a clear photograph of me was featured, smiling for the camera, windswept hair but perfectly and fashionably dressed in a suit.

Is that really me?

His hand under my chin tilted my head. Then he said in that gravel-deep voice, "That's you, a gorgeous, smart woman, but I like you better how you are here. With my cum on you, mostly naked, and that pretty, tear-stained face."

God. Those words should have repulsed me but they didn't. They stirred me. My pussy clenched.

I'm smart, remember? Maybe I needed that too, like armor against these foreign emotions he was evoking in me. With those brown eyes of his observing me, I gathered my scattered thoughts.

I used to be a writer. Write something. Be intelligent.

A headline emerged: *Jazmine Foulkes kidnapped and enslaved by virtue of her weird naive emotions and being made to eat off the floor.*

Ugh.

"What are you thinking? Hmm." He tidied my hair, tucking it behind my ear.

"Nothing, Sir."

"Nothing? Again? Do I have to cane you? Or spank you? I expect an answer when I ask you."

And now he was trailing his fingers over my lips like they were some forbidden fruit he'd discovered. I shuddered when he dipped one inside my mouth, left it there for a few heartbeats, then pulled it out, but I knew I'd dampened.

The nonchalant ownership of my mouth…

Mindfuck alert. Inhale. Exhale. I cleared my throat. "I was imagining the headlines about me."

"Sir," he prompted.

"Um. Sir."

"Why did you lie to me about your name and who you were?"

I frowned, but he was playing with my hair and it mesmerized me in a way only my hairdresser had ever managed. "I thought it would make you…" Why had I?

"What?"

"Hate me? No, it wasn't that. I was worried because I didn't trust you with my real name, with knowing how to find me if I ever escaped. Sir." *Escaped*, my favorite word.

"Trust. I thought so. I never really believed you were a librarian but you know what?"

I shook my head, barely catching myself before I sighed as he kept on combing my hair and patiently untangling knots. So tired…

"It still hurt when I found out this was who you were." He pointed with his chin at the paper. "I lost a finger for you, killed for you, kept you alive when someone else would've pandered to Gregor. You repaid me with a lie. Do you think that was good, *meisie*?"

Oh, man, play with my guilt why don't you. Slowly, I shook my head. "I did it because I was afraid of you."

His smile was a stark one. "And you were right. Why did that man want to kill you? What did you do to his son?"

When I tried to duck my head he waggled my chin from side to side. "No. You're not allowed to look away. Tell me it all."

Fuck. I sucked in my lip. I wasn't sure what was on those pages, so I took a deep breath, and said it straight. "His son was my boyfriend, only I found out he was married, with a wife and daughter." *Who must've died. How much should I say?* "He was odd. We never had sex."

Especially not like you make me. I never even knew anyone could really, outside of porn fantasies, have sex like this.

With him holding my face, I had an urge to squirm. "He used to tell me all these secrets. Including that he was ripping off the government for millions through his plastic surgery practice." I wound down. "And that was it."

"If that's not all, my girl, I will hurt you."

He couldn't know. Couldn't. But he kept staring…and staring. I should tell. My mind filled with crazy thoughts…

And I broke.

"He had a fetish for my underwear and when I wrote up the story, I mentioned his kinks too." To embarrass him, for lying to me, the bastard. "Last I heard, he was being charged and going to be arrested."

"Yeah. He suicided and killed his family on a Monday. They kept it covered up according to the news until three days later. You were taken on the Wednesday."

"Oh."

"If I'd known," he set his mouth in a line, "It would've made no difference. Except I would've thought you callous. It was the sexual allegations that made him suicide. He wrote a note, and a journalist as nasty as you leaked it in a story."

As nasty as me.

My heart thumped slowly, painfully. Everyone likes to think they are good deep down. Making someone want to die, and to kill their family… I'd heard what his father had said, and swept it from my memory. Because I didn't want to be that person. Besides, what had been done to me had cancelled it out, right?

Wrong.

"I never wanted him to die. Or his kid or his wife. I was just doing what I do."

It was never worth this. I was stupid. Vengeful. I'd hated that I was only some bit on the side for him, and not even worthy of intimacy. Being scared of sex had only made me think about it incessantly.

"You were bad and you lied to me about it. Were you planning to write a story about me?"

I did not want to answer this. Ever. I'd thought he'd plumbed the depths of my soul with what he'd already made me confront. He had no lie detector – not that they worked. But people made the best readers of body language. As an ex-cop, he'd know that. I was afraid and the fear was overriding my instincts. In a way, lying had been my life. The best way to get ahead. It always was.

"Pieter, I mean Sir. I…"

My forehead was pounding from the strain of trying to second guess him.

"Tell me. From the length of time you've taken to reply, I already know."

I slumped. "I was, at first, but then I wasn't."

Pieter snorted. "And when did you change your mind?"

Late. Way late. Shit.

"In the taxi. After you found me, I felt guilty." And how silly was that, considering what had happened since?

"Uh-huh."

Then he sat, with his hands between his knees, obviously thinking. I waited. I could do nothing else, except wait for his judgment.

After a while, he focused on me again. "What you did was terrible, and so was what his father ordered done. But you've paid. Too much if anything. As for me, I've already punished you for lying.

"From now on, every day, you're going to tell me more about yourself, until I have all of you, up here." He tapped his head then he tugged on the leash and beckoned me to climb into his lap.

Oh, that appealed. I always did like his hugs, once I had them. Though it'd taken a while to see that.

He tugged again.

Feeling like a penitent soul pardoned by a benign king, I climbed up and rearranged my legs when he urged me to, until I curled there. The similarities to a cat struck me yet again, especially when he began petting me.

For a few minutes I tensed. I was damn well never going to purr. Then the stroking wore me down and I breathed out, relaxed into him, and closed my eyes. Exhaustion flooded in.

When he spoke again, I was half asleep.

"There, *meisie.* Consider this your new life and today the first day of that life.

My last hazy, crazy thoughts drifted in like clouds on a warm summer's day. I'd always been the one who looked in on other's exciting lives but now I was the one looking out. Eyes closed, I snuggled up to the warm man under me. Funny how good this felt.

Chapter 31

Jazmine watching was my favorite occupation. I sat on the sand, with a baseball cap pulled low to shade my eyes.

I'd brought my resume of her past with me to see if I'd missed clues. From what I could sense, the woman still wasn't disclosing everything. The rising wind grabbed at the pages and I set them aside under a rock. The gray clouds gathering above meant we were in for some rain tonight.

Without the internet to lean on, I figured I was getting good at weather prediction.

The wind flicked her hair, as she waded into the foot-high waves on this corner of the island furthest from the hut. The sun beyond glittered through her black tresses. Since she wore them so often, her blue pair of underwear had faded and her skin was tanned despite the sunscreen we used. She'd looked skeptical when I first rubbed the lotion into her. I'd had to inform her that sunburn wasn't on my sadistic list of activities.

If there was one chore I was happy to do, it was rubbing lotion on her, especially when I could follow the red lines of whip marks with my fingers.

After a week, the salt spray was getting into everything. Our hair, our skin, our clothes. We couldn't afford the water to wash clothes, though every day I had us both use a water-dampened washer on our bodies.

With all the sex I was subjecting her to, we needed it. With all the spanking and light whipping, she needed it. Pain slut that she'd turned out to be, that wasn't punishment, but it was showing her my physical dominance and that was crucial in my plans.

I'd found the appeal for me wasn't just the sex or the sadism – it was *everything* about owning this woman. I was beginning to understand my addiction. I'd do almost anything to keep her. Whatever I had to do to break her to my will, I would, or this would be a never-ending struggle.

Was I an expert at breaking women? No.

But I wanted to be.

Did I have a perfect solution? No again, but I could see how it would happen.

During the past, she'd reacted perfectly when dominance interwove with the pain. She was almost there when we arrived – almost mine. I only had to get her to wrap her mind around the concept.

Maybe what I needed here wasn't breaking but bending, because why would I want a broken woman?

My only need was that she obeyed me one hundred percent, without question, no matter what I wanted. And she was changing, even if she didn't comprehend it. I could see it in the small ways she deferred to me, in the tiny reactions. Whenever I spotted one, I had the urge to do a fistpump.

But it was time to up the ante. I toyed with the small butt plug in my pocket. From my questions, she'd never had anal sex and found the concept horrifying. An ideal activity then, especially since I'd been keen to fuck her little hole ever since I first saw her.

What a surprise to hear how little her previous lovers had satisfied her. I'd interrogated her day by day only to hear her reinforce her story until I knew it was truth. She hadn't come with a single lover before me. By her own words though, they'd been pussies. I smiled. Good to know, because I sure as hell wasn't.

I scanned the horizon again with the binoculars. No signs of thieves today, though two days ago I'd had to warn off a fishing boat by shaking my rifle. They were likely just islanders on their way elsewhere. The fuel here was aviation fuel and most of the gear would take expertise and cutting tools to get loose from the locked shipping container.

Of course the poor often stole what they had no use for, hoping to sell it to some clueless fool.

The rifle lay on a crate beside me, loaded, ready. The odds were that one day it would be required. How much I'd have to use it depended on how much the thieves were willing to risk, but I wasn't dealing with a special forces squad here, just petty theft.

I clambered to my feet and brushed off the sand. "Stop there! I've something for you."

She rose from where she'd been crouching in the water and waited, arms by her sides, wet sand cascading from one hand.

Seawater might make an okay lubricant to pop in the plug? I'd find out soon enough. I had a tube of lube but it'd be more fun to try something new.

I stood and waded out after her, to where she'd been wandering among the rocks in this inlet. A few black sea cucumbers lay bloated and slopping to and fro, and schools of silvery fish shot away from me as I sloshed through the water. This was the first time we'd come over this way. With the rocks obviously came more creatures. Near her foot, a blotchy underwater shape caught my eye.

"Don't move!" I snapped. "I think that's a stonefish next to your foot."

"Where, Sir?" Jaz glanced down.

The paling of her cheeks said she knew about stonefish.

"Just come this way and you'll be fine." Once she was close enough, I scooped her up and set her behind me then bent to peer at what the thing. "No. My mistake. It is a rock."

Stonefish were deadly and stepping on one here might mean death. Medical help was hours away. It was one of the drawbacks to a deserted island, apart from pirates, tsunamis, and a lack of hot showers.

I thought back. She'd said *sir* automatically. Well, well. None of the little hesitation I often heard or the distaste, and she was waiting, saying nothing, despite looking like she wanted to blurt something. "You can speak."

"They paralyze you, don't they, Sir? I visited a North Queensland resort once for a travel article and we were given a whole speech about poisonous underwater creatures."

"Yes. Give me your hand."

I drew her back to the shallower area then reached into my pocket and drew out the plug. "Bend over."

"Umm." She took a step away.

I hadn't seen rebellion for days.

My smile wasn't that evil, surely, but she frowned at me. "Please, Sir. No."

"Say one more word and I'll do full anal on you with my cock, here and now." I wouldn't get far into her but it was cute seeing the fear arrive. She knew about anal needing lube and that no one did it that easily, first time. Jaz wasn't naive, just inexperienced.

At her hesitation I lunged for her, pulled her forward by a wrist, and tripped her into the water. Wrestling hit the adrenalin button, even if I had her down with her face in the water in seconds. All the fish zipped away from the flurry of splashing and the burbling scream she let out after arching her neck and grabbing a breath. With all her thrashing, it was lucky my finger had healed well.

I calmly put the plug back in my pocket, locked her wrist cuffs together and hauled her onto her knees. She gasped, dragging in no doubt much-needed air. Her underwear was dripping, her hair soaked. I yanked down her underwear at the back to bare her butt then kept her elbows in a lock while I fingered her hole. She squirmed but got nowhere.

Whoah. The water did help. With one knee down in the sand and the water, steadying me, I wormed the little finger of my good hand an inch deep, past her entrance ring, feeling it clamp onto me.

"Ohhh baby. Do you know how much men love fucking these tight little holes?"

Her glare then wince when I rotated my digit was an awesome catalyst for a sadist. We were both sopping wet but I was the one with the grin and the hard on.

"The things we can do with this." I nipped her ear and removed my finger, then pulled the plug from my pocket. "Going in, *meisie*."

Fok, she started wriggling like mad and I nearly dropped the thing, but there was one thing I was good at and it was hand to hand fighting with an already wrist-cuffed woman. I dropped her back into the water – she could grab air if she arched high enough – and found the leash in my opposite pocket.

"Up you come." I pulled her head from the water and her onto her knees again. While she was recovering from vaguely drowning, I wrapped the leash around her thighs a few times and clicked it onto itself. "Got you."

"Sir, no. Please."

Her protests were amusing as I dragged her into even shallower water, rinsed the sand off her butt and lubed up the little black plug. If there were any sand grains left on her or my straining cock, I didn't notice. The lube tube floated away with the waves and it started to rain, the drops smacking into the water at our knees.

So much for my weather-reporting prowess. I needed to get it inside her before the rain washed off the lube.

But Jaz. Oh my. Now I had her where I wanted her.

She kneeled before me in a foot of water, her thighs bound, her wrists at her back, and my arm locked under her elbows.

I smacked her butt a few times then pinched her nipples until she moaned. So predictable. It was the next bit she'd not like.

"Relax." With great concentration, I wiggled the tip into her hole, fraction by fraction, with her squealing and gasping, until the biggest part disappeared inside. The last of it went like magic as her muscles claimed it. I tugged as if to pull it out and she squeaked again.

"Now I'm going to fuck you with that in. This might seem crowded."

When I leaned her forward, her pussy lips were so engorged, pink, and pushing out between her legs, that I knew something had worked for her. The pain or the wrestling, or both.

"Little bitch, that's step one for cock-in anal." Then I squeezed my cock in past those inviting lips. With her thighs crammed together by the bondage, my cock seemed in heaven. Tight, wet, and every thrust made her whimper.

"Sir! Too tight. Hurts!"

Had I found a pain she found overwhelming? I stuck it deeper into her again, slamming in hard, and she descended into animalistic noises. I fucked her until both of us were panting and crying out louder than the noises of the squall. The rain poured down on us in a mad accompaniment.

I reached around and found her clit, massaged that little female button as I pumped slower, in and out. The clutch of her pussy on my cock was enough to make me come in ten seconds if I didn't keep it slow.

I gasped and stopped, tensing for a few seconds, holding back from erupting. Then I worked at her clit while only thrusting an inch in, an inch out, until she stiffened, mouth wide open, and cried out *oh fuck oh fuck oh fuck* in a high-pitched voice, while shaking through a long climax.

"My turn," I grated through my teeth. The base of the plug down there reminded me of what I could do to her. One day. My cock in her there. Soon. But right now, this minute…

With the plug in her ass and her thighs squashed in there was almost no room for my cock. Damn. It would probably come out two sizes smaller.

Holding back any longer wasn't happening.

As I hammered into her cunt, the squall hit us full force, blowing me sideways a bit and whipping up the water. I came so hard I didn't notice the rain thudding into us until she bowed her head and slowly collapsed forward. I had to use serious muscle to keep her upright.

I spent a while just leaning on her neck, breathing there, before I popped out the anal plug, undid the leash, and helped her stand. Washing us off was easy with the rain and the sea.

The only problem, when we reached the beach, was that all my pages were wet or blown away.

When she wobbled on her feet, I decided to let them go where the wind took them. Letting her snuggle head first into my chest, enclosing her in my arms, feeling her sighs and mutters of *that was good, sir*...far, *far* better than chasing her past.

Maybe this was the tipping factor. She loved these hugs. From now on I would dole out both daily spankings and hugs.

I had this in hand. Everything was working out well.

Chapter 32

Fishing had always been a great hobby – relaxing, a way to think of nothing. Here, it was also a way to provide food for us both and more satisfying because of that. I'd left her back in bed at the hut, but tied up enough to keep her out of trouble. She'd been sleeping. We'd played under the stars last night with the flare of gas lanterns flickering light across her curves as I beat her with the flogger. I wanted to catch something for breakfast. With no fridge, fish didn't keep for long.

That little inlet with the rocks had looked promising, but when I reached the top of the dune above, there was a small, dilapidated boat rocking in the waves.

Fok. No rifle. Keeping the salt, sand, and rust off it was a full-time occupation here and I'd left it behind for once. The only time, really. Murphy's law.

I set down the fishing rod on the beach but kept the canvas satchel with me. The fishing knife would do, for now. A man snored in the stern, a bottle rolling back and forth at his feet as the sea tossed the boat. At least he'd remembered to throw out an anchor. Sails and a motor. I hadn't heard him arrive, so he must have sailed in.

I waded out and checked in the cabin. Nobody else. Good.

So I gently woke him up, standing in the water with my hand on the gunwale and saying howdy like some American. Most couldn't place my accent. If he didn't speak English, I'd figure out an alternative way to scare the shit out of him.

His snoring choked to a halt and he blearily opened his eyes then jerked fully awake.

"You scare me!" His hand was on his heart.

"Sorry." I nodded at his boat. "What are you doing here?"

He shrugged then clambered to his feet and staggered to the side. "Hey, I don't know. I'm going to fish here. There's a time to get away from your lady, some days. You know?"

The grin splitting his dark-skinned face invited me to smile back.

"Ahhh. I get it. You're in trouble?"

"Yes!" He half fell, half climbed over the side, landing with a splash, and I caught his arm. "Yes. That is it."

So the poor guy had gone on a drunken bender in his fishing boat to get away from his woman. It was hilarious in a way. God knows how he got this far without sinking.

I guessed he was fortyish and his face, teeth, and clothes were as battered as his boat but I hadn't met anyone so cheerful in a long while.

We sat on the beach exchanging silly stories about women and fishing for half an hour before I managed to tell him the island was off limits and private. I hadn't conversed with anyone for days, apart from a few times on the sat phone with Glass. Sad to have to shoo him off the island, but necessary.

"You got any friends coming here, looking for free stuff?" I gestured at the beach in front of us.

"No. Nobody I know comes here. Why?"

"Ahh. I'm having trouble with a few. Make sure people know. Okay?"

"Sure. Sure." He shot me another gap-toothed grin. "I'll do that. I have something of yours here, maybe. I found this on the beach last night." He shoved his hand in his pocket, pulled out a folded-up piece of paper. Though wet, he managed to uncrumple it, and smoothed it on his thigh. He tapped it. "She looks like your woman maybe? This one? I see woman last night when I sail past. All lit up. You play rough?"

I'd had a couple of gas lanterns out last night, with Jaz tied under the roofed shelter at the jetty. Crap. With all the light, I'd not seen a thing outside the circle. I was getting careless.

"I guess I do."

He had the first page on his knee and there was Jazmine's picture, clear as day. *Damn.*

"You read English?"

He shook his head. "No. No. Not much. I read little." Then he gave the paper to me.

Little?

I tucked it away. "Thanks. *Shh* on this though. Okay? It's just what she likes me to do to her."

"Yes? I guess I can shush but…" He shook his head while looking down at the sand. "I don't know. It don't seem right."

Where was the line between reading *little* and reading enough?

I rubbed my forehead.

Words could be powerful when said to the right people.

I shrugged, annoyed, tired, and feeling sad about where my accidental decisions were taking me.

"My mother always told me to take care of my wife. You think you do that? By beating her? But hey." He held up his hands and gestured, pushing the air outward. "Don't want to interfere in your marriage with her. No. Your business, for sure, but I feel for your soul." He thumped his chest.

This fisherman had principles. He was right, of course.

Drunk old bastard that he was. Like most people he deserved better than life had delivered to him.

That familiar tug awakened and pulled me between caring for Jazmine, loving her, and wanting to hurt her. I'd sat out by myself a few nights trying to reconcile this new facet of myself. Being a sadist was old news, wanting to do things the woman didn't want and then doing them anyway? New. This freedom was making me have second and third thoughts.

"We have souls that gather dirt as we live our lives. Mine has many spots, I know this." He nodded, lower lip curling out. "Is bad. Yours? Is yours dirty?"

For a drunken fisherman, he was giving Aristotle a run for his money.

"A soul?" I smiled weakly. "Sometimes I think I don't have one of those."

"You do! Some of you is a good man!" He snuggled his arm across my shoulders and breathed fumes in my face for a moment before his arm slid off. "Don't want you going to your death with bad things weighing you down."

"Uh huh."

In the middle of nowhere and I was getting into a philosophical discussion with a fisherman.

"So why are you here? Hmm? This is nowhere." He pulled a horrible face, wrinkles folding on wrinkles as he surveyed the beach. "Is pretty but shithole. Storm will blow you away, if the waves don't get you."

"A shithole? Damn, I could show you worse than this." I chuckled despite everything." I came here with her to…" I had a compulsion to tell him some of the truth. "Make sure we agreed on things." Inside, I laughed again. That was sort of it.

"By beating her until she screams?" His eyebrows shot up. "Wow."

"Wow?" What was wrong with giving this guy some of my time on this beach? Nothing. It wasn't like I had an appointment to get to. "What's your name?"

"I am Miok."

"I'm Pieter." I shook his hand. "Okay, here's a pretend puzzle for you. Something bad has happened. If you do one thing, all your friends go to jail. Maybe for the rest of their lives. But…" Why was my heart beating so fast and hard? "One woman is freed from prison. Do the *opposite* and she is in prison but your friends are free. Which do you choose?"

"That's a moral puzzle." He took a swig from his bottle. "I know what morals are. Shit. And I know answer. I think."

"Go for it."

A late ghost crab scuttled past my toes along the sand. The waves gently shushed back and forth, shifting the gravel and sand. I was missing the best fishing time arguing morals with this guy but it had become important to me.

Swaying, he held up his finger. "Depends. Did she do anything bad? Did your friends?"

I thought a while. "Both. Her, it was accidental badness with some bitchiness too. The friends have done many deliberate bad things, but they've also done good."

"*Ahh.* Hard one. You try to trick me, but...but, the rights of many really bad people should not mean more than the rights of one little bit bad person. I say let the friends go to jail. Okay? Fixed?"

His was the viewpoint of the average good man. And well said too. Clear as day, none of the wishy-washy stuff I told myself.

"Fixed."

"S'not just me saying this. You know? My son shot a man once and he wanted to run but I told him no. He was good boy. He got out of prison and now he's got a good wife, a little baby coming. Hmm?" He peered at me. "See?"

"I see. Yes."

I let him talk for a while longer before I decided I'd spent enough time being his new friend. Jaz was tied up at the hut. It'd be cereal this morning, not fish. I drew in a long breath and stood up. My offer to help get the boat out to sea was accepted.

"It's going to storm again today. But late," he said as we trudged down the sand.

I waded out after him and we pulled up the anchor.

"Get in."

I gave the poor guy a shove to help him climb into his boat, while I steadied the vessel with my hand.

He peered back at me, saluted sloppily. "Thank you, sir. Small storm. Little one. I'll be fine. I hope your moral problem is now fixed."

"It is. Yes."

The people you meet in the middle of nowhere. Life isn't always a box of chocolates. Hand still on the hull, I fingered the paper in my back pocket.

"Sit down. Let's get you out into deeper water."

Chapter 33

I'd been dying to pee and managed to wriggle out of the straps, since they were looser than normal, and to go outside to pee. If I didn't get back in them, I might be in trouble. My head was telling me that even as I held his rifle across my hands.

The fucking thing shone where the morning sun lit it up, but the metal of the barrel was cold and oily on my palms.

I had the means of my escape in my grasp. *Shit, shit, shit. Deep breath. Think.* I peeked about, terrified he'd return and find me like this. Past the shipping crate, the huts, toward the beach and the palm trees on every side. The fishing rod was missing. *No. Nowhere in sight.*

Kill him? God no, my soul shrank at that idea. He'd know that too. I wasn't a killer. He'd been kind as well as scary. *Shit.*

Decide. I had to do this properly and with courage, or not at all. And fast.

Could I shoot his leg? That might kill him anyway. I'd seen plenty of gunshot wounds in my early days as a reporter on the police beat. But...yes, I think I could.

I could.

Check if it's loaded.

As I looked for the catch to release the magazine, a shadow moved in front of me, coming up from the beach. Him.

He'd seen me, what I was doing. As he advanced, the stark expression – rigid mouth and eyes as still as stone – said a nuclear holocaust was a minor disturbance compared to his fury.

"What are you doing, girl?"

Dumb question. He was trying to get close enough to grab the gun, or me.

Shit.

Clutching the rifle, and aiming it at him as I backed several yards, I shored up my crumbling willpower. *I can do this!*

"Stay there or I shoot!"

He stopped level with the box and held out his hands. They dripped water and his hair and clothes were wet too. "I come in peace."

"Sure you fucking do." My words shook, and my heart beat hard enough to make me worry it'd explode any second.

"That's sure you fucking do, *Sir.*"

"Not anymore." I resisted the need to wipe my face. Sweat had prickled up on my brow, probably due to my stomach turning into a block of ice. When nervous, confuse your inner thermostat. "Turn around and put your hands behind your back."

How was I going to do this? He'd grab me still. Were there handcuffs that fi –

"Before I will do that, let me tell you something important. A story."

A what? "A story?" When I hesitated, he sat on the box.

"See. I'm no threat to you. Besides, I don't think you know much about guns, do you?"

Was he trying to decide if I could shoot? "I can pull this trigger fine. I didn't say sit, I said *turn.*"

His monotone delivery continued. "If you shoot me and kill me how will you get off this island? The sat phone is locked away. You going to wait for Glass and shoot him too? Let me talk then you can think about these orders again? Maybe I'll cooperate?"

His logic was impeccable. Bastard. He was setting a trap here, but what was it?

"Talk. Two minutes."

He shifted his feet, rested his forearms on his thighs. "I remember, *meisie*, how much you like what I do to you." His eyes narrowed. "Last chance to give me the rifle without fuss. I'll only punish you a little."

My grip crunched in enough to strangle the rifle, if it were alive. "One minute forty." Pity I had no watch.

"Suit yourself. I wanted to tell you who I met on the beach just now. An old fisherman, drunk, lost. He ended up here by accident. Was a nice guy with a boy of his own. His son has a baby coming too."

He went on with more detail about his talk with the fisherman. Now and then, as he spoke, he would study the rifle in my hands then look away, then stare at it again. It made me think he respected what a bullet could do. But then he stopped looking and I agonized that it wasn't loaded at all. Damn him. He'd been in combat and been fired on many times. Were there bullets in this thing or did he scorn the threat of me with a loaded gun?

I frowned. And why was he saying this? Was his new friend sneaking up on me? The tension of wondering if there was someone there, about to jump me, became a compulsion. I did a quick scan behind me then whipped my head back around to check Pieter. He hadn't moved. Thank god. My heart stuttered back to life and he smiled at me.

"So?"

"So he told me his life story. I told him some of mine. He'd found a bit of paper on the beach, from your resume. It had your picture on it and I was worried he might have read your name. He said he could only read a little English. Then he went on to tell me he saw what I did to you last night."

That…I recalled, all the pain, all the climaxes Pieter had forced from me. In his strange way, he cherished me, yet here I was ready to shoot him. Why? Was what I was doing right? If it wasn't… An unwelcome tear rolled down my face.

Fuck it. I was right. I must be.

Except I sort of, kind of, loved some of him. How was that possible?

The rifle seemed heavier every second. Where was this heading? "And? Sixty seconds left."

Only I was the one dreading the end of my countdown...and I had no clue why. Just something about how he regarded me. As if being held down and hurt a million times while he fucked me into nirvana wasn't going to have psychological impact. Be strong.

"Not giving me the gun?"

"Fuck off."

"I don't think so. He gave me this big speech about being good in this lifetime, which I agreed with. He's right about what is morally correct. I agreed that what I'm doing to you is wrong."

Stunned, I rearranged my fingers on the rifle. Was he saying he was going to let me go? Did I dare ask him that? My vocal cords wouldn't function for all of half a minute. If I never said it, I'd never hear him say no.

"Are you...are you saying you're going to free me?"

He nodded, looking sadly at the ground between my feet.

This couldn't be.

"I'm saying that after I pushed him out to sea, I climbed aboard, and I strangled him, and then I dumped his body overboard."

Blankness filled my head as everything seemed to jerk into stillness, then I kicked over into horror. He'd killed a man. Just now. A complete innocent. Was this a lie? I stared into his eyes, concerned if I looked away for a second, he would pounce.

"You're lying."

"The day my brother died, I ran through the crowd of demonstrators to Aden, my fellow officer, planning to, I don't know, just stop him. My brother was curled in a puddle of blood at his feet, dead, brains spread out in a splatter. I pulled my pistol and shot Aden's face off.

"I lost a brother, a country, a wife, and for a long while, my respect for myself, but I've come to terms with who I am. Killing is what I do."

Stated so blatantly. I blinked, my thoughts running about like freaked-out mice. Truth then.

He'd killed a stranger. A fucking stranger.

A dark purpose emanated from him, and his feet moved under him, ready.

His large hands rested on his knees. The damage those could do…if he managed to seize me.

Caged and concealed behind the swayed locks of hair, his eyes lurked. The crack and rustling thump of a palm leaf falling to the sand behind him distracted him not at all. I was his only target.

I was playing a dangerous game with a dangerous man.

"Why?" I croaked. "Why today?" Black specks danced across my vision. My lips numbed. The gun seemed lost in my thick fingers.

"Because I want you." He rose to his feet, heavy muscles sliding on arms and thighs, ominous as a dread instrument of war about to attack. "Because I will kill to keep you. I will kill a man on the bloody *whisper* of a suspicion to keep you. That –" He nodded at the rifle. "– an empty gun, will not stop me from taking you back." He took one step.

All my fears crashed in.

"Stop. Stop there. It's not empty." My finger tightened. It couldn't be empty. He was bluffing. I didn't want to shoot, but he took another step then leaped for me. One, two strides. Panicked, I pulled the trigger while scrambling back, half tripping, unsure where I was aiming, the barrel swinging in little arc. *Click. Nothing.* I yanked the trigger madly. *Nothing. Nothing.*

I stumbled and my heel hit something. Just as I was on the verge of toppling head over heels, he was on me, snarling, one hand on the middle of the rifle and twisting it aside, the other hand had my throat.

"I wanted to see if you'd shoot. Three, four times, you pulled that trigger? You are in so much *fokken* trouble. Did you really think I'd leave it here loaded?"

Still off balance, but with both hands hanging onto the rifle as if it were a life jacket, I gaped at him.

Terror stampeded my mind.

I had to act. Had to do *something.* If I let him have this I was done for, his victim again. If I kept it, he was going to half kill me. Frantic, barely able to think, my fingers stayed locked on.

"Let it go. *Now.*" In the rumbling threat in his words, I could hear the *or else* like the music cue before the beast eats the teenagers in a horror film.

Something, probably that irrational terror, along with having him snarling down at me like that movie beast, made me attempt to swing the rifle around to bear on him. An empty rifle.

And fuck me, if I didn't tear it from his hand. It was the left, hurt one, of course. I sat down abruptly.

He ripped the gun from my grasp.

I swallowed past the tightness in my throat, my eyes watering purely from the anxiety of facing him down. "I… I'm sorry, Sir. I didn't mean to…" But I had.

His eyes narrowed, darkened to what seemed pits-of-hell level.

Doomed, was putting it mildly.

"You spoke."

The next *sorry* died on my tongue.

He rarely gagged me, but he hauled me to my feet, marched me over to the box, and held me facedown over it while he connected my wrist cuffs at my back. The leash clicked on, then he wrapped it around and around my face and knotted it somehow. My tongue met the metal links if I swallowed. While still behind me, he twisted my head back until I bent like a bow…*god.* That black stare – so impersonal. I floundered, crazy scared.

"You will learn never to touch another weapon. One lesson only because that's all I need. Down."

He shoved me to the sandy concrete and made me kneel with my face to the hard surface then he sat. The box creaked under his weight. With my head low, I could only see his feet before me.

"Turn your head to the side and look at me."

I did that, blinking up at him, and his foot descended on my neck. The weight pushed my cheek into the grit.

"Being bad means bad consequences."

I sobbed once. It was a little wretched, and he would see it, but what did it matter now? All I'd done had come to nothing. I was his again.

Chapter 34

I was incandescently angry. She'd tried to shoot me several times. The trigger pulls had been obvious. Another man might have beaten the crap out of her over what she'd done but that wasn't going to be me. I'd unleash my anger, yes, but it would have purpose. After weeks of this, I'd thought we were nearly there. I'd thought she wanted to be with me.

That notion she'd just dragged through the dirt. I figured that meant I could drag her through it too.

Tears trickled from her eye and over her nose then dripped to the concrete, making wet splotches. I kept my foot where it was while I calmed.

"Crying? You should have thought. You should never have done this. I need to remind you of your place. Down there." I tapped her neck with my foot then reached down to run my finger over her cheek and collect some of those precious tears.

My wet fingertips slipped over one another as I rubbed them together. "These are mine," I murmured. "Like you are. Understand?"

She nodded, her lips trembling and her eyes communicating misery.

This was hard. Even with my anger, this was hard to do. This couldn't be a relationship where we were equals in any way, at all. I had to have all the control in my hands, to her mind, her body, her heart, her soul. I couldn't do that by continuing on the way I had.

I'd thought being on the island would help us become a loving couple. Wrong.

I couldn't have a woman with so much knowledge wishing to escape whenever I looked away.

I had to come down on her with brutal precision. There was no question I could dominate her or that she loved it when I did, but now…now I would dom her ass out of existence until she didn't take a breath without thinking to ask my permission.

I stood then pulled her up by a grip in her collar and her hair.

"When I'm done training you, you will beg me for proof of my ownership of your body. It isn't just my cock that has rights to your body. For every time you pulled that trigger, I will pierce you."

I would pierce her irrevocably with my metal. I could taste that. If I didn't nearly come in my pants doing that, I'd be damn surprised. Growling, I shook her neck.

"What I did to you before was nothing, girl, and what comes next is only the beginning."

Chapter 35

His declaration repeated in my head, yet I dared to hope. Being towed over to the jetty and the shelter with his hand clasped on my neck was no worse than other times. I could take pain. What could he do that was worse?

My cuffs were unclicked and fastened with rope to the roof, high above. I swung on tiptoes if he pushed me to the side. I remained there stretched out, while he went away. He came back carrying multiple implements, a whip, a flogger, and a stick of some sort?

Those I could handle, but when he attached the leash to the ceiling with a fine piece of rope and tightened it enough to force my head up and put pressure on my neck, goose bumps trickled down my spine and I grappled at the floor with my toes. I could die of asphyxiation if things went wrong.

My gurgled squeaking as I tried to tell him were met by a whip across my breasts and I jerked, coughed, and ceased talking.

"Be. Fucking. Quiet."

He whipped me again, making me screech. Already my drool soaked the rusted chain.

The end of each sentence, he punctuated with the whip.

"You touched a gun that you knew you should not."

Whip. The hard crack as it hit my skin made me dread my nipples splitting.

I choked out a gasp.

"Whatever you thought you might do..." Whip. "...you will never think that again, little bitch."

His speech ended but he circled me, laying it on so fast that I wrenched myself everywhere in an attempt to escape. My arms ached from the strain. I'd thought Gregor was harsh but I'd have bruises on my breasts already.

The fire laced me, seared me, and sent me spiraling into a litany of muffled screams.

Then he halted, leaving me dangling and shuddering.

Something hard and lubricated probed at my ass, squeezing into me inexorably, as he wedged me in place with his legs and a hand on my stomach.

In...further, I felt myself stretching though I was crying again.

"A size bigger than I planned. It fits. Just." With teeth, he claimed a big chunk of my shoulder then pushed the plug all the way in.

Too big. Keening from the hurt, I attempted twisting sideways and got exactly nowhere. His palm smacked onto the end of the plug, jolting it deeper.

Pieter came around to my front and tucked his fingers into the chain of the leash either side of my mouth so that I had to look into his eyes. The pressure on my neck increased. Air rasped in my throat.

Panicking, desperate not to be strangled, I went up high on my toes, but he screwed the leash tighter.

The violence I saw in his eyes. The lust for hurting me.

This monster couldn't be the Pieter I went to bed with. Something had happened. Just me? Just putting my hands on the rifle? I wished I'd never gone near it. This fear unraveled me, tore me to shivering pieces, until my legs trembled and the blood in my veins seemed to become worms of dread.

I had no savior here. My savior had become my torturer.

"I'm going to fuck you there later and you won't like it, then I'm going to make you like it and come hard, then I might hurt you again. And not in a good way. You're going to bleed. Learn from this. Are you learning? Nod."

Though tears streamed down my face, I nodded and nodded, until he stopped me.

"Good." He untangled his fingers and slapped my face, twice. "Good."

Then he flogged me and caned me, covering me everywhere with a fetish artist's playground of welts and bruises. More, and more again. He stalked past, studying his work.

I wanted him to stop, pleaded in my head for some impossible rescue, please, please, please, and knew no one was coming.

"Pretty, pretty stripes."

Then around again, I heard the dance of his steps, the swish of leather and stick. I swayed, spun. Distantly he muttered *no blood.*

The last strikes of the whip were like leaves drifting silently onto a mountain of leaves. They didn't register in significance. I was gone, *elsewhere.* Only the gasps and rasping sounds of my breathing came to my ears.

A whisper: *Yes.*

Then he pulled that plug from me and his cock shoved in. Red-hot pain. That made me scream and awaken.

"You're fine," he said, his words thick and harsh. "I'm in. Just." Another shove, rocking me on my toes, then a grunt from him, and my inhalation became a whine. "A little more."

The implacable surge of his cock as he slowly thrust further must rival childbirth. Burning, tearing pain. The circle of muscle seemed to stretch beyond what was possible. My teeth clamped onto the leash and I bit down as if I thought to crunch through the metal. The hold of rope, metal, and his hands on my hips made getting away impossible. I wrapped my fingers in the rope above and whimpered as he began fucking me in earnest.

A millennium later, his fingers clawed my stomach and I felt the swell of his cum inside. Then he released me from all the bindings except the leash in my mouth and laid me gently down on a blanket on the concrete.

My arms flopped at my sides and I groaned, eyes half open.

On his knees and arms, he leaned above me. "Have you learned properly or do I have to do that again?"

Oh god, no. No more. My eyes surely wide and full of fear, I nodded.

"Say yes, I learned."

Though the gag made it a gurgle, I obeyed.

His smile crept out like the sun emerging after a storm, but this had been no ordinary storm. This had been an implacable assault on me, meant to devastate absolutely, and meant to make me obey him without question.

He rose and brought back the rifle, offered it to me, slowly advancing it toward my hand. Tears slipped down my face as I scrambled to avoid the weapon. Though my arms ached and could scarcely hold me off the ground, I dragged myself away. If I touched it even by accident, he would beat me, I knew this. I'd learned. Fuck. I had.

"Very good." His lips quirked up. "Good, *meisie*. Now hold your ankles and be still. I'm going to eat your pussy and then fuck your ass again. Hold your ankles as long as you can. Say, yes, sir."

My asshole clenched in at the suggestion of more, but he had me. I'd become nothing more than his owned thing and I knew it. I hadn't even the will to be disgusted at myself. I blinked, sniffling. I could no more deny him than a rabbit deny the teeth of the wolf.

My drooled, "*Ess, ssrr,*" clearly made him happy. I wriggled my hands onto my ankles and held on tight. Like this I was so exposed, and he could slide into me easily.

I was terrified he'd rip me this time when he violated my ass.

Yet at his first lick across my clit, I dropped my head backward. Pleasure washed over me. I closed my eyes to let him do as he wished. His fingers entered my pussy. Other fingers made a V either side of my clit, isolating it for him to lap at and suck on, to flick with the tip of his tongue, to bite softly.

I groaned, squirmed, and prayed he'd suck all of my clit into his hot mouth.

Within minutes, I approached the bliss of climax. Such a betrayal of my own self – after all he'd done, that he could bring me to climax so fast.

A final suck and I hit the orgasm explosively, my muscles taut and the scream so exuberant, I felt the burn in my throat. I writhed on his fingers, arching, awakening the pains and finding those pains and his continued sucking setting me off on yet another climax. When he'd milked enough from me, he ceased, gave me one final exquisite lick that made me squeal, and sat up.

He undid the leash gagging me. "Keep yourself there."

God. How? Sweat covered me and made my skin impossibly slippery. My fingers slid on my ankles and I was exhausted. I had my mouth back again but the indentations on my face and the corners of my mouth felt deep enough to be permanent. I ran my tongue over my lips and worked my jaw to lessen the hurt.

My grip kept my legs wide and as Pieter worked lube down his cock, his focus was on my pussy. Then he centered himself down there. The head of his cock poked in a fraction, pushing into that constricting circle. Already I had to bite my lip not to shriek.

Slowly, with a look of immense concentration on his face, he entered me.

"Hurts! Hurts! Hurts!"

But he kept going. For once my speaking seemed to please him.

The relentless advance of what seemed an immense cock, in that place I'd never thought to allow a man, cemented his dominance. I held myself open as he reamed me, squeaking with every fraction of an inch that he took.

When I almost released my ankles, he growled a stark *no*. Somehow I fumbled with my numbing fingers and found the energy to tighten my grip.

Once his balls met my ass, he leaned on his arms over me, pressing my knees to my belly, and fucking me a little as he spoke. "This ass is mine now. Every part of you, every hole I can fuck, every thought you have, is owned by me. Do you understand that I will do anything to keep you? Anything?"

I nodded through the sear of the hurts. Despite the fatigue, the scratches, the dread that perhaps he'd torn me open, I still whispered a *yes*.

In the storm, something had been obliterated, and I feared it was me.

"Good. That's what you needed to say."

By then my arms were shaking, I was dedicating so much effort to holding my ankles. Before my grip failed, he extracted himself and put me on my side and lay down behind me

"This time, you're going to like it." His cock brushed my asshole, found the center, and he pushed.

I whimpered, waiting for that burn again.

"Relax. Push out."

Trembling, I feared what would happen next, but he entered me slowly until only the first part of the head of his cock seemed inside me. The pain was there but I could stand it. With his palm on my lower stomach, he kept me in place and when I cringed, his hand slid lower, over my mons. Using one fingertip, he played with my clit, feather light, and in the tiniest of circles.

"There. Are you feeling that?" His cock sneaked in some more, the pressure widening me by increments. "You smell like a bitch in heat. Taste like one too. Damn, I could fuck you harder again. Next time I will."

Talking in that dirty way and playing with me, it made me center on what he did, on his hold on me. On the sensations he was coaxing from my abused flesh. Now I knew he was satisfied. He'd dominated the fuck out of me, and if this was what he wanted, he would get it.

I breathed in, breathed erratically out. His other hand cupped my breast and toyed with my nipple.

My clit swelled under his tender ministrations. When I moaned, he clamped on finger and thumb and began a rhythm that would take me to climax.

More squeezing of my clit, more cock, more dirty words. Mouth parted, eyes rolling back, I was gasping, lost in that sexual haze, that eternal moment, seconds from coming.

"Oh. Oh."

"There. Come for me, girl."

He sucked on my neck, while his fingers kept working their magic and his cock penetrated me, all…the way…in.

Panting, straining onto his fingers, and aware of everywhere he touched me with mouth, fingers, and cock, and of everywhere I stung and ached, I soared into the climax.

When I was still shuddering through the aftershocks, he began to fuck my ass properly.

"You're mine," he said into my neck, "*Mine*," as he bit me and thrust hard into his own climax. "Mine."

No one had ever said that and meant it like he did, ever. No one.

I finally understood. I was. I was completely his. My world was him.

*****

"Do not touch the rifle, the knives, or any weapon from now until forever."

That was his first command on arising the next morning.

As if I would forget. I bowed my head from where I kneeled on the floor. I'd slept curled on the floor all night. I had a blanket, but sleeping away from him was because I needed reminding when I woke up, that I'd done something bad.

I understood. It had been lonely on the floor, and my bruises hurt. Worst though, I craved him, his body, his pain, even his distorted love.

I should detest him. I knew this logically. But I didn't.

I think I pouted, certainly I was looking miserable, because his mouth twitched and he beckoned. "Come here."

Like I had the first time, I crawled up onto his lap, and I cried unashamedly as he rocked me and whispered sweet words.

"It'll be better today. You just need to behave for me. In a minute I'll check your marks, then we can have a swim, then breakfast."

He put me back on the floor and clicked his fingers. A little déjà vu shock travelled through me. Gregor's signal.

"You know what that means, girl."

He wanted me to kneel?

I shuffled into position then peered up at him through the smudge of tears. Then it struck me, he wasn't calling me *meisie* anymore. I felt the pang of loss, and how twisted was that?

Though it pained me, I said it. "Sir, may I ask a question?"

A pause, then he nodded. "Yes."

God. Why had I wanted to say this? I shut my eyes for a second. *Do it.*

"Sir, why aren't you calling me *meisie*?"

"Because you haven't earned it. When I call you that again, you'll know you've earned it and that I'm happy with you. Also, you are never to call me Pieter again. Sir will do." He caught my chin. "Understand?"

Fuck this. My perception of him, me, the world, seemed to stutter. Never, ever to call him Pieter again? It was as if the color orange had been outlawed. That he dared to…no, that he could do this. It rattled me as much as, or more than, any of the humiliating things he'd already done. It was a nail in the coffin of my old life.

"Why do you look so stunned? Hmm?"

He'd seen that? *Crap.*

"I…" I swallowed.

"Say it. Or do I need to spank you?"

Wetness, instant wetness. I wanted to squirm on the spot. The threat of spanking had caused that. What had he done to me?

His eyes narrowed.

"I don't know why exactly, but it bothers me. I like calling you Pieter. Please?"

"No. I asked if you understood."

Oh. He had. "Yes, Sir. I do."

"Fantastic." He patted my head then kept caressing me while studying me as if to see how it affected me.

I tried to shut down my reaction. I was ashamed, turned on, and absolutely confused. To my consternation, I felt a building ache in my pussy. After a while, I gave in and shut my eyes again. As his hand ran over me, I lowered my head, relishing the sensations and drifting into his touch.

I wanted this Sir, so much, but not the one who punished. I wanted to be free but I also wanted to be with him. I'd been willing to kill him. So stupid. If I'd succeeded, would I have been able to move even? I could see myself standing over his body forever, like some pet that had lost its master, fading away to nothing.

"I'll be good, Sir," I whispered.

"Mmm. That's what I need to hear. Come here, little bitch."

Then he dragged me back onto the bed, shifted my legs apart, and entered me, ever so slowly, with his eyes on mine.

It was a quiet fuck, more like making love than his normal, but it reaffirmed who was who in this relationship. I didn't get to come but that familiar feeling of being used because I was his and available, and maybe even loved, was welcome.

Chapter 36

We waited at the jetty as Glass took the seaplane around in a big circle. The sea was a little choppy and spray drifted off the tops of the waves outside the sheltered bay. Even the few seagulls that had made it to our island looked windblown, with their feathers ruffling in the gusts. Sand spattered against my legs. Any rougher and we'd be waiting for this oncoming storm to die away before leaving.

I had Jazmine kneeling by my side. It was a cooler than normal and her dress fluttered in the breeze. I could even see goose bumps on her arms, but I kept her kneeling as much as possible now. All part of the constant reinforcement of what I needed her to do, to think, to *be*.

The roar of the plane intensified as it cruised toward us. Glass steered in to a few meters out, then cut the engine. The pilot's door swung open and he jumped down into the water. "Got much to take back?"

"Some."

His progress through the sea slowed as he studied Jazmine. He popped up his brows. "You seem to have her well in hand. I find that strangely attractive."

I nodded. "It is. Man after my own heart."

"Yeah. If I find a girl like this, you can train her for me."

Half serious? I wasn't sure.

"Come, girl. Let's load the gear."

The weeks that had followed my sadistic blowout had been useful in asserting my dominance. The rifle was out in plain view on top of the boxes but I had no doubt she'd avoid going near it.

I'd left out knives and the rifle on occasion and watched her behavior. Letting her closer than a few yards was dangerous, I'd decided. Besides, how could I train it out of her, if I had to be certain she'd touched the weapon? So I'd made new rules and punished her if she went within ten feet. It worked well. She tended to make a fifteen feet circle around them, since my idea of ten feet and hers didn't always tee up.

And now, Glass was eyeing her since she'd stopped short of the pile of our stuff. I strode over and removed the weapon, then gestured to her.

The power at times like this, with Glass watching, it was an indescribable rush, a haunting feeling that made me ten feet tall. Even with another man watching, I could've bent her over the boxes and fucked her and she'd do nothing except take it and moan when I made her come.

The curve of her bottom under that short dress...why not?

"Want to truly understand how well she's trained?"

He shrugged. "Sure."

I gave him the rifle, beckoned to her then clicked my fingers again. She kneeled before me, eyes widening as I unzipped. "Here."

The little *V* on her brow and her glance at Glass said it worried her but after a few seconds, she shuffled forward. Her pink mouth opened and my cock twitched in my hand. Memories had me anticipating. The feel of that moist little tongue and her throat pulsing around my dick was always riveting.

I let her lick me. Her tongue tip curled up and around, then I stuck myself all of two inches inside her before I gradually pulled out, took a long breath and zipped up.

From her smile, she knew how good that had felt. Her tongue slid along her upper lip then went back in.

"Whoa." Glass chuckled. "I tell you what, I wouldn't have stopped. Damn. I'm going to have blue balls all the way back."

He wasn't the only one, but the storm was coming.

"When we get back, I'm fucking that mouth," I murmured.

"Yes, Sir." When she went to grab another piece of gear, she leaned over so far I could see her wet slit.

Behind me, Glass coughed. "Damn!"

Was that a deliberate tease? I smiled, finding it strangely enticing that she still might have enough fire in her to tease.

After we'd taken off and reached a good height, the plane banked as we altered direction. Her lips were pale and I recalled her worries over landings and take-offs. "Here. Hold my hand." When she wriggled her fingers underneath mine, I squeezed.

"Have you still got a job for me, Glass? And a house?"

"Yes. I do." With the plane level, he glanced back. "You still happy to take it?"

"Absolutely, boss." I grinned.

"Great. Couple of things. My IT guy tracked the emails from the main guy running that House back to a place in Australia. Long way from us. But at least we know. Second. There's been someone sniffing around the city. The cops on loan from Australia found Jazmine's DNA. You can imagine the uproar over that. The local cops are helping them, digging around, interviewing people. That makes things even hairier if anyone links her in any way at all to us. Plus some friend of hers has brought a private detective over. They're talking to a man tomorrow and he has relatives in the raskols."

"Okay. You need an emergency plan?"

"I think so. I don't want them linking you or me to this. To her."

"Sir? May I speak?"

She'd be wondering who this friend was and about their fate.

"No. Not at all."

I mused while staring out the window. How far could we go with this?

A dark shadow below in a stretch of shallower sea caught my eye. The shape and size made me think it might be the old man's boat. If that was it, the vessel hadn't gotten far at all before sinking. The hole in the hull had been small but there had been the storm that night. They'd never find his body there anyway because I'd dropped it into the current separately.

Risk exposure because he had read more on that page than he admitted? No. My decision had been cold and logical.

I would not let his face haunt me. Not this time.

The wreck was far enough from the island. Soon with the weather and all, no one would think we'd been there, ever. In a month, six months, if anyone waded ashore on those little beaches they would find paradise. White sand, blue sea, scuttling ghost crabs, and sun. No one would know what had happened.

Events sometimes made it necessary to do monstrous things, even when you were not a monster.

If I had to deal with this friend and the detective, I would. Like Jazmine, I'd learned. Sometimes unusual decisions were necessary to survive and regretting them was foolish.

My motto popped up in my thoughts. *Never give up. Never give in.*

That motto was a good one. One I'd lived by much of my life. I'd always strived to be a good man, no matter how many awful decisions I'd made. Like shooting Aden. Like keeping Jazmine as mine.

I grimaced. My problem was clear. For once, that motto wouldn't do.

She was almost asleep, nodding off, her eyes closed, her body snuggled up against mine. My balls and my chest ached just thinking of her. I could see her automatic arousal when I did certain things to her but it affected me too. I had a boner most days – but I was lucky that I could get her to suck me off or open her legs at the click of my fingers. *Ja*, I was a lucky man, but also a nasty one.

I was never going to be a good man, not if I wanted to keep her.

Today was the day I officially gave in on being good and moral and righteous.

I smiled and tucked a wayward curl away from her eye. After wrinkling her nose and sniffling, she snuggled even closer. The prickle in my eyes surprised me. I couldn't afford to be sad; I had to be her mean-ass, cold-hearted trainer – the man who would fuck her sideways and hurt her for the most minor of infractions.

Ja. It was the only way I could save her life. Glass would never let her go. Neither would I.

When we landed off the coast, it was at a small, unwatched beach with the shore almost mangrove swamp to the very edge. We waded up onto the short stretch of beach and waited for Glass to come back with word of our transport. The first thing Jazmine did when I deliberately took my eye off her, was to head toward the villagers at the far end of the beach, who were stacking crates to take to the plane. Glass was going to fly back to Port Moresby while I drove in.

Unloading a slave woman in the middle of where he had to land there was never going to work.

I nabbed her before she drifted more than two yards up the beach. "Where the fuck are you going?" I clicked my fingers and she dropped to kneel in the wet sand.

Chewing on my lip, arms folded, I examined her. "Answer me."

Her swallow was obvious. "To see those people."

"Why?"

"I don't know, Sir. It just happened." Her gaze seemed to hold as much confusion as I felt.

"You don't know? Guess."

"I don't. It was automatic." Her head shake and misery-packed frown said it was the truth.

If she wasn't trying to escape… No. I was going to send myself crazy.

Training, training, and more training – that's what was needed.

"Whatever the reason, it was wrong. I'll punish you in the car."

And so it went. I knew now how much and what sort of pain she liked, and what she didn't. What worked as punishment. None of them were likely to work in a moving vehicle. I knew how to get her off fast when I wanted to. So I tried something new.

The window tint was so black we could've fucked the London Philharmonic Orchestra and nobody would've noticed. I tied her to the seat and the safety belt and stopped every half an hour to give her G spot orgasms with digital massage. It was novel and messy but it kept me amused when she squealed while thrusting onto my hand. I improvised. The bull-dog clamps from a clipboard in the car made things even better for the sadist in me, especially when I placed one on her tongue as well as her nipples. Temporary but intriguing.

I eyed her after the fifth time I got her off, leaning over her as she panted down from the *O*. I'd cuffed her hands to the struts under the headrest to keep her from interfering in my exploration of her pussy and her fingers were still wrapped around them. The clamps were still on her nipples, squashing them a little flat.

A car zipped past on the small roadway, rocking us in their backwash. First one for ages.

The scenery was cock-erecting territory and my dick was about to poke a hole in my pants. Was it wrong when the Dom had to do orgasm denial on himself? I took another tour of my prize – where I'd pulled down the neckline of her dress to reveal her boobs, where I'd rucked up her dress to get my fingers up into her cunt. At her parted lips as she struggled to suck in enough air, even at the sweat sheening her breasts and her face.

"I'm not quite sure this is punishment," I said quietly. "But I sure as hell *fokken* like it."

Her eyelids drifted up and she seemed surprised to see me.

"Yes, I'm still here. I did say I'd fuck your mouth."

I plucked off the bulldog clamps, fascinated by her moans and flinches, by the red and white on her outthrust breasts.

After a few delicious gasps, her eyes opened wider and I could see that flicker as she searched my face for clues. The tiny smirk of her lips and creasing under her eyes said she liked something. "Yes Sir, you did."

When I unzipped, she smiled and wriggled her hands. She probably thought I'd free her to do this. Instead, I dragged her lower into the foot well space, stretching out her arms and bringing her mouth down to cock level.

Anyone passing us might catch a hint of movement, but I kneeled up and into position, anchored my fingers in her hair, and brought her mouth and my cock together.

"Open wide. I need to check you out from the inside."

That first whispering touch of her lips on the head, then the swirl of her tongue across the slit and I was gone. Suppressing a groan, I thrust further in and she began to suck.

"Damn, woman. Your mouth is made for this."

Though making this last for longer than a few minutes was tempting, she was, technically, abducted and this was almost public. I fucked her mouth quickly – fast, slobbery, wet and deep, until she gagged and lost the ability to breathe. The rhythm built, I slid to the very back and jammed myself there, feeling that exquisite rush as my cum choked her, and her tongue, and all those other moist parts of throat and mouth, created suction around my cock.

I pulled out, cupped the back of her head and leaned in to kiss her like the animal I was. I could taste her and me both.

It was a feral, violent kiss, all mingled and insane – crushed lips, cum, drool, penetrating tongue, and male possession. I dragged her up the seat and slapped her legs apart when she went to close them.

"Keep that pussy where I can see it."

She whimpered and wriggled her lower torso, playing the part of innocent victim so well my cock twitched, getting ready for round two.

I grunted, smiled malevolently, and draped my arm above her, along the headrest.

Her soft eyes and the way she lay where I'd made her, said submission with a big huge *S*.

"Coming in your mouth with you my prisoner, where you have no choice but to swallow...*fokken* incredible. You are..." I sucked in air, considering what I'd been about to say – that she was the best thing in my life, ever, but I couldn't, not without seeming weak.

For much of the drive, I reminded her of her vulnerability by keeping my hand between her legs. Her squirms and delicate moans were a great accompaniment to driving, though I had to dig up the gag when we drew nearer the city. I pulled her hat down over her eyes and let her recover...apart from clipping her clit hood with the clamp.

Those whimpers made me evil. I let it stay on for the maximum safe time before I pulled over and removed the clamp.

By the time we reached the housing compound, and drove inside Glass's garage, the seat cover was thoroughly damp.

"Look at that mess," I murmured while biting her ear, then her neck, then constructing a three-bite track down to her nipple. I admired the red hickeys springing up while she whimpered, and took the opportunity to twist her nipple, hard, in a half circle. "Not done with you yet. That was just the start of punishment."

With the gag still in, she could only blink at me through those pretty tears.

I exited, went to her door and undid all the ties, then clicked my fingers and pointed at the floor.

Watching her almost pour off the seat and then kneel with her head down, drool dripping from the ball gag, and her palms on the concrete because she needed them there to stop herself from faceplanting... A sweaty, bedraggled woman devastated by too many climaxes.

I grinned. Today would be interesting.

Why hadn't I given up on being a good man earlier in my career?

*****

Standing in the corner with my nose to the wall in the dining room, with my hands laced together at my back and headphones muffling whatever talking was going on...I had time to think. The men were eating. No doubt they were staring at my ass since Piet... Since Sir had only deigned to let me wear lacy underwear. It was true what I'd said to him. I hadn't registered why I was gravitating toward the people at the beach. It had simply happened automatically, like my body knew I should be trying to escape even if my brain had lost the plot and neglected to remind me. I sighed and leaned my forehead on the wall.

I was losing it.

So tired. I'd never known orgasms could be a punishment but between my legs throbbed, and not in a good way.

Crazily, from the flurry of montaged images from the drive here, the one that kept coming back was of his face just before he kissed me. He'd seemed exultant? Like I was something special. That had impressed me. How many times had I ever seen that on a lover's face? Never, ever, ever.

I'd felt as if I'd won a victory too, in making him so happy. Being face fucked had blissed me out for a while.

I sighed. Clearly I was sunstruck. Or lovestruck. Life was just fucking wonderful when you were fangirling your captor. My Dom. Because, really, that's what he'd be if he wasn't my abductor.

The man should be in prison.

My heart did a fancy *dub, dub* as if it knew something I didn't. I loved being at his feet and I was beginning to see that if I was anywhere else I'd be miserable. If I was back home right now I'd be pining for him.

That simple. That crazy.

"Here."

As if by magic, Sir's hand appeared holding a glass of milk and his other hand rubbed my back.

"Drink. I'll get you food soon. You're pleasing me."

I'd had water already but I was starving too. After I drank, he took the glass, gave my butt a pat, and walked away.

The wall was hard against my head. My interlaced fingers were wet from the condensation on the glass, and I was about to cry. Not from being tired. No. It was because his praise had sunken in and made me glow with warmth.

I was indeed losing it.

*****

"What are you going to do with her now?" Glass was next to me at the table. He stuck another piece of steak in his mouth. "I mean I know you're going to fuck her silly later, 'cause who wouldn't. I mean now, what now? She's still trying to get away?"

I stared at her – all mute and meek, hands at her back like I told her to.

"I'll be training her still. Be good and don't distract her too much. No touching her." I nodded at Jurgen, who was leaning back in his chair, with his head twisted around so he could eye her. The man had enough tattoos on him to give him ink poisoning, enough piercings to make a surgeon jealous, many of which were self-inflicted, and a libido any other pushing fifty-year-old man would envy. "No touching, Jurgen."

Unless I said he could. It was a possibility I'd considered, sharing her just to imprint on her how much I owned her.

Only that idea gave me such a twisted-up gut I doubted it would work.

"Sure." He wiped his nose with the back of his fork carrying hand then rubbed the same hand through the dark stubble on his scalp. "Cute one though. I'm *fokken* fascinated." He sat up and leaned on the table, coming in close. The corrugations on his forehead said he was serious. "If you've pulled this off with a woman like this, from what I've heard of her background... A journalist with awards and all. Kudos."

"Pulled it off." Was that really a compliment? I sucked on the inside of my cheek while looking at Jazmine. "She's not fully my slave yet."

"You're closer than you think."

Glass nodded then added quietly. "I agree. She's close. You just don't see it. The change since you left here is enormous. Another few weeks of whatever you're doing to her and you're set."

Were they right? She hadn't moved an inch.

I decided. "One month from now let's have another dinner. A special one. Unless I don't think she's ready. I'll need a few things. I need to see if you can do something to her, for me. Piercings."

"Yeah. No problem. Can I do her nipples?" He chuckled. "I won't even charge for those."

"I bet you wouldn't. No." I checked her out again, the little wriggle she did every so often, when she adjusted the position of her feet, and that white lacy underwear, it made me yearn to drag her upstairs immediately. "What I want you to do, you might have to pay me for the privilege."

What I wanted from him was maybe too personal for me to let him.

I thought through it. I'd enjoy it. So why not do it myself? It wasn't as if the government had legislated that owners of slaves couldn't fuck with their bodies.

"What if I asked you to teach me how instead?" I raised a brow at Jurgen.

He sniffed. "Damn. Meaning I miss out?" His shrug was accompanied by a grin that said he knew why I wanted this.

"Pieter."

I looked to Glass. "What?"

"I need a test on that day. You're going to need to pretend to let her go and see if she comes back.

I couldn't swallow for a second. "*Ja*, I know."

Chapter 37

For the next week, I concentrated on what some in the BDSM lifestyle would call protocol. Kneeling on command and on my entry to a room. Crawling on command. Saying Sir without hesitation, and any hesitation was punished, severely. I could do pain that she didn't like as well as pain that made her scream her loudest climaxes and left her trembling with need for the next. Averting her eyes from mine for a week, and then at the end of that week, always meeting my gaze, unless I ordered otherwise. She slept on the floor by the side of the bed, unless I wanted her with me. Sometimes, though I never said, I drew her to me simply because I wanted to cuddle.

Cuddling…nothing wrong with that in a normal relationship. Or pillow fights. Or flowers. I couldn't see us doing the last two. I'd turned that over and thought about her and me in that situation and came up with a blah reaction. I'd only want to wrench the pillow off her and make her bite it while I bent her over and spanked her until her ass was red. But cuddling, yeah.

That was the bastard thing of all this. I needed her unquestioning, a robot, and yet I could see and feel much of her that I loved draining away. It was heart breaking, but if she tried to escape again, the punishment might well be death…if I allowed Glass to do it. I was a mean man but Glass was even meaner. Or so it seemed. What would he do if he too adored a woman like this?

From small things she did, I could see fire still lurked deep inside. Would it be smothered entirely if I kept this up?

I had no clue. For the next week, I blindfolded her whenever we slept. In the morning she had to wait for me to remove it before she could rise. It made waking up every morning like a birthday. My present awaited me, wrapped however I'd arranged it.

I sat on the edge of the bed and admired her for ages as the sun's rays strengthened and striped the ivory walls. Like the work of some ancient painter with an eye for beauty, the rays lay across my lady where she knelt, waiting. One wrist was attached by a long and fine steel chain to the leg of the bed nearest my pillow. The silvery chain crossed the timber floor then climbed to her wrist where the cherry-red cuff circled her. Her lips pouted, glossy as a ripened apple, and begging to be molested.

Rembrandt would have done her justice.

I rubbed at the whiskers on my chin and thought about standing but a stripe of sun approached her breast. It slanted across her areola, kissing it. I imagined my tongue there, or my mouth, and hardened. I remembered my cock in that sweet mouth but she was so perfect sitting down there on her quilted mat, with the black blindfold wrapped over her eyes and the long tails of the knot tumbling over her shoulder, that I still didn't rise. Such soft elegant curves. My gaze travelled over her thighs and breasts and down to her waist, to where the swell of her succulent bottom showed. The *V* where her thighs met her body hinted at her pussy, a place I meant to explore soon.

"Part your legs, girl."

She slid them aside.

"More."

Ahh, mouthwatering. My cock was fully at attention.

I wanted to keep her like this – as my gorgeous prize – and I wanted her as a woman, in my bed, because she wanted to be there. I needed more than her flesh; I wanted her, whole.

I also wanted her alive.

Fok this. "Stand and come forward."

When she reached me, I unclipped the chain then took her hands and guided her until she straddled my legs and my cock settled in place at the very start of her sweet little cunt.

"Give me your wrists, *meisie.*"

Her intake of breath alerted me. As I linked her cuffs at her back I asked her, "Do you think you've earned that?" I smoothed my hands up her arms to her shoulders then down to her warm breasts. The weight of them in my hands prompted me to grip both in the circle of my fingers. I pulled her deeper onto my cock, absorbed in how her mouth fell open and she sighed.

"Answer me." I kissed her mouth and pushed my cock all the way in. The squirm as she wriggled herself in place was so cute. I nipped her lower lip. "Answer."

"Uhh, Sir?"

Pumping up and down slowly seemed to space her out even more.

"Have you earned being called *meisie*? Are you my good slave girl now?" My hoarse voice betrayed my own passion. The ripple of her around my cock demanded more action. So I turned, toppling her onto the bed, rolling her to her stomach but keeping her knees on the floor. Then I fucked her properly making the bed shudder and protest with almost as many squeaks as she.

At what seemed a word gasped from her, I halted with my cock halfway out. Her juices had spread and made her thighs glisten. With my forefinger, I dipped into her cunt entrance, sliding it in alongside my cock. I pulled my finger out and drew a long curvy trail with her moisture to her butt.

Inserting my digit again made her quiver and her pussy tighten on my finger and cock. I watched the squeeze of her entrance where my shaft disappeared into her. Sexy fucking sight. Next time I'd get pictures.

"What?" Had she gathered her wits and recalled my question? I slipped another inch of cock into her. "Did you want to answer my question?"

*****

Question? What question of his? I'd missed something. When he'd entered me, my mind had plummeted into arousal space.

"I'm sorry Sir, I forgot your question. Punish me if you wish to."

His reply was incredulous. "You're asking for punishment?"

And that had hit the heart of the matter. I hesitated then blurted it out. "Yes, Sir. And I wanted to ask you something too."

"What?"

He stayed dead still while he waited.

I crammed shut my eyes, wanting him to shove his cock in again, but my gentle bowing of my ass earned me only a smack. Having to say this was excruciating. I held my breath a second then plunged onward. "Can you hurt me, please Sir?"

I blushed, the heat flaming across my cheeks. Thank god, I was face first in the sheets, staring into the blindfold.

"You want pain?"

"Yes." My affirmation squeaked out. I'd never asked him this and it seemed so wrong.

"Next time, ask me before I'm about to explode in your hot little cunt. Before I'm inches deep in your sopping wet pussy. Then I will. I'll bruise you so hard your screams when you come will scare away the damn birds in the trees."

The bed shifted and I felt his breath on my neck and he bit me there, hard enough to make me gasp. Hard enough that my pussy compressed onto his cock. Delicious pain.

"I felt that, little slut."

Then he pounded me into the bed with his thrusts, ignoring my cries, which only made it more delicious. He came partly inside me before he pulled out. The rest of his cum splattered on my back and my hands where the cuffs held them behind me.

I lay with my eyelids at half-mast, staring into the darkness of the cloth, feeling his solidly muscled arm draped over my back. When he moved in closer, I was pinned by the weight of his leg also, with his chin beside my ear. His inhalations and exhalations warmed my hair.

Oh god. This I loved. I didn't care whether he made me come or not. I just wanted to be his after he fucked me. I released a long joyous sigh.

*****

I made sure not to call her *meisie* after that. It hadn't been right even though the revelation of her asking for pain had startled me. I experimented and made her beg for pain at least half the time before I gave it to her. It worked. Sometimes she begged for it on her knees, the need intense.

Please Sir, hurt me. Those words had such power. I'd never been so hard.

Pain and pleasure had become entwined for her, almost inseparable. Perhaps that and dominance had been the missing ingredients for her past lovers. Whatever, I had the magic. I bet Merlin never used canes, whips, or needles. Needles almost became her favorite, sending her flying so easily.

The night I made a train track of them snake from her nipple to her mons, she blissed out entirely. With some candles for lighting up my needy victim, I took a gallery of pictures of her naked, needle-decorated body.

Such a tasty little girl she was when she begged.

Begging for cock was the obvious next step. She took to that like a duck to water. Then, of all things, she asked me to fuck her mouth. I found out that making her drool and cry a few tears turned her on even more.

Was I transforming her into my sex toy, or my perfect lover?

She wasn't a robot, not by any stretch of my imagination. Not when I leaned over her after coming, with her sweaty and semi-comatose from orgasming, her hair tangled and thrown in a crazy halo about her head. But I guess she'd had nothing from her other lovers, while I served her up a feast.

The day arrived, a month after that first meal, and Jurgen and Glass and I sat down at the dinner table. It should have been a celebratory feast but it felt like a wake.

We were letting her go, with that lethal clause…if she truly walked out, she died.

I'd left her here alone, numerous times, while on jobs for Glass, locked up mostly, though sometimes with instructions for one or the other of the men to care for her. I trusted them in combat. I trusted them with her. Except now.

I'd taken her to the entry foyer, uncollared, uncuffed, clothed in a cute red dress and with underwear on for the first time in days, with more clothes in a small suitcase and some money. I'd kissed her and told her she could leave if she wished to. Now, we watched her on CCTV. If I had to sum her up, out there in the hall, it would be small, alone, and pretty.

And fucking mine. What was I doing?

My heart ached. She hadn't moved in these few minutes apart from turning her head to check the room. She hadn't been in there by herself since the day when she'd escaped.

Though the camera lens was tiny and up next to the light in the ceiling, she looked directly at it a few times. In her eyes I recognized fear. I'd seen that often enough, and caused it many times.

I was sure I also saw plain anxiety. She'd been my girl for so long. Had I crippled her? Though honestly that had been my aim.

The guard at the gate was alerted to keep the gate locked and Randall was waiting with him. She couldn't actually get out without turning into a spider and climbing the walls. If she screamed we'd be on her in seconds and no one in this neighborhood would bat an eyelid.

The chair creaked as I sat back in it, thumping into the timber.

Glass eyed me sideways. His white blond mohawk looked sharp enough to attract a whole flock of women today. "What?"

"How long?" I asked sourly.

"Before we grab her again? Another five? You've done a thorough job on her head."

I grunted and resisted grinding my teeth. Time ticked past. Without sound what I saw in the monitor seemed dreamlike or a nightmare. She walked to the door and opened it. I tensed, only relaxing when she stayed there, looking out toward the guard.

What the *fok* was she doing?

"Time." I rose, shoving back my chair with a screech.

Jurgen took a handle of nuts from a bowl on the table and threw them in his mouth. "Thank *fokken* god. Go get her. If you'd tried killing her, either of you, I'd have whacked you both. I like her. Fucking waste as well as damn shocking to kill her. We'll figure something, Pieter." He crunched onto the nuts then pointed a finger. "She's moving."

Glass grunted. "You better go." I stared and he shrugged. "So? Figure out something."

Was that him bending? If she ran, she broke his rule.

Words with him seemed pointless. I strode to the door and headed after her.

She'd made it as far as the driveway where she'd deposited the suitcase. At the sound of my boots crunching closer, her shoulders slumped a little, but she said nothing, took no step, just waited. I went around and stood before her and stared down at her bowed head. A breeze stirred stray tendrils of her black hair, wafting them over her bared shoulders. My pretty siren. For a moment, I saw her naked and wrapped in barbed wire.

Slow as the moon rising, she raised her head. At the first sight of her liquid greenish eyes, I raised an eyebrow. Now to see what she would do. Her lips trembled…

Chapter 38

He was here.

I didn't want to leave. Whenever I thought of stepping into the outside world I felt the ache of loneliness sweep through me, cold, raining on my soul, making me less than I was.

As his, I was someone. Out there, I was nothing but a cog in the machinery of society, doing my little job, growing old, growing less, dwindling day by day.

I was afraid he meant to truly free me. I knew it was bizarre and despite all my knowledge of the psychology of people in captivity, I also knew I was right to stay.

All that had happened these last few months had slowly disintegrated my sense of self and now I felt the tattered remnants of my ego unpeel from my bones and blow away, dust on the wind.

What was left was the essential me, stripped bare of trivial things. I had everything to lose though it was something I'd never valued before – my worth to a man.

Sir was like a gruff bear standing over me. I managed to hold his gaze for all of a second before I wavered and then he'd draw me again, because I knew he was still looking. Big. A powerful man. And he cherished me no matter what he'd done. The way he stared down with that eyebrow cocked, waiting to see what I'd do…I melted. Just melted.

I slid to my knees and clutched his leg through his jeans.

I was vulnerable because I'd surrendered completely.

With one simple word he could destroy me: *Leave.*

Please, please, don't say that.

My words came out strangled and miserable, a few caught in my throat. "You didn't mean to let me go, did you, Sir?" I looked up, pleading terribly.

Pitiful and I didn't care.

A pause, as if he wondered whether to be truthful.

The world poised on the verge of fracturing.

When he spoke, each syllable was measured. "No. I was never going to let you go."

"Thank you," I whispered.

Then his hand encompassed my head and he ran his fingers along my scalp, parting my hair. I shuddered, unravelling from the emotions tearing through me.

Bliss settled in as his fingers did their sorcery.

Embarrassing, but I could no longer deny how much this turned me on.

"What would you have done if I'd run through the gate?" I had to know. Even if it hurt.

Around his eyes crinkled just a little. "Glass planned to kill you, but that was long ago. None of us would do it now." His fingers scrunched in on my hair until pain pricked through my skin. "I'd rather lock you up in my room, chained to my bed, for a hundred years, than let you leave me, *meisie.*"

Breathing in *Him* through the denim, I whispered my reply. "I'd rather be there in your room, forever, than be made to go, Sir."

Then I shut my eyes, needing to say more, but this was so contrary to what should be true and so repulsive to my old self, that it was torture to squeeze the words from my brain to my tongue.

"I…know logically that what I'm doing is crazy, but it is what I want. I want to be yours, owned, your slave. I need to be." My arms slid around his leg and I held on as if an earthquake might be about to shake me loose.

He tightened his fingers some more. "Good. Keep your head up." His voice rasped with raw emotion.

Still with my eyes closed, I did as he asked. I felt his collar encircle my neck and he buckled it on. Then came the small click as he fastened the leash. Peace settled on me. I was *His* again.

"Look at me now." He nudged my chin and I looked up into his brown eyes. The intensity there was scary. "I see you, *meisie.* Never forget from now on, that you are mine. You answer to only me. I will keep you, and care for you, but I will also punish you when you need it. You are my beloved slave."

My vision blurred with the tears flooding my eyes.

"And now." His smile turned ferocious as he raised me to my feet. "I'm going to claim you with metal. I'm going to pierce you. You can scream if you like. That will only make it better."

I knew that. He loved my screams. Anticipating that moment of cruelty, my toes curled and I shivered the teensiest amount. "May I ask where, Sir?"

"No. You'll see soon enough. I'm going to enjoy this."

The leash jingled as he stepped away and let it sway between us.

Oh. The evil in that statement. I shuddered and felt my pussy dampen. At the tug on my leash, I followed him back into the house.

Whether he didn't trust me not to move, or he maybe he just liked me bound, Sir strapped me onto the bed in his room, my arms above, my legs spread. When he shoved pillows under my lower back and my bottom, I guessed where he meant to pierce.

My clit? Nooo.

I'd never heard him speak of having done anything like this. Jurgen, yes, but not Sir. Was he bluffing?

The slow and tidy assembly of a whole collection of instruments on a tray on the other half of this king-sized bed seemed aimed at scaring me more than anything. My heart beat louder. There were at least six fat metal rings over there. Big shiny ones.

I sucked in my lower lip then cautiously cleared my throat. “Sir?”

“Yes?”

I was used to him studying me but this, when I figured he was going through some procedure in his head – far worse. When I squirmed, he smirked.

“Sir, surely you don’t need all those…things?”

“I might.” He kneeled on the end of the bed and began wiping my pussy and clit with an alcohol-moistened swab.

I squeaked at the cold and lifted my butt, only to have him glare.

“Be still or I’ll rope you down and pierce your tongue as well.”

Oh fuck. I glued my butt to the pillow, even when he picked up a long, silvery pair of forceps.

“Sir, do you know how to do this? Whatever it is you’re doing?”

“I do.” He snicked the forceps open and shut a few times then approached me. I was sure my eyes were as wide as they could go. I squeaked but stayed in one spot by virtue of tensing every muscle and curling my toes. Clothes pegs, needles, sure, but violating my lady bits with some big fat pieces of metal was past my limits. “Sir!”

“Shhh. No more talking. I need to concentrate on putting these in. Three rings on each side of your pussy.” He glanced up and grinned. “The outer lips if you’re curious.”

“Not curious,” I whispered to myself. Then I plonked my head back on the pillow as the forceps closed with a *click, click. Ow!* Sharper pain lanced in and I hissed, then it settled into a throb that infused me, slowly, and became that odd mix of arousal and ache. He used some other instrument then pierced me again. I breathed through it, panting, appreciating the sensations more. Pain and I had come to terms with each other and this was only another rung up the ladder from needles. The ritual of the piercing sank in. By the third one, the little spears of hurt were spacing me out.

I raised my head to see.

Though a sadist, my Pieter, my Sir, seemed as engrossed in the technique and getting this done right, as in observing my reaction. That was reassuring.

"You're being good." He stroked my thigh. "This is looking damn sexy."

Ugh.

Another ring was inserted. The regular *click* and *clack* of metal things being played with calmed me and I stared upward, lowering my eyelids.

I fuzzed out, the haze taking me until all I registered was the clink of instruments, and the distant bites on my pussy. The ceiling was miles above and drifting sideways.

As the straps were released, I came back to earth and focused. Then I realized he was sitting between my legs and smiling smugly while staring at what he'd done.

My mouth ran away before I could think. "You look like a boy who's just built his first house from blocks."

That skeptical eyebrow rose.

Something pulled me over the cliff, maybe my journalistic streak. "The cat that's got the cream?" I moved to draw my legs up and he grabbed my ankles.

Oops. Memories of punishments returned. I caught my lip in my teeth.

"Not so fast. More like the wolf that's caught the girl skipping naked through the forest." Still holding my legs, he sneaked up the bed and leaned in mouth open, heading for my newly tortured pussy. When inches away he dived, his teeth snapped together, and I screamed.

"I'm sorry, Sir!" Funny, but I almost giggled. It was the expression – an evil glee that seemed to glitter in his eyes.

After months him being super strict, I sensed a change. A tolerance for bad behavior that hadn't existed before. Because he was certain of me staying? It must be.

"I hope so, my slave." After a long, sadistic silence, he let go, came around the side of the bed and sat next to me. I rolled over, winced at the sharp reminder as the rings pulled on my pussy, then I dared to snuggle in with my head on his lap and my arms around his waist.

Without saying more, he caressed my cheek then piece by piece, a few strands at a time, he rearranged my hair. If there was one thing he loved, it was playing with my hair. Lazily, I watched it slide through his fingers while he studied me so closely, I wondered if he was memorizing my every detail.

"Now, you're really mine. Permanently, irrevocably, forever mine."

Oh, the arrogant satisfaction in that. All those words he'd used meant forever to my little writerly heart but I loved the repetition; it was as though he stamped his ownership on me with words as thoroughly as the three pairs of rings in my labia. With every surge of blood in my veins, the ache down there reminded me that I was his, absolutely.

"Yes, Sir. I'm yours, forever and ever." There was nowhere in the world I would rather be. "Does this mean you won't need to cane me anymore?"

"Hah. It means I get to do it more."

I tried to hold back my smile but failed. "Mmm."

He was my sadist and I never wanted him as anything else. On some days I knew he would come to me, in need, with the million shards in his eyes, to whip me and pierce me until I fell into the abyss before him, but on others he would be merely my Sir. I would dread the storm days, but those others, I wanted to lie at his feet and be his.

He bent to brush my forehead with his lips then he shifted onto the bed to lie with me, with his chin on my hair. Where I was, tucked into his chest, I felt safe and surrounded and his.

*****

From now on, I would be her protector as well as her master, I would make her feel loved, because she was, terribly so. I hugged Jazmine closer to me and kissed her. I buried my nose in her hair, breathed in her natural perfume, and sighed.

Paradise was not the island, it was this, having her as mine.

Later I'd have to help Glass decide how to deal with this not-so-friendly friend of hers, Wren. The fallout from crime seemed never-ending but I could handle it. Making people do what I wanted them to was getting easier day by day.

I'd learned my lesson. Bad men got what they wanted. Fuck being good. I was going to be a bad, bad man, because that way I got to keep my beautiful pet.

Teaser for Book 5, Own me Until Forever

Moghul shut off the phone and swung back to the naked model his rigger had suspended from the ceiling by hooks. Her frantic pleas to be let down were worrying his men but the film crew kept to their task. Randy was working methodically to get her down.

The ropes lowered the last foot. Her bound breasts, then the rest of her front, gently kissed the floor.

"Way to go," he muttered. Maybe he could salvage something from the footage.

Not all the scripts worked, especially when they tried something new, like hook suspension.

The crew relaxed and Randy went to one knee beside Mel to extract the shiny hooks.

"Thank you, Randy!"

The Texan gave him a thumbs-up then resumed soothing and freeing the girl. The man was a find and a half with all his skills – big attitude, bad jokes, and big dick. If anyone else had been handling the submissive, she'd have been screaming the room down.

His second phone buzzed and Moghul walked carefully backward until he found the wall.

He did a last check on the scene.

There was nothing sexy about the next part. Not with her panicking. Maybe if they were a torture snuff porn site but Kinkaverse was a straight up BDSM porn site. Domination, humiliation, and bondage of every sort while the models got fucked every which way. All above board and legal.

He pursed his lips, and just for a second allowed himself the leisure of imagining Mel being made to stay up there. Enticing situation. Suspended on hooks, with her arms bound and anchored to the wall by other ropes, blood trickling from the points of entry, gagged maybe. Then she could be fucked by the Texan, and one or two others.

He smiled and let the little vision slip away.

It wasn't often he let himself to dwell on the possibilities. Not while at work. His employees would be aghast, but not at his fantasies, at his realities.

"Got ya sweetheart." Randy removed the last hook then cuddled her to him.

Moghul snorted and glanced down at the message on his BlackBerry. Military-grade encryption but it never hurt to be careful. Someone reading over his shoulder could be as disastrous as it being sent in plain text.

The woman in Moresby is not a friend of Jazmine Foulkes. She's Gavoche's daughter, Wren. She's trying to figure out her father's death. Dangerous if she links you and the House.

"Fuck," he said softly.

The spotlights in here were overcoming the aircon. He wiped his forehead with the back of his arm then stared up at the ceiling for a while.

The House, he'd written off. The place was being closed down anyway and the only liabilities, his men there, had been killed. The systems in place meant no one could link him directly. Vetrov was a name he kept in quarantine from his other businesses.

What were the odds she'd connect him to the House? Low, as in very.

He should have her killed. It was final. It was sensible. People were loose ends because of their nosiness and Wren had met him, even if she knew nothing of her father's fetishes. Once all the immediate family was gone, no one was likely to see anything except an old man's kinkiness exposed in a tawdry fashion by his death in Papua New Guinea.

He grimaced. What a waste. The last time he'd seen her, the girl had blossomed into a beauty.

The hooks called to him. Someone needed to try them out properly.

He rarely, ever, took things this far on his home turf.

Yet a woman caught on those hooks, for him, just for him… Definite possibilities there. It would be karma in a way, considering Andrew's proclivities.

*****

Wren played with the napkin next to her plate. The late afternoon sun came in low, glinting off the tableware and making the place so glary it was difficult to see the man weaving between the other empty chairs and tables. For a little roadside pitstop eatery up in the New Guinea mountains, the décor was…cute. Her napkin had Bart Simpson on it and none of the chairs matched. And the waitress had vanished.

She glanced at her hulking bodyguard and he nodded reassuringly. Not a single black hair was out of place. James Bond and Hugh probably exchanged texts and anti-villain plans, but her father always employed the best. Hugh had insouciance down to an art. Nothing fazed him, except maybe the tropical heat. He had a thing for being properly dressed in at least long pants and buttoned shirt. Today was a day for sweating.

Even in her pink tank top and denim knee-length pants she was feeling the heat. More sweat dribbled down her spine. If they stayed any longer, she'd melt and stick to the timber. Wren took up the napkin and used it for a fan as the new arrival reached the table. Surfer shorts and T-shirt. Good. She hated being the under dressed one. Student life at university had been like diving into her ideal environment. No one ever dressed up except at parties or functions.

A flight of parrots shot past a few yards away, squawking alarmingly.

"Hello." He put his hand on the back of the chair beside her. "Wren Gavoche?"

The British accent sounded wonderful and never failed to give her an instant rapport with the speaker. It was just…cute, even when attached to an alarmingly large man. Despite her instinct that looking more pointedly might give him the wrong impression, cause really he was not within light years of being inscribed in her little book of possible bf's, she looked…and looked.

She let her gaze cruise over the swell of his biceps with the mysterious tatt peeking from under the sleeve, took in the breadth of his chest, his scent, the solid *don't fuck with me* way he stood, those huge hands, and those palest ever blue eyes.

Ooops. Caught staring. His minimal yet knowing smile seemed to rivet her to her seat.

"Hi." She pasted on an innocent grin. "You're Richard? No last name?"

That was so odd but she had Hugh. Safety in numbers, and concealed firearms.

"No." He removed his baseball cap, revealing a perky light blond mohawk, pulled out the chair, and sat.

Then he waited.

"You contacted me, Richard. You said you had information." About what she had no clue but this search for what was behind her father's death, at a place designed to turn women into sex slaves, had so far gotten her one step past the starting post. "Do you know anything about my father's death? About this woman Jazmine Foulkes? I think she escaped."

The chair squeaked as he reclined. His focus was entirely on her, as if the menacing Hugh wasn't sitting beside her. "Perhaps. I don't know her whereabouts but I can help you find the man who set your father up to die."

"Oh." She tensed. This was what she'd been looking for. A breakthrough. "Who?"

He gestured at Hugh. "Get your watchdog to move away and I'll say more."

Damn. Was this safe? Hugh shook his head, grimly. But she dived in. Nowhere was where she'd gotten so far.

"Hugh, please?" She raised her eyebrows.

"Ma'am…" But he took in her expression then nodded.

Once he'd risen and seated himself at a distant table, one with the wall behind him, she nodded at Richard. Clever Hugh though. Always seeking out the safest places. Could he read lips?

Richard, or whoever he was – she wasn't believing his name for an instant, leaned his forearms on the table. His nearest hand ended up resting inches from her left hand. Her breaths turned ragged. Just that proximity had made warmth suffuse between her legs. This man attracted her, no matter that he was clearly out of bounds. Fantasy territory – like lusting for the tatted-up, muscle-bound biker stalking through the pub on a Saturday night.

With her friends, she'd ogle after this type of man then turn aside and giggle about what he'd be like in bed.

"Well?" She pulled her hand away a fraction but the electricity of his presence drew her still.

"The man you want is called Vetrov." Ugh, and even his voice seemed to stroke between her legs. Testosterone concentrate.

She swallowed and made herself listen.

"He organizes human trafficking. I know where to find him."

To business. She'd get the person who had done this and to hell with her life until she did. No brother, no mother, no father – only she remained. Most days she wanted to weep despite the millions Dad had left her. Her vet science degree could wait. This money, what better thing to do with it than destroy the man who'd killed her father?

"Give me his name, where he lives, and I'll pay you very well. Once I know for sure he's the right man, one hundred thousand is yours."

For the first time he truly studied her. When his eyes lowered, her breasts tingled, her nipples tightening until they were aching and hard. They'd be showing through her skimpy shirt. *Focus. Business.*

His mouth twitched and he lifted his hand and trapped hers. What the hell?

"Remove your hand." She tugged but he held on tight. The creak of the chair warned her that Hugh had noticed. She shook her head at him and he subsided into his chair.

"First hear my terms. Two hundred thousand. You're going to need me with you to help fine tune the location of Vetrov."

She frowned and was still considering when he spoke again.

"Also I want you."

Time shivered. "What ?" She'd heard wrong.

"You." His smile was hard, uncompromising, and so lethal every hair on her body stood on end. "I want you in my bed. Once. After that, you won't want to leave. No you. No deal."

He didn't wink or move in any way, just waited while examining her face, and that floored her. Arrogant bastard.

Was this blackmail? Yet he intrigued her. She shook her head, jarring herself out of the state of shock. "Ummm."

One eyebrow rose. "Dare to take a chance for once, Wren. Life is better with surprises."

One night. Why was she even thinking it was possible?

She blinked, running through crazy thought after crazy thought. What would it be like to have sex with such an overtly dangerous man? All her lovers in the past had been students. Young *safe* men who'd never done more than go to university, parties, maybe the beach.

Insane to say yes.

She opened her mouth and was caught by how he stared at her lips. His large hand squeezed down harder until where his thumb pressed hurt. The pain brought another level of scariness to this. Now she was aroused and afraid in equal proportions.

The words seemed to blurt out without her mind having much say. "Once, only. And it's one hundred thousand if you want me as part of the deal." *Let's see what the smart ass thinks of that.*

"Done." He drew her hand to his mouth, kissed her knuckles like a gentleman then he singled out her forefinger and sucked on it.

She could feel the movement of his tongue.

In one second, her finger became hot and wet and his.

Tremors ran through her pussy. Breathing halted. Her eyes must be so very wide. The man had turned her on so much with that simple action, as if it were a button to her sexuality.

Holy fuck.

His murmur rumbled past her last defenses. "Keep looking at me like that and I'll bend you over this table now, pull down your underwear…"

…and fuck you. She could hear those unsaid words in her mind.

He released her hand. Wren snatched it away.

What had she just agreed to?"

About Cari Silverwood

Cari Silverwood is a New York Times and USA Today bestselling writer of kinky darkness or sometimes of dark kinkiness, depending on her moods and the amount of time she's spent staring into the night. She has an ornery nature as well as a lethal curiosity that makes her want to upend plots and see what falls out when you shake them.

When others are writing bad men doing bad things, you may find her writing good men who accidentally on purpose fall into the abyss and come out with their morals twisted in knots.

This might be because she comes from the land down under, Australia, or it could be her excessive consumption of wine.

Freaking out readers is her first love and her second love is freaking out the people living in her books. Her favorite hobby is convincing people she has a basement…though she really doesn't. Promise. If it existed it would be a terrifying place where you would find all the dangerous things that you never knew you craved.

To escape you'd need to get the key you can see through the grate in your cell door. A key that's hanging from the ceiling by string. The light above is flickering on…off…and you can hear feet dragging along the corridor floor. Your door is locked.

Anyone know how to get blood stains out of concrete?

My website, if you're curious about my other evil pursuits: http://www.carisilverwood.net/

Connect with Cari Silverwood

To join my mailing list and receive notice of future releases:

My mailing list
http://www.carisilverwood.net/about-me.html

Books by Cari Silverwood
http://www.carisilverwood.net/books.html

Connect with Cari Silverwood on Facebook
http://www.facebook.com/cari.silverwood

Cari Silverwood on Goodreads
http://www.goodreads.com/author/show/4912047.Cari_Silverwood

Also by Cari Silverwood

Pierced Hearts Series

(Dark erotic fiction)
Take me, Break me
Bind and Keep me
Make me Yours Evermore
Seize me From Darkness

Preyfinders Series

Precious Sacrifice
(Published in the anthology, Kept. Also released as a solo book)
Intimidator

Squirm Files Series

Squirm – virgin captive of the billionaire biker tentacle monster
Strum – virgin captive of the billionaire demon rock star monster

The Badass Brats Series

The Dom with a Safeword
The Dom on the Naughty List
The Dom with the Perfect Brats
The Dom with the Clever Tongue

Cataclysm Blues Series

Cataclysm Blues

The Steamwork Chronicles Series

Iron Dominance
Lust Plague
Steel Dominance

Others

31 Flavors of Kink
Three Days of Dominance
Rough Surrender
(Re-released by Momentum, an eBook branch of Pan Macmillan)

Made in the USA
Lexington, KY
30 March 2015